His Wrath

Erin Michelle Katherine

PublishAmerica
Baltimore

© 2006 by Erin Michelle Katherine.
All rights reserved. No part of this book may be reproduced, stored in a retrieval system or transmitted in any form or by any means without the prior written permission of the publishers, except by a reviewer who may quote brief passages in a review to be printed in a newspaper, magazine or journal.

First printing

All characters appearing in this work are fictitious. Any resemblance to real persons, living or dead, is purely coincidental.

ISBN: 1-4241-2951-6
PUBLISHED BY PUBLISHAMERICA, LLLP
www.publishamerica.com
Baltimore

Printed in the United States of America

Dedicated to anyone who has ever been raped.

Acknowledgements

I would like to thank all of my family and friends for believing in me and always pushing me to do better.

Special thanks goes out to my parents Valerie and David and my brother Matthew, my dear friends especially Douglas Whitcher, Dr. Ginger Miller, Coletha Cox and Julia Huprich.

Thanks also goes to: my grandparents, aunts and uncles, cousins and all my other family members and friends.

Table of Contents

Chapter 1 9
Chapter 2 21
Chapter 3 28
Chapter 4 38
Chapter 5 41
Chapter 6 50
Chapter 7 59
Chapter 8 73
Chapter 9 84
Chapter 10 93
Chapter 11 108
Chapter 12 117
Chapter 13 135
Chapter 14 141
Chapter 15 151
Chapter 16 164
Chapter 17 167
Chapter 18 169
Chapter 19 173
Chapter 20 178
Chapter 21 186
Chapter 22 197
Chapter 23 206
Chapter 24 209
Chapter 25 212
Chapter 26 214
Chapter 27 222
Chapter 28 233
Chapter 29 247
Chapter 30 255
Chapter 31 257

Chapter 32 262
Chapter 33 266
Chapter 34 269
Chapter 35 271

Chapter 1

Another Thursday morning, Laura stretches her arms out as she awakes.

Another day in the life of me...

Laura Lynn grew up in an upper class society. Luxurious houses with 16-year-olds receiving brand new cars on their birthdays surrounded her. These cars would be awaiting the child's birthday in the driveway with a big, red bow. Laura's family, however, sneaked their way into this society. Therefore, Laura was ostracized on a regular basis, but she swore her senior year would be different.

Laura walked into her history class as Miss Jingle was taking attendance.

Late as always, she sighed. The only seat left was next to her friend, Nate. Nate had always been there for Laura. They lived right across the street from each other.

But something grabbed attention as she sat down in front of Nate. She wasn't the last one to enter the class. This nice looking fellow, whom she had never seen before, entered after her.

Mmm. Look at that piece of Chocolate. He has got to be new here, she thought.

"Class, I would like you to meet Keith Holcomb," Mrs. Jingle said.

Keith took a seat. Class is about to begin.

Laura Lynn had a hard time concentrating and instead spent most of the time staring at Keith's bicep.

Laura, having no spine, had of course no intentions of talking to Keith.

"Hey Laura," Nate said.

"Hey," Laura responded.

"I saw you looking at the new kid," Nate said.

He never missed a chance to pick on Laura.

"What new kid?" she asked.

She said trying to look innocent.

"Right. Right. So should I get his number for you? You know he happens to be walking this way. Hey new kid," he said as he raised his voice a little.

"Quit it. He better not be…oh hi, you are Keith right?" she asked.

"Sure am. How are you doing?" he replied.

"Well I will leave you two kids to talk," Nate said, as he walked away.

"Nate um.um. I'm fine," Laura answered.

"You sure are. What would your name be?" Keith questioned.

"Laura Lynn Timberwood," she answered.

"While I have to run to English class, but I'll be seeing you around," he replied.

Laura Lynn gasped as she realized not only did she talk to a boy, but also she got a compliment. She was glad he was new here, because that means he didn't know how the middle class and the upper middle class students treated each other.

She realized she was again late for math class and ran off down the hall, thinking about Keith and wondering if he would say hi to her tomorrow.

High School girls will go through a bunch of crushes, but the first one they will remember the most. That is also the one that has the ability to cause the most pain.

That night, Nate called Laura to get some juice for more picking on her.

Laura always wondered about Nate's motives. Does he like me? Is he a spy for the upper middle class students? Mmm…

"Hi, Nate," Laura said.

"So how did go?" he asked.

"How did what go?" she asked.

She was hoping he was referring to some other incident.

"Oh come on. You got his number didn't you? And you have memorized all of the digits," Nate laughed.

"Not quite, we just talked," she said.

She said feeling embarrassed.

"Sure. You know I will get the whole story out of you sooner or later, but for now. Have you done your homework yet?" he asked.

"I only had history homework, since our quiz is tomorrow. Do you need my flash cards or something?" she asked.

"No, just making sure, he wasn't the only thing on your mind. Bye," he replied.

Laura thought, now what is he up to? Why is he always pushing me into the arms of other men? Does he have a complex?

Laura's and Nate's relationship started when they were playing Danish Rounders at Eastland Elementary School in fifth grade. They both ended up on second base together. Danish Rounders is similar to the old-fashioned game of kickball, but the players may stay on the base as long as they can. However, in their situation the boy on third base was afraid of getting tagged out and only went when he was sure he could reach the next base. Laura and Nate ended up standing on second base for around ten minutes, before the teacher made Bobby run home. During those ten minutes, Nate managed to say, "Look at that Bobby, slow as a turtle. The turtle and the hare is one of my favorite books. What's yours?" Laura just stared at him before she realized that he was actually talking to him. Trying not to lose her attention on the game and being a bit of a tomboy, she just smiled and said "see you later" as she noticed Bobby had finally ran home.

Ever since then Nate and she had done homework together, held joint parties for their friends and developed an interesting friendship by the time they entered high school. This was about the time Laura Lynn developed and became a young woman. Needless to say, Nate noticed. He began to look at Laura, a little differently. He began picking on her and shoving her onto other guys. Laura never quite understood why his personae around her changed, but she never asked either. She looked at Nate as a "brother," and not one she would ever date.

Laura arrived to history class early the next day, looking forward to seeing Keith. She sat in front of Nate like she always did.

"Early today, huh?" Nate asked.

"Yeah. I'm sure I have run out of tardies," she replied.

She said trying to look innocent.

Nate just smirked.

Keith strutted in and sat next to Laura.

"Well hello there? You've been taking this class for the past few weeks? Right? You think you can catch me up? I'm excused from the quiz today you know, but that test next week, killer," he said.

"Mmm. Me?" she said, looking confused.

"Yeah, Cutie," Keith answered.

"I guess so," she replied.

"I mean you are smart right. You got an A?" he asked.

"Yep. I've got an A. I'll talk to you after class about it," she replied.

Laura being nervous walked out of class a little faster than usual and went directly to her locker, which was located on the same hall.

Laura was petite, fit, 18-year-old African American, who was going to graduate in two months. She had already been accepted to a public liberal arts college in Georgia.

She hid behind her locker door hoping Keith didn't notice.

"Hey you. Trying to lose me?" he asked.

"Nope. My math class is just three halls away, that's all," she replied.

"Alright. Well I won't keep you; just give me your digits," he ordered.

"Umm. Umm. Well you got the phonebook? I'm listed," she replied.

She shut the locker door down and ran off.

She said feeling so embarrassed.

Nate walked up to Keith.

"Hey, Laura is a good friend of mine. You better treat her right," Nate told Keith.

"Relax kid. I'm just trying to get her notes not a date. Hey listen she ran off without giving me her number, you think you could provide me with it," he said.

"I don't know. I mean there is a tough screening process you need to go through to get those digits," Nate commented.

"Okay. I can take a hint. Bye," Keith responded.

Nate thought maybe, I should have given it to him…that would have been an interesting story later…

Nate was a tall, muscular 18-year-old African American, who was also going to graduate in two months. He had also been accepted to his first choice of University of Georgia.

You know, he thought to himself, I'm going to miss picking on that girl in a few months.

Keith opened the door to his brand new convertible. After getting tons of questions for talking to Laura, he sighed. She is cute, and I obviously have the market cornered since everyone else here is stuck on this "rich guy dates rich girl deal." He turned up his rap station and rolled down the street and onto the driveway of his parents.

Keith's dad was a U.S. senator and his mom was president of the local bank office. She had just been transferred from the Atlanta office to the local office causing the family to move a matter of 15 miles—meaning he now resided in the city as Laura and also attended Eastland High School.

Keith rushed upstairs to his room passing by the servant thinking about where the phonebook would be.

Mmm.Mm.Mmm. He hummed one his favorite rap tunes as he turned the pages of the phone book. He thought of his old friends and how he only saw them on the weekends now. His family owned a $400,000 home near the high school. He was one of the few sons of rich African American parents in the area.

Keith was thought as the big man on campus at his last school and wasn't about to give that up. He of course would describe himself as a buff, hot young man. He had no idea where he was going to college and didn't quite care. He only cared about the pretty girls, and the one on his mind was Laura. He had just broken up with his ex, Janelle. That virgin, he thought.

His finger finally ran across the "T's." Timberwood…

"Hello is Laura there?" Keith asked.

"Hold on. I will get her, Nate," Laura's mother said.

"Um. This isn't. Oh well," he whispered.

"Oh hi, Nate. No, he didn't take my number. I'll talk to you later. Big quiz in math tomorrow," Laura said quickly.

"No wait," Keith pleaded.

"What?" she asked.

"This is Keith, sweetie," he said.

"Oh. Oh. I bet you are looking for my notes," she replied.

"I was hoping you could come home with me tomorrow and help me to catch up with my homework. What do you think?" he asked.

"I can't, but if you really need to be caught up. When's your lunch hour?" she asked.

Knowing that if she keeps this relationship on the down low so she won't be embarrassed and likely to screw up.

"Block A, you?" Keith replied.

"Me too. See you then. Bye," she said hanging up.

She hung up the phone abruptly and breathed a sign of relief. Why me…she thought as her cheeks blushed.

Keith listened as the dial tone rung in his ear.

"Damn it. I always choose the shy girls," he thought to himself. The shy girls are always the smartest and the hottest. What is up with that?

He slammed the phonebook back in his top desk drawer, knowing he needed Laura's help to pass history class and go to college like his parents wanted him to.

"Damn parents, trying to make me study and bring up my average," he thought to himself.

He knew even if he brought up his grades, he would still be starting college a semester behind everyone else his age.

"We'll just see what happens at lunch," he murmured as he closed his eyes and drifted off later that night.

Laura stretched out her joints. She glanced around her realizing that today at lunch…she would have to figure out how to react around Keith.

At least Nate won't know, she smiled. He ate lunch during a different period.

She threw on jeans and a t-shirt knowing exactly how hot today would be.

She strolled into lunch block A and sat down at her usual table with Ginger and Sally. Ginger, Sally and Laura have been eating lunch together since the semester started. Ginger and Sally were in Laura's math class. The three of them were assigned seats next to each other on the first day of class. Her math teacher always made sure everyone found out at least three things about each classmate and reported them back in "Meet and Greet" portion of the first class of each semester. Laura had had Mr. Sandler for other math classes before and hated this part of the class. Ginger, Sally and Laura met each other first and put together a plan so they could talk to fewer kids each by sharing the facts they found out. Ever since then they have been studying for quizzes, eating lunch together and passing notes.

Keith stood in the back of the lunchroom, seeing the group of popular students he had eaten lunch with the past two days. The annoying girl whom had an obvious crush on him, Lisa, waved and motioned for him to come on over.

Keith smiled and walked up.

"Sorry I can't join you all for lunch today. I must bother some smart girl for her notes in history class, being behind and all. Bye," he told them.

"Oh. Don't be long. Come back for some dessert," Lisa said.

Keith had always liked the girls who played hard to get. He liked the excitement of the hunt. He enjoyed feeling like a tiger figuring out how to pounce on his prey. Spotting Laura and her friends in the corner, he rehearsed his opening as he walked over and tapped her on the shoulder.

"Nate, are you cutting class again?" Laura asked.

"Nope. You know sweetie that is the second time you have mistaken me for your friend, Nate." Keith said.

"Oh, hi Keith. Listen why don't you give me just a second okay," she asked.

Laura turned to Ginger and Sally as Keith nodded and went to the line to grab his lunch.

"Explain your gentleman caller. Your very hot gentleman caller," Sally ordered.

"He looks like some famous rap star or something. Is he new here?" Ginger asked.

"He sure is. He wants my help in history class. You know another one that needs to borrow my brain," Laura replied.

"Most of them aren't this cute, though. You should give him a chance, Laura," Sally said.

"I'm so embarrassed, every time I see him. I'm afraid I'm going to scare him away. Besides, he is rich I'm sure he will find out that I'm not and move on. It's just that easy," Laura said.

"Wait a minute. Now what's his name?" Sally asked.

Sally was always up on the new gossip, since her sister had somehow squeezed her way into the "in" crowd. Her sister, being a freshman, just had to bat her eyes and deny relationship to Sally, and she was in. Sally had learned how to listen in on her sister's late night phone chats.

"Keith," Laura answered.

"Keith Johnson? His dad is a U.S. senator, and they bought some expensive house on Oak Lane, I think," Sally said.

"See. I knew he was rich," Laura added.

"I have to listen up for his name next time it enters the conversation," Sally said.

"Excuse me," Keith said.

"Back so soon," Laura chuckled.

"I can't stay away from you long. Looks like we don't have much time left of lunch break. We can meet later also," he said.

"I guess. In the library after school? I'll just have to find a ride home," she said.

"No problem. Sweetie. I'll take you home. Great. I'll see you then. I'm going to go eat over there," he said.

He motioned to another table. Laura knew that was a table where the kids with money ate together.

"Well, he ran off fast. Interesting. He talked mainly business, yet flirted with you. He sure is an interesting character. You'd better watch out," Sally recommended.

"You know we can't trust them. They have screwed sweet girls like us over too many times," Ginger said.

"I guess, but he is so dreamy. He seems too new, maybe he hasn't been corrupted yet," Laura said.

"Maybe. I would stick to public areas to begin with though. Good thinking on the library," Sally said.

Ring. Ring. As the class bell rang, the girls parted and ran off to class.

Laura collected her notes together as she waited for Keith to arrive. He was only five minutes late, but she figured he might have forgotten and then worried about how to get home.

Keith tapped Laura on the shoulder.

"Sorry I'm late. I brought you something, but you can't get caught with it. Let's move to a more hidden spot," Keith said.

"What? Why? Here is fine," she proclaimed.

"Trust me. It will be better over there," he said.

Keith helped Laura gather her stuff, and they moved to a table located in the back of the library.

"Here," he said.

He handed her a soft drink and box of candy.

"I wasn't sure what you wanted, but we should be here awhile. You know," Keith said.

"We'll get caught, you know. There is no food allowed here," Laura said.

"You have to be squeaky. Don't worry about it. I'll take care of it," he said.

"Alright. So where did your class leave off for history?" she asked.

Keith and Laura got down to business and concentrated on history for about 30 minutes before Keith distracted her.

"Thanks, I think that helps a lot," Keith said.

"Well, we just got started," Laura said.

Keith interrupted her.

"Well we can take a little break if you don't mind. What your plans for prom?" he asked.

Prom was around two weeks away. Laura had missed her junior formal, knowing that you only went if you had a date. Laura, who had never had her first kiss or a real date, had no plans for prom.

"Nothing yet. You?" she asked.

"I was hoping I could take you. What time should I pick you up? I'll take care of all of the details," he said.

"Well, let me think about it and get back to you on that one, but we should get back to history. You have a lot to catch up on," she said.

Laura knew it was obvious that she changed the subject because she was nervous, but she didn't care. This could be her first date ever. She had goosebumps running up and down her arms. She was having trouble composing herself in front of him, as they continued to discuss the missing history he needed to pass the next test and probably the class. Two hours later, she realized they talked very easily, and Keith was actually interested in her and paying full attention. Not only was he planning on acing history, he was planning on dating Laura soon.

"Well honey, I think that is plenty for today. Why don't you come over for some dinner? You must be hungry. I'll take you home right afterwards," Keith said.

"I guess dinner would be okay," Laura said.

Meanwhile...

Sally was home waiting for her sister to get on the phone. She thought to herself I need to find some dirt out on this new kid before he turns my friend into a popular girl. Then it will just be Ginger and me. That would be boring.

Keith opened the car door for Laura. He walked around to his door and climbed in.

"Ready? What are you hungry for?" Keith asked.

"I bet your mom has already begun something, right? Whatever has been made is fine," Laura said.

"No. No. You get whatever you want. I'm going to call in our orders to our cook right now," he said.

Keith reached for his cell phone. Laura had only seen cell phones being carried by popular kids, but never this close up. She smiled.

"What about chicken? Does the cook have any special recipes?" she asked.

"I'll surprise you. Hold that thought. Cover your ears, while I order," Keith said.

Laura pressed her hands over her ears, trying not to laugh. She hadn't done that since she was in elementary school with Nate. Laura loved surprises. She couldn't figure out why Keith was being so nice to her. Keith knowing how good his family's cook was with Chinese cuisine ordered two plates of sweet and sour chicken. This recipe was one of his favorites, and he hoped Laura would like it. He hung up the phone and turned his attention to driving to his house.

She removed her hands from her ears.

"All set?" Keith said.

"I've got everything," Laura said. "You?"

"Sure thing. Dinner is ordered! I hope you are hungry," he said.

"You bet. How far do you live from here?" she asked.

"Oh about 10 minutes, in one of those new neighborhoods," he said.

"WOW," she said.

She gasped as they pulled up into his driveway.

"Your house is huge," she said.

"Yeah. Ridiculous, really. I'm an only child, and my parents work all the time. Most of the time the only people home are the servants," he said.

"Well, it is beautiful. It's just larger than I expected," she added.

"Come inside. I'll give you the grand tour," he said.

Keith and Laura stepped into a three-story house. It opened with large foyer and a grand staircase. Off to the left was an open doorway leading to the kitchen and a dining room. Off to the right was an open doorway opening to a living room. The living room featured beautiful maroon couches and decorative pillows and blankets. A brick fire place topped off the room's effect on Laura. She knew she was out of place and very uncomfortable. A door in the back of the room led outside to the pool and deck area. The second floor featured Keith's large room, office and bathroom on the left side. On the right side, was a bonus room and a den. On the third floor, his parents had their bedroom, a bathroom and an office on each side, one for each of them. Keith didn't take Laura to the third floor. She could only imagine how those rooms looked. He ushered her into the dining room for dinner.

"The house is so quiet. Where are we supposed to sit?" she asked.

"We'll sit together at this end. No need in spreading ourselves out," he said.

"Do we need to help them with anything?" she asked.

"Of course not. You will get served on hand and foot here. They will make you feel like the princess you are," he said.

"That's sweet of you, but it's not necessary at all," she said.

"I'll be right back," he said.

Laura smiled. She felt overwhelmed. She waited patiently, but wished that this whole situation would end soon. She knew the pressure was getting to her. Is this for real? Does he really like me? Is he playing games, in order to embarrass a poor girl? What's going on here? Should I run away? Should I stay? Do I trust him?

These questions filled her head, as the servant set the table with dinner.

"It looks delicious. Thank you," he said to the servant.

"Yes, thank you," Laura added.

"Well, dig in," he said.

The two began to eat. Laura loved Chinese food and thought this was just scrumptious.

"What do you think?" Keith asked.

"You sure know how to please a girl's appetite," Laura said.

Laura smiled. She couldn't believe how calm she seemed now. That remark just rolled off her tongue.

"Thank you, darling. I knew you would like it. She is a great cook especially with Chinese food," Keith said.

"I agree," she said.

"You are welcome for dinner anytime. I usually eat alone with the TV on," he said.

He pointed towards the corner where the TV was located. Laura smiled and picked up her fork to continue eating the food. Keith smiled as he thought about the possible future of their relationship. What could happen next?

Chapter 2

Laura rolled over and continued to dream about Keith. Friday night dinner was just delightful at his house. She was in the middle of an endless dream...

It was prom night, and Keith and Laura were dancing in middle of the dance floor. The floor sparkled. Lights reflected off of the dance floor. Everyone was standing in a large circle around the dance floor staring at the happy couple in amazement.

Laura and Keith smiled and twirled around and around in each other's arms. Laura's long light purple dress and Keith's black suit with purple tie complimented each other as the background music played.

Laura finally woke up around 11 a.m. Saturday morning with the biggest smile on her face. She awoke to the phone ringing.

"Hello," Laura said yawning.

"Did I wake you?" Sally asked.

"Yes," Laura answered.

"From anything important, I want the juice," Sally said.

"Just this dream, about me and Keith," Laura answered.

"Fantasy, I hope. I have the 411 on him," Sally said.

"Spill," Laura said.

"Well, his dad was just elected to the U.S. Senate and will be living up there during the session, while Keith and his mom continue to live here. He went to Southberry High School before transferring here. He dated a lot of girls there, but most recently he dated this girl for three months and broke up with her before being transferred," Sally said.

"So he is a big man on campus?" Laura asked.

"Sounds that way, but this is the juiciest part. He broke up with his last girlfriend because she would not sleep with him. This piece of evidence was heard from the mouth of one of his old friends, who passed it down to my sister. Therefore, you better watch out," Sally said.

"I don't know Sally. He has been nothing, but a gentleman towards me. I mean I had dinner at his house, and he never laid a hand on me. I was there for like four hours before he took me home. We ate dinner and talked forever. Before that we met in the library for two hours to study history. He has been a perfect gentleman. Are you sure about that information?" Laura asked.

"Well, I mean what I hear on the phone is sometimes gossip, but usually it's true. What if it is true? This could be dangerous," Sally said.

"Really? I don't know it's just sex," Laura commented.

"It would be your first time, silly. That's huge. It should be with someone you love. Not to mention, with all the diseases that are out now," Sally said.

"I want it to be with someone I love, but what if Keith is the one? Besides we could get tested first," Laura said.

"Guys usually have a hard time with the idea of getting tested. I have researched that one, not only online, but through the grapevine," Sally said.

"I guess. I have to think about it as our relationship continues. Oh. He invited me to prom," Laura said.

"What did you say?" Sally asked.

"I said I would think about it. I just met him, you know," Laura said.

"True. Have you asked your mom?" Sally said.

"No. I haven't even thought about it till now. You are the first one I've told," Laura said.

"Oh. Wow. Me before Nate. That's a first," Sally said.

"Well you called first, so I guess you get first dibs on everything new today," Laura said.

"Yeah. So anything else?" Sally asked.

"Keith lives in this huge, elaborate house," Laura said.

"I bet. According to my sources, only his close friends have visited, meaning you are a 'close friend.' How close?" Sally asked.

"We are just friends and possible dates for prom. No kiss, no hug, well there was a handshake," Laura said.

"Well, I have a feeling he will start putting the moves on you soon. He digs you. He was flirting with you at lunch," Sally said.

"Yeah. He flirted with me all night last night," Laura said.

"See. Be careful. I don't want you to get hurt like his last girlfriend. I need to find out who she is and get some insider information," Sally said.

"That would help. You sound like an investigative reporter," Laura said.

"Yeah. I enjoy doing this stuff," Sally said.

"Maybe you should pursue it as a career," Laura said.

"Nah. There is no money in journalism. I'm going to use my brains and go into engineering instead," Sally said.

"Interesting. I'm not sure what I want to do yet. I guess I'll figure that out in college," Laura said.

"You know Ginger and I got accepted to Georgia Tech. We will have to keep in touch. You can't split up the girls," Sally said.

"No. I'll have big phone bills because of you two and Nate, too. I can't wait. But in the meantime, we'll enjoy high school," Laura said.

"You bet. Well, my mom is calling me for breakfast. Keep me updated. Bye girl," Sally said.

Laura hung up the phone. She knew Sally was trustworthy and usually collected true information, but her experience made her want to give Keith another chance. She knew she would have to watch her step, because all of this was new territory. Laura had never even had her first kiss. All of it pretty much scared her, which is why she tried to play off sex as not being a big thing, when in fact; she didn't even want to consider the possibilities of this relationship.

"Laura, are you up yet?" her mom yelled.

Laura heard her mom from a distance. She hurried to get dressed and ran down the hall for breakfast. She knew her mom was cooking her Saturday favorite, blueberry pancakes.

"Yummy! Yummy!" Laura exclaimed.

"Well, good morning, Sleepyhead. So do you want to tell me about this boy, who kept you out till 10 p.m. last night?" her mom asked.

"I guess so. Well. Keith is this new kid in school. His dad serves in the U.S. Senate," Laura responded.

"What's his last name? Maybe I know the senator," her mom asked.

"Johnson," Laura said.

"Oh, yes. I do. Nice guy. I voted for him," her mom said.

"Keith was behind in history, so I agreed to help him catch up, and we became friends. He asked me to go to prom with him. I really want to go," Laura said.

"Well, I will have to discuss it with your father, and if he says yes, you and I will have to do some budget shopping. Not to mention. We need to meet this boy. When is prom?" her mom asked.

"Two weeks away. But I have to tell him my answer so he can buy tickets on Monday," Laura said.

"Well, eat your breakfast, and we will call him later today. Your dad should be available for a discussion soon," her mom said.

Keith rolled over and got up. He was hoping the phone would ring soon with a phone call from Laura. He walked down to the kitchen and ordered eggs, sausages and biscuits. He waited sipping his orange juice and staring at the television. He realized his parents wouldn't be home this weekend. His mom had gone up to Washington D.C. for some conference and to be with his dad. He frowned. He needed to figure out some stuff to do as soon as possible. Keith hated sitting in the house with just himself and the servants.

Meanwhile...

Sally was trying to plan how she was going to get a hold of Keith's ex-girlfriend. She knew she had heard her first name last night, but she had trouble remembering it. She never took notes or tape-recorded her sister's phone calls, because then there would be evidence of her listening in. She was forced to be able to remember everything that was said. Therefore, it was easy for her to forget a name.

Hmmm.

Jessica, no Rachel. Oh what letter did it start with? Come on think. Think Sally think.

It started with a...

Yes a J.

Jennifer no. It was more original.

Janelle.

Wait that's it. Now I need a Southberry phone book. Wait, my cousin, Jen, goes there.

"Hello. Is Jen there?" Sally asked.

"This is she," Jen answered.

"It's your cousin, Sally. Listen I don't have much time to talk. This is very important. Can you look someone up in your school directory for me?" Sally said.

"Yeah, let me get it," Jen said. "Okay, I got it."

"This might take you a while. The girls' first name is Janelle. I don't have a last name, and I don't know what grade she is in," Sally said.

"I'm going to have to call you back for that. Why do you need this?" Jen asked.

"Well, I'm sworn to secrecy. Please. I'll owe you one," Sally said.

"Give me a few. You owe me big. Bye," Jen said.

Sally hung up the phone and began pacing back and forth. She knew if she told Jen the story, her sister might find out. She also knew that Jen might know more details, but she could not risk losing her only source.

Pace. Pace. Pace.

Sally decided she had to get her mind off of this, so she went to eat breakfast.

Twenty minutes later. The phone rang. Sally jumped up and grabbed it.

"Hello," Sally said.

"Sally. There are three girls with that name," Jen said.

"Okay. I've got a pen. I need the name, phone number and address," Sally said.

Meanwhile...

Laura waited patiently in her room. She was doing homework at the same time, while her parents discussed the possibility of her going to prom for two and a half hours.

She pondered question of why it was taking so long, several times while she was doing her homework.

Meanwhile...

Keith was home making a list of homework to do, friends to call in order to fill his weekend agenda. Although he was busy planning, he kept pondering why Laura had not called yet. It was driving him nuts. He had been up for only a few hours, but it seemed like forever for him.

Meanwhile...

"Thanks, Jen. I owe you," Sally said.

"I want a meeting with you next weekend. Got it. I'll call you later to set it up. At the meeting, you better fill me in. Bye," Jen said.

Sally thought to herself—I can't fill her in. I'll have to be crafty to get out of that one. But what am I going to do with this information now. Maybe I could pretend to sell Girl Scout cookies or I could call and be selling prom tickets. Wait. That is brilliant. I'll sell prom tickets and be a nosy girl.

Sally wondered if her plan would work. She wondered if the girls would talk to her at all, let alone tell her why their ex-boyfriends left them. She knew this was a hard scenario and would require reinforcements. She needed Ginger.

"Is Ginger there?" Sally asked.

"Hold on. Ginger pick up the phone and make it quick," Ginger's mom said.

"Hello," Ginger said. "Sally, my mom is taking me to a debate practice soon. What's up?"

"Okay. Let me fill you in quick. Keith asked Laura to prom, but I found out that he broke up with his last girlfriend over the matter of sex. I got numbers for all the girls at Southberry named Janelle, being that was his girlfriend's name. I need to get to the bottom of this and find out the truth for Laura's sake. Can you help me?" Sally asked.

"Wow. That's tough. You bet. I'll call you back later tonight. Don't do anything till you hear from me. Some of the people on my debate team go there. I'll see what I can find out. Bye," Ginger said.

Sally smiled as she hung up. She knew that she and Ginger made a good team. It was time for them to work their magic for Laura's sake.

Meanwhile...

Finally, Laura got a knock on her door.

"Laura, honey, open up," her mom said.

"Yes. Please, say it is a yes," Laura said.

"In order for it to be a yes, we must meet him first and then we will decide. That is the best deal I could get out of your father. I know how first crushes are. I remember my first crush," her mom said.

"Well, thanks mom. I better call him," Laura said.

Laura cut off her mom and dashed for the phone.

"Keith?" Laura asked.

"Yes. Who is this? Such a sweet voice," Keith answered.

"It's Laura. I have an answer for you on prom," she declared.
"Really?" he said with surprise.
"My parents said they must meet you first before they decide. Want to come over for dinner tomorrow?" Laura asked.
"Sure. How's six o'clock?" he asked.
"Let me check. Hold on," she said.
Laura put down the phone and asked her mom.
"Sounds good. Do you remember how to get here?" she asked.
"Yes. I'll see you then. I have a lot to catch up on with all of that history you gave me yesterday," he said.
"Okay, bye," she said.
Laura hung up and continued working on her homework.
Keith hung up the phone. He picked up his pen and the agenda he was making and added his new Sunday plans. He circled them with a smile. He knew he would have to put on a show and win their approval, so he could move forward with his and Laura's relationship.
He was very excited. He finished the rest of his list and started making phone calls in order to make plans for tonight.
Ring. Ring. Ring.
Keith finally reached all of his friends and put together exciting plans for his Saturday night out.

Chapter 3

Sunday…

"Ready, Laura. Time to go," her mom said.

"Coming," she answered.

Laura's mom was a professional budget shopper. She had done research for sales and put together a list of places to hit and when to hit them. Knowing the family's budget, she was prepared to find everything Laura needed for prom for under $150.

Laura and her mom arrived at a local clothing store. Knowing her daughter's size, her mom quickly scanned the room for sales racks and started fishing for nice dresses.

"You take that rack. I've got this one," her mom said.

Laura nodded.

Laura felt so embarrassed having to dig through racks for clothing. She wished her family wasn't on such a tight budget. Her dad had worked for Georgia Pacific for years, and mom was a budget buyer, otherwise known as a housewife. Laura thumbed through the selection on her rack, looking for something.

"How's this?" Laura's mom asked.

She was holding a dark purple dress with a rather simple sparkle design.

"It's nice," she said.

Laura was not excited by the poor selection, even though the dress was nice enough for prom.

"Go try it on. It's only $42," her mom said.

Laura nodded.

"I know you are embarrassed by what we must do, but I would appreciate it if you would at least try," her mom said.

"Be right back," Laura said.

Laura stood in the mirror of the dressing room thinking to herself about the dress she was wearing.

"Hmmm. This is nice, and I do like the color. It's not overly stylish, but it will work, if there is nothing better," Laura walked over to see her mom.

"Was that so hard? You look very pretty in that dress. I found two others while you were in there," her mother said.

Laura picked the two dresses out of her mom's hands and walked back into the dressing room. She slipped into the next dress. This one had navy blue with spaghetti straps; black patch across the breast and then the navy blue material cascaded down to her ankles. The next dress was red. It had also had spaghetti straps and then it crisscrossed back and forth with the material making the dress rather form fitting and appealing to Laura's body.

"Mom, how's this one?" Laura asked.

"I like that one the best. Let me see the tag. That's a steal for $55. It's a winner. What do you think?" her mother asked.

"I like it," Laura said.

She smiled.

Laura removed the dress and put back on her regular clothing. Her mom paid and the two of them drove off for a shoe store.

Meanwhile...

"Hey, Ginger. Thanks for coming over today," Sally said. "Any luck on finding out who we should call first?"

"Yes! Janelle Thompson," Ginger said.

"I've got her number," Sally said.

"Well, I have a plan," Ginger said.

"Come down the hall to my room. Would you like something to drink?" Sally asked.

"Sure," Ginger said.

Sally went to the kitchen and grabbed two soft drinks and her list of phone numbers. She ran down to her room.

"So what's the plan?" Sally asked.

Sally was excited about getting to the truth. She enjoyed investigating issues like this.

"A friend of mine attends Southberry High School and has an English class with this girl. I was thinking we use her as an insider. I explained to her our situation and how we are concerned about Laura and how this guy could hurt her. She agreed to call Janelle and ask for help in English class, meet with her and try to get on the subject of ex-boyfriends. She should be calling here any minute with an update," Ginger said.

"You are brilliant. I hope this will work. Laura is probably out shopping for a prom dress right now. You know that guy has been nothing but a gentleman. I fear it is an act," Sally said.

Ring. Ring. Ring.

"Hello," Ginger said.

"Ginger?" Jamie asked.

"Yes," Ginger said.

"It's Jamie. I just got off the phone with Janelle," Jamie said.

Ginger nodded.

"She agreed to meet with me in an hour at Starbucks down the street. I told her since we had a quiz this week that I wanted to meet as soon as possible. I'll call you back in a few hours. I have to get my notes and thoughts together in order to this. And Ginger, you owe me," Jamie said.

"I know. How about this? Coffee is on me; just tell me later how much I owe you. Okay?" Ginger asked.

"Thanks. I'll call you later," Jamie said.

Jamie and Ginger hung up, and then Ginger explained to Sally what was going to happen later tonight. Sally screamed with joy. She loved the excitement of an investigation.

Meanwhile…

Laura had found a dress, shoes and arranged to pick up a boutonnière all for under $150.

"I guess we are done. I'll do your hair, and we can do your make up together. I guess that just leaves transportation up to this boy. Let's get home for dinner. You know Keith is supposed to be coming over," Laura's mom said.

"Right. Mom, can you pick up some magazine or book for different hairdos tomorrow? I want to try something different," Laura said.

Her mom nodded.

Laura and her mom left the store and hurried home to fix dinner. Keith was due for dinner in an hour and a half.

Meanwhile…

Keith was trying to decide what to wear in order to impress the parents. He had been working and reworking the future scenario out in his head. He thought back to other times he had met girls' parents and impressed them with his charm. He remembered the remarks he said and the gestures he made. He smiled as he continued getting ready, knowing he was ready for this task.

Meanwhile...

Jamie climbed into her car and drove over to Starbucks to meet with Janelle. Jamie arrived and sat down at a table, waiting for her to arrive.

Meanwhile...

"Mom, the salad is ready," Laura said.

"Good. Set it over there," her mother said.

She pointed to the countertop.

Laura's mom pulled out the pork chops to glaze them. She glazed each pork chop and set the pan on a hot plate next to the salad. Laura pulled out all of the salad dressings and arranged the cooked platters on the counter. She then set the table.

The doorbell rang. Ring. Ring.

Laura's dad, being one for intimidation, jumped up and opened the door.

"Hi, there. You must be Keith. Did you bring a dessert?" her dad asked.

"No, sir. Sorry. Was I supposed to?" Keith asked.

"No. I just thought you might be that considerate," her dad said.

"I'm sorry. I brought flowers for Laura, though," Keith said.

"I guess that will have to do," her dad said.

"Leave him alone, dad. Keith, come on in. Thank you for the flowers. My dad likes giving people a hard time," Laura said.

"Well. He does a great job," Keith replied.

"Thank you. I am a master at raising three kids," her dad said.

"Right," Laura chuckled.

She rolled her eyes.

"Dinner's ready," her mom said.

"Sounds like we are being summoned," her dad said.

"Right this way," Laura pointed.

"Mrs. Timberwood, everything looks delicious," Keith said.

"Thank you. Grab yourself a plate," she said.

"No, Ladies, first. Laura, can I make you a plate," Keith said.

"That's not necessary, but okay," Laura said.

"I'll go last. I need to get some things from down the hall," her mom said.

"Want to grab me a plate to, while you are at it?" her dad asked.

"Walter, get your own plate and leave the boy alone," her mom yelled as she walked down the hall.

He nodded.

Meanwhile...

Jamie spread her notes on the table along with her coffee. Janelle tapped her on the shoulder.

"Jamie?" Janelle asked.

"Yes. You recognized who I was," Jamie said.

"Yeah. I can't stay long hon. I have to get back for dinner," Janelle said.

"Well, have a seat. Did you want anything? It's on me for dragging you out here," Jamie said.

"Sure. I'll have an espresso," Janelle said.

Jamie nodded and got up to go get it.

Janelle looked at Jamie's notes while she waited. She was trying to figure out why Jamie would ask a C student to help her. She looked like an A student.

"Here, you go. Got an important dinner date tonight?" Jamie said.

"Yeah. My new boyfriend is coming over for dinner," Janelle said.

"How long have you two been going out?" Jamie asked.

"Two weeks," Janelle replied.

"Are you two ready for him to meet the parents?" Jamie asked.

"I think so. He's a sweetheart. He really respects me, unlike my last boyfriend," Janelle said.

"What do you mean?" Jamie asked.

"Don't tell me. You haven't heard the rumors. I thought everyone knew why Keith broke it off with me," Janelle said.

"No. I missed that gossip," Jamie said.

"While, he was my first boyfriend, first kiss and almost my first. He tried to rape me at prom last year. I was able to scream loud enough for my friend, Brad to hear me and beat up Keith. It's taken me this long to move on," Janelle said.

"Is he a sexually active guy?" Jamie asked about Keith.

"I would imagine so. He's an actor and a user, if you know what I mean," Janelle said.

"That's horrible. I didn't want to drag up old memories. There was a reason I asked you here," Jamie said.

Janelle nodded.

"Were you in class Friday?" Jamie asked.

Janelle nodded.

Jamie had missed English class due to a doctor's appointment. Janelle explained to her the discussion done on Friday, and Jamie copied her notes even though her best friend, Karen, another A student had already faxed her copies. Jamie said thank you, and Janelle ran off to go home. After Jamie gathered all of her notes and the receipt, she left for Sally's house.

Meanwhile...

Laura's family and Keith sat down for dinner. Her dad had decided to continue giving Keith a hard time in order to get his questions answered.

"So Keith. I understand you invited my daughter to prom. Why?" her dad asked.

"Sir. I beg your pardon, but think the easier question is why not. Your daughter is a beautiful, smart woman. I also enjoy her company," Keith said.

Laura smiled and then quickly turned blank noticing her dad was just getting started.

"Uh huh. You are quite the charmer. So tell about yourself and your family," her dad said.

Keith started on his life story, while Jamie pulled to Sally's driveway. Nate and his mom also pulled in across the street. He had just gotten home from visiting his dad for the weekend. His parents had been divorced for three years now. He noticed Keith's car as they pulled in. Knowing it would be rude to run in, even though he wanted to, he just made a mental note to call Laura later and harass her.

Jamie rang the doorbell. Ring. Ring.

"I'm coming. Hi. Jamie," Sally said as she opened the door. "I didn't expect you to come over."

"Well, it's not out of my way. Besides Ginger owes me money, and I'm low on gas," Jamie said.

"Come on back. Can I get you anything?" Sally asked.

"I can't stay long. But I have big news," Jamie said.

Ginger ran down the hall.

"What do I owe you? What's the big news?" Ginger asked.

"He attempted to rape her prom night and didn't succeed because a friend of hers rescued her. You owe me roughly six dollars," Jamie said.

Ginger handed her six dollars.

"I have to run. I have so much homework to do. Nice doing business with you," Jamie said.

"Thanks," Ginger and Sally said.

"Oh my God. Rape," Sally screamed.

Her mouth dropped staring at Ginger.

"We have to call Laura right now. Where's the phone?" Ginger asked.

"I'll get it," Sally said.

Ring. Ring. Ring.

The phone rang at Laura's house.

"Keith, do you mind if I grab that?" Laura's mom asked.

"Not at all. Go right ahead," Keith said.

Laura's mom picked up the phone.

"Hello?" she asked.

"Is Laura there?" Sally asked.

"I'm sorry, but we have company over for dinner. Can she call you back?" Laura's mom said.

"I guess, but this is really important," Sally said.

"I'll have her call you back right after dinner, unless it is an emergency," Laura's mom said.

"Oh. It's not an emergency, but make sure she calls Sally right away," Sally said.

"I will. Bye," Laura's mom replied.

Laura's mom hung up the phone and glanced over at Laura. She was drooling over Keith as he continued answering her dad's questions.

"Laura, that was Sally. She said it is important that you call her after dinner," her mom said.

Laura nodded.

"Interesting. Now that we know all about Keith, his life story and his parents. What are your intentions for prom, young man?" her dad asked.

Laura's mouth dropped as her dad finished his sentence. Keith knew this question was coming, and he was ready for it. This question was on of his favorite parts of the hunt.

"Well, sir. I was planning on picking up Laura in my car around 6 p.m. with flowers. I was going to take her to dinner before the prom and right home afterwards. But my intention as you say is to make sure Laura has a wonderful time. She told me that she didn't go to her junior prom, so I want to make sure she has a remarkable senior prom," Keith said.

Laura smiled. Keith knew that no one knew what he really meant by "remarkable." Laura's dad appreciated that he said he would bring Laura right home afterwards and that her happiness was his main priority, but he wondered about his sincerity as he tried to figure out his next question. Keith waited quietly for his next question. He knew that fathers appreciated the time to think their questions through.

Ginger waited patiently for the phone to ring, while Sally paced back and forth. Nate stuffed down food while he waited for Keith to leave Laura's house.

Laura waited with a scared look on her face, as her dad thought of a way to intimidate Keith.

"Walter, leave him alone. You have quizzed him enough. He seems like a gentleman and genuinely cares about Laura. He has my approval to be Laura's date for the prom," her mom said.

"Thank you, Mrs. Timberwood," Keith said.

Laura looked over at her dad and stared at him trying to give him to his approval.

"Alright. I can't disappoint my little girl. You can go with him," her dad said.

"Thank you, Mr. Timberwood. What time would you like Laura home after prom?" Keith asked.

"I guess I can let her out until midnight. I'm being generous though, so make sure you are on time," her dad said.

"She has no school next day, so I guess that is okay," her mom said.

"Thank you!" Laura smiled.

Keith smiled back.

"Laura, What is your favorite color, you know for your corsage, and would you like me to rent a limo?" Keith asked.

"Red will match my dress. You don't have to rent a limo. I like riding in your car, but can we put the top up? I don't want my hair to be blowing in the wind," Laura said.

"Of course," Keith said.

"Would anyone like dessert?" her mom asked.

Laura's family and Keith enjoyed the dessert. Laura's sibling had been rather quiet during all of dinner, which Laura was happy about. Her younger brother sometimes made rude and annoying remarks, but her older sister was away at college. After dinner, Keith knew it was time for chitchat, unless he got that look. Laura's father gave him that look. Keith was referring to the look of I want you to go, so I can discuss what just happened with my wife and daughter, because I've lost control.

"It was nice of you to come over, but Laura has a lot of homework to do before tomorrow," her dad said.

"Yes, sir. Thank you for dinner. I enjoyed meeting your family, Laura. It was a delicious meal," Keith said.

"Keith, you are welcome to come back anytime," her mom said.

"Dad, my homework is done. Keith can stay longer," Laura said.

"Oh. It's okay. I believe your dad has something he would like to talk to you about. I'll show myself out. Thank you again," Keith said.

Laura walked Keith to the door and gave him a hug. He kissed her on the cheek and then left out in his car.

"Laura, I don't trust him. He is a rich boy," her dad said.

"He acted like a perfect gentleman the whole time, and Laura said he has yet to lay a single hand on her," her mom said.

"Alright. Fine," her dad said.

Her dad walked off mad, after seeing he was overruled. Her mom followed him. Laura wandered down the hall and put her backpack together for school the next day.

A few minutes later, Laura lay down on her bed. Her door was closed so she didn't hear her parents argue about the potential of Keith being a typical high school boy and wanting to only date her for sex. She had also closed her door so no one would bother her.

She laid there for 20 minutes, before she remembered she was supposed to call back Sally. She finally got up and grabbed the telephone and began dialing Sally's number.

Nate had fallen asleep after dinner and just woke up to notice Keith's car missing from Laura's driveway.

"Hello. Is Sally there?" Laura asked.

"Can you hold? I'm on the other line. Sally, one of your dumb friends is on the phone. Use dad's phone to call her back," Sally's sister yelled.

Laura hung up.

"Laura?" Sally said.

Chapter 4

Call waiting beeped on Laura's phone.
"Sally, can you hold for a second?" Laura asked.
"I guess," Sally said.
Laura switched lines.
"Hello," Laura said.
"Hey it's me," Nate said.
"Can I call you right back? Sally said it was important," Laura said.
"Yes," Nate answered.

Nate hung up; disappointed that Sally was taking precedent over him. Laura knew it was Nate since he is the only one that says it's me to her.

"Sally? You there?" Laura asked.
"Yeah. Keith tried to rape his ex at the prom last year," Sally said.
"Are you sure?" Laura asked.
"Yes. Ginger and I used a spy to talk to his ex and find out the truth," Sally said.
"He just seems like such a gentleman," Laura said.
"I know, but guys can play tricks with your mind," Sally said.
"I guess. I just like him so much, and so did my parents, I feel like I should give him a chance. Besides I already brought a dress," Laura said.
"Okay, but Ginger and I will go and keep an eye out on you. How's that?" Sally asked.
"I can do that. We can go shopping Friday night," Ginger said.
"That works. But don't be obvious. I don't want to scare Keith away. Besides Nate should be there too," Laura said.
"True," Sally said.
"Thanks. I really appreciate you two caring about me enough to do this," Laura said.
"No problem. That's what friends are for," Sally said.

Laura, Sally and Ginger changed the topic of their conversation and continued talking. Laura hung up around 20 minutes later and called Nate back.

"Nate?" Laura said.

"Hey girl. How was dinner?" Nate asked.

Laura filled Nate in on dinner with Keith and her parents' reaction.

"Are you going to prom with the kid?" Nate asked.

"Yeah," she said.

"What did Sally say?" he asked.

"She said according to his ex, he tried to rape her," she said.

"Wow," he said.

"I don't know. I really want to give him a chance," she said.

"Well, I'll be there, and so will Sally and Ginger. Don't worry. We will be your bodyguards," he said.

"Just don't be obvious," she said.

"Like I said, don't worry. Listen I have a bunch of homework since I spent most of the weekend at my dad's," he said.

Nate and Laura hung up. Laura got ready for bed.

Meanwhile...

Sally and Ginger set their schedules in order to go prom shopping, and then Ginger left to go home.

Keith arrived home a couple of hours ago, proud of himself for gaining Laura's parents' approval. He sat and watched television studied a little and then hit the sack.

Keith awoke later on from a dream. He sat up thinking about prom last year.

He remembered how Janelle had promised that the night would be special. The two of them proclaimed their love, and he wanted the night to be special. However, she didn't agree with his desires later that night. He felt betrayed after waiting patiently for her to want a serious relationship. He hoped that Laura knew that he honestly liked her and that he cared about her and just wanted her prom to be unforgettable. He rolled over and went back to sleep.

Meanwhile...

Laura kept having nightmares about Keith and prom. She sat up in her bed fed up with the nightmares. She wondered what she should do with the new information. She wondered if it was true or if it was an exaggeration of the truth. Keith was so passionate and open with his feelings. She wondered if it was an act and if he had been sexually active before. She also wondered if it was part of a game like she saw in a movie one time. Laura didn't sleep much the rest of the night.

In Washington D.C...

Keith's mom was visiting his dad. She got to visit him once a month during the session. She wasn't used to the change. They used to see each other every day when they owned a company together not too long ago. That was where they earned their millions.

She was worried about Keith having to handle a new school on his own. Now she worked a full-time job, and his dad was always out of the state. She knew that high school was tough. She hoped he was making new friends and maybe a girlfriend. She also hoped that he was getting by all right in his classes. He really needed to pull up his G.P.A. to make it into a good college. She wanted her son to go to college and find a career and be successful. She figured that she and his father had set a good example of success, but she just regretted not giving him enough of their time. She sighed as Keith's dad arrived home.

"Honey," Keith's mom said.

His dad nodded.

"I think I'm going to take off this upcoming weekend and spend the whole weekend with Keith," she said.

"Keith's a grown man. He can take care of himself," he said.

"True. But I'm his mom, and we have never spent any time together. I've been up here more weekends lately," she said.

"I guess," he said.

"High school is tough especially since it's a new school for him. I just think he might need someone in that big house," she said.

"I guess so," he said.

She nodded.

Monday morning came quick. The kids jumped out of bed and got ready for school. With prom only weeks away, tickets were being sold. Stores experienced long lines and an extra load of phone calls.

The school bell rang as classes began a new week.

Chapter 5

A new week began as Laura crawled out of bed next Monday morning.

Prom was this Saturday night. Laura was excited as she prepared for school.

"Good morning. Can I walk you to your first class?" Keith asked.

"Sure. This way," Laura said.

Keith walked Laura to her science class as they began their week together looking like a couple like last week. Classes started Monday and for Keith, everything went slow until lunch. He walked into the lunchroom to find his normal seat taken.

"What's up with this?" Keith asked.

"You're dating the poor girl," Lisa said.

"Listen, you know the deal. Don't you?" Keith asked.

"Yeah. Everyone knows the deal, but I didn't make the decision. Talk to Corey," she replied.

He nodded.

Keith walked down to the other end of table where Corey sat.

"Hey, Corey," Keith said.

"You are getting too close to the poor girl. You were just supposed to even the score," Corey said.

"I had to earn her trust," Keith said.

"Yeah, but you are falling for her," Corey said.

"I'm not sure about that. However, I know I have played this game before, and in order to win, you have to play it right. That means moving only when you have the right information and making sure you have the trust of all of the players," Keith said.

"I understand you are the expert, but this girl destroys the curve along with her friends every year. Every year, we lose out to them, and it's time they felt some pain. I know you already know this, but I am having trouble waiting. I could see interest in your eyes as your arm went around her this morning," Corey said.

"Don't you know a good actor when you see one. I don't understand, you have never played the game, so how can you tell me what I'm doing wrong. I have her and her parents' right where I want them. Trust me," Keith said.

"I don't know if I can wait any longer. I'll have to think about it," Corey said.

"You can't call the deal off. I know that this will work besides I need the answers to pass my exams," Keith said.

"Then do your job and do it right. Tell, Lisa, you can have your seat back," Corey said.

"I won't fail you," Keith promised.

Keith walked down to the end of the table and spoke to Lisa. He sat down and ate his lunch.

Meanwhile...

Laura was enjoying her lunch with Sally and Ginger.

"Ginger, how's Wednesday night for you?" Sally asked.

"Fine. I'll meet you at your house at six. Do you think we can get a dress and shoes in one night?" Ginger asked.

"Sure. If not we can go back out on Thursday," Sally said.

"Okay. Laura tell us about your dress," Ginger said.

Laura filled Ginger and Sally in on her red dress, her red shoes and the flower she ordered for Keith. She also filled them in on her and Keith's plans for Saturday night.

The lunch bell rang, and they rushed to math class.

The rest of the week continued slowly as Laura, Sally and Ginger waited for Saturday to arrive. Keith spent most of the week with Laura studying and getting to know her better.

On Wednesday night...

Laura went home with Keith, instead of Keith going home with Laura like Tuesday night. At Keith's house, the couple was all alone.

"Laura?" Keith asked.

Laura nodded.

"No studying tonight. Okay. It's just us. What would you like for dinner?" Keith asked.

"Something with meat," she said.

Keith ran downstairs and ordered some pork chops and vegetables. He grabbed a couple sodas and ran back upstairs.

"Laura?" he asked.

Laura nodded.
"Close your eyes and lie down," he ordered.
"What for?" She asked.
"I just wanted to give you a back rub," he said.
She nodded. Laura lay down on her stomach. Keith placed the sodas on the table by the bed and sat down next to Laura. He reached over and began rubbing her back. Laura closed her eyes and allowed the rub to relax her.
But in her head she could hear Sally's voice about the rape. She opened her eyes once again and jumped up.
"Everything okay?" he asked.
"Let's just talk okay," she said.
He nodded.
Keith and Laura spent an hour talking before heading down for dinner.
Meanwhile…
"What do you think of this?" Ginger asked.
"I don't think that is your color. But how about this?" Sally asked.
Ginger and Sally spent three hours shopping for dresses and shoes, before finding matching dresses with shoes.
Sally settled on a sky blue sparkling dress with spaghetti straps and black-strapped shoes. Ginger decided to go with a black dress with a white slash and black shoes.
Satisfied with their choices, the girls arrived home at 10 p.m. and crashed.
Meanwhile…
Laura and Keith finished dinner and walked over to the living room. Keith popped in a video.
The movie began with coming attractions as Keith's arm reached over. Laura saw it coming and wondered what she should do.
In her head, the voices started again. She thought about how there was a maid here, and she was a strong girl. But would Keith do anything to her?
She let the arm rest behind her and just kept an eye on it. She didn't want to push him away, because she was rather interested in Keith. However, the information that Sally and Ginger passed down to her made her nervous to be alone with Keith.

Laura was a virgin in every area of a relationship, not mention that Keith had only kissed her on the cheek thus far. She had no idea what to do in most of these situations. She was excited about the possibility of considering Keith as her first boyfriend, but she didn't know how to handle it or how to act.

She wanted to consider him a boyfriend, but she wanted his approval. She was excited about the possibilities of their relationship and its future.

He is so hot and sweet, she thought to herself.

Finally the movie began, and Laura turned her attention to the movie.

Keith watched her facial expression as the movie began. It hadn't changed. Laura seemed to be deep in thought. He considered all of his options before reaching his arm over. Part of him wanted to stop the movie and directly move their relationship full drive to the intimate level, but he decided that slow was a better option. He wondered what Laura was thinking about. He worried about his deal with Corey.

Can I go through with this? Will it work this time versus last time? Do I need to go through with this? Is it worth it? Should I hurt Laura like that? Do I truly have feelings for her? Can I wait?

Keith looked over at Laura's face, noticing that it still lacked expression. He smiled at her catching her eye, and she smiled back.

His smile caused Laura to feel more comfortable. She could see truth in that smile, which causes her to question Sally and Ginger's news. She continued to focus on the movie hoping it would take her mind off of all her questions.

Keith thought to himself, well my smile seemed to relax her. He hoped that meant that he could jolt the relationship just a little later.

The movie continued to play.

Meanwhile…

Nate decided he needed more information from Sally and Ginger in order for all of them to protect Laura on prom night. He picked up the phone and called Sally.

"Sally?" Nate said.

"Yes, who is this?" Sally asked.

"It's Nate," he answered.

"I meant to call you. We need to plan out our spy plan for prom night," she said.

"We sure do. Can you tell me everything you know first though?" he asked.

Sally explained her investigative reporting occurrences from the beginning.

"So it is true, the rape I mean?" he asked.

"Straight from the horse's mouth. I don't know if she reported it or not though. I doubt she did," Sally said.

"I doubt it too," Nate said.

"So, if we are to assume she is telling truth. We have a rather large load to carry," Sally said.

"You bet. I'm very worried about Laura. She spends a large amount of time with him, and she is really new to the relationship world, you know," Nate said.

"Yeah. But I don't think any of us know anything more than she does," Sally said.

"Well, I had a girlfriend last year for around three months. I don't know if Laura told you about that or not. Otherwise, I have had a few dates here and there," he said.

"No. She never mentioned any of that. Maybe you should talk to her. You know guys and their games being that you are one. You also know how a relationship works first hand. Ginger and I have no personal experience in either one of those and while otherwise there is just Laura's family, and I don't want to scare them unless I have concrete evidence like a videotape or cassette tape with voice recordings," she said.

"I agree. I'll call her tonight. She is too good for us to allow some guy to corrupt her. We need a game plan for prom night. We need a map of the facility, and we need to know where they are going for dinner. We also need to know where Keith lives," he said.

"I can take care of all of that. Did the three of us want to meet in order to set up roles?" she asked.

"You bet. Friday night?" he asked.

"Yeah. I'll talk to Ginger and get back to you on that. What's your number?" she asked.

Nate provided Sally with his number and wrapped up the conversation, so he could call Laura.

"Is Laura there?" Nate asked.

"No, Nate. She is out with Keith. She should be home in an hour," Laura's mom said.

"Just tell her I called. Thank you," he said.

Nate hung up and crossed his fingers that Keith would keep his hands to himself that night.

Meanwhile...

"Ginger?" Sally said phoning Ginger.

"Hold on," Ginger's mom said.

She ran down the hall and told Ginger to pick up the phone.

"Hello," Ginger said.

"It's Sally. I just got off the phone with Nate and filled him in on everything. He plans to sit down with Laura and talk about relationships from a guy's point of view, and we decided that we needed to meet Friday in order to plan prom night operation," Sally said.

"Good. I'm open all night. Just call me. I have to get off the phone though. You and I have so much homework," Ginger said.

"I know, but I figured this was important," Sally said.

"It is. I'm just worried," Ginger said.

"Don't worry about it. If you don't finish, we can do some together at lunch tomorrow. Talk to you later," Sally said.

Sally hang up the phone and went back to her homework assignments.

The movie continued to play in front of Keith and Laura's eyes as the doorbell rang.

Keith paused the movie and jumped up to get the door as his mom was turning the key. He ran back to the living room.

"It's my mom," Keith said.

Laura nodded.

"She wasn't supposed to be here until this weekend," he said.

His mom walked in the house and heard the talking. She began walking towards the living room.

"Keith?" His mom asked.

"In the living room," he said.

"Well hello," she said.

"You're early," he said.

"Yes, I thought you and I could spend some time together tonight and tomorrow night," she said.

"Sure. This is Laura," he said.

Keith's mom was surprised to find a girl home with her son.

"Hi Laura. Keith, I don't think you should have your girlfriend over while I'm not home," she said.

"Mom, let me take Laura home. We'll talk later," he said.

"It was nice meeting you," Laura said.

Keith and Laura walked away. Keith drove Laura home.

"I'm sorry. We can finish the movie later," he said.

"Don't worry about it," she said.

Keith and Laura arrived at her home. Keith walked to the door and went in for the kiss. He planted a nice juicy one right on her lips.

Laura smiled afterwards.

"Keith, does that mean?" she asked.

Keith cut her off.

"Yes, we are officially dating," he said.

"You mean like boyfriend and girlfriend?" she asked.

"Yes. I have to run back. My mom doesn't like to wait," he said.

He planted another one on her lips leaving her speechless and ran off to his car. Keith sped off. Laura just stood there watching the street for a few minutes before opening the door.

Nate had watched the entire incident from his bedroom window.

Laura opened the door to her house and attempted to walk down to her room. Her mom cut her off.

"It is about time you got home. I'm sure you have a lot of homework. Nate called," her mom said.

"I have lots of homework. I'm going to go work on it now," Laura said.

"Wait a minute. Did he kiss you? Your lipstick is smudged," Laura's mom said.

Laura chuckled.

"My little girl is growing up. Maybe we can talk about that later. Okay?" Her mom said.

Laura nodded.

Laura walked down to her room, hoping her mother would forget about the remark she just made. She was not willing to sit through any mother-daughter bonding time about boyfriends and kissing.

She opened the door to her room and locked it behind her. She lay down on her bed, dreaming about the incident that just occurred.

She kept repeating a saying in her head.

He kissed me. He kissed me. He kissed me.

Ten minutes later she decided to move. She got up off the bed and gathered her homework together.

She reached in her backpack and started on her homework.

She had spent 20 minutes on her homework, when the phone rang.

"Is Laura there?" Nate asked.

"Hold on. Laura, pick up the phone," Laura's mom yelled.

"Laura?" Nate asked.

"Yes. Can we talk later? I have a lot of homework," Laura said.

"Come over after school tomorrow. We need to talk before the prom rolls around," he said.

"Okay. Bye," she said.

Nate hung up the phone and turned back to his homework. Laura was up late working on homework and felt sleepy the next morning.

Meanwhile...

Keith arrived home after dropping off Laura with a smile on his face, but he quickly hid his feelings, realizing his mother was inside. The two of them have never been that close. She was preoccupied with her full time job and left little time for them to bond. With his dad, always being in Washington D.C. and before that in Atlanta when they owned their own company, Keith was forced to be raised by the family's maid and butler.

Keith opened the door and shut it quietly behind him. He was not looking forward to talking to his mom. She didn't know how to talk to Keith, since she had been absent from so much of his life. She probably didn't even know his favorite color. He was nervous. He knew his mother had good intentions and loved him simply because he was her son, but he didn't know how to handle the fact that she was here. Keith was used to being on his own and making his own decisions and not caring what others thought, but his mom had just caught him with Laura on the couch watching a movie.

"Keith? Is that you?" she asked.

Keith decided maybe if he went to her now and bailed out for homework, he wouldn't have to suffer much. Keith walked into the living room.

HIS WRATH

"There you are," his mom said.

Keith nodded.

"Are you going to explain yourself, young man?" Keith's mom said.

"Laura and I are friends. She is catching me up on history class, since I started in the middle of class, because I changed schools. We were taking a break when you arrived. I was not expecting you," Keith said.

"Well, the rules have not changed, and in the future, you still can't have the opposite sex over without me or your father home," Keith's mom said.

"But you are never home, which would leave me no social life," Keith said.

"You can take her out and go to her house. However, if you are going to continue seeing this girl, I need to meet with her. We don't need her making rumors like your last girlfriend, you know," she said.

"I know. I'm taking her to prom Saturday, and I can invite her over for dinner Friday, so you can meet her then," Keith said.

"Good idea. She can come over at 7 p.m. I'll make sure I am home by then," she said.

"Good. I have a bunch of homework to finish, so good night," he said.

Keith began walking up the stairs to his room.

"Wait," she screamed.

She realized that Keith has not happy to see her home. He also didn't respond to her call. She just frowned and sat down on the couch.

She wondered how she was going to be a better parent, but she thought it was too late. Keith was going to his high school senior prom Saturday night, meaning he was going to graduate from high school in a matter of a couple months and go off to college. She realized she had missed 18 years of her own son's life, because she was devoted to her work. She also realized that she may have killed any possibility of them being friends in the future. She walked upstairs to the master bedroom and closed the door. She lay down and began crying herself to sleep.

Chapter 6

Keith woke up the next morning to get ready for school.

His mom decided to go into work late in order to make an authentic breakfast of pancakes.

"Want fruit on yours?" she yelled at Keith as she heard him run downstairs to grab his backpack.

"Got to go. I don't want to be late. I have a quiz this morning," he said.

"You have plenty of time," she said.

But Keith had already slid out of the door and into this car, put up the garage door and pulled out, by the time his mom realized he didn't even respond to her last comment.

She sighed. She stopped cooking and rushed out the door to head to work, knowing traffic was already beginning to pile up on her Marietta route.

Keith drove to school. It was Thursday morning. He breathed a sigh of relief as he pulled into a parking space.

I made it out, he said under his breath. Why is she here, he wondered?

He grabbed his bag and headed on to class.

Laura avoided Keith, knowing that he was probably embarrassed about last night, and so was she. Nate had seen the kiss, and she was lucky she had gotten out of a phone call, but why did she have to go over there tonight. She wasn't sure what Nate wanted.

Keith ran up to Laura and knocked her gently after history class.

"You scared me," she said.

"I had to. You seem as if you are on another planet, girlfriend," he said.

Laura had been just called girlfriend for the first time. A feeling of happiness crept over her as she stood in surprise next to Keith. She didn't have the will to respond.

"You know my mother is in town tonight, and she wants to spend some time with me. I guess we can't hang tonight then," Keith said.

"Oh yeah. I have to meet up with Nate for something," she said. Keith nodded.

"Don't go cheating on me during the first week now," he chuckled.

"No. Oh yeah, good one," she said.

She realized he was kidding in the middle of her sentence. The whole idea of having a boyfriend made her too nervous to speak.

The lunch bell rang.

"I'll let you have lunch with the girls. I have to go to the library today," Keith said.

Keith had decided he wasn't sure about his feelings on the deal that he would avoid Corey and study instead of going to lunch.

Laura nodded and smiled. She walked off to her lunch table.

"There's a weird smile on your face, Laura," Sally said.

"I see it too," Ginger said.

"Let me think. I know this look," Sally said.

Sally sat back for a minute before sitting forward and studying Laura's face for a few minutes.

"Uh-huh. Uh-huh. I believe our Laura has fallen in love with this boy," Sally said.

"I think you are right," Ginger said.

"He called me girlfriend today," Laura said.

Erica had been sent as a spy from the popular table. She was walking by at just the right time to hear the entire discussion. She walked a little faster back to her table.

She tapped Corey.

"Corey?" Erica asked.

"Fill us in," Corey said.

"She's in love with him, and he called her, his girlfriend today," Erica said.

"Interesting. It could be too serious or it could be just right. Good work. Same assignment for the rest of the week unless Keith shows up," Corey said.

Erica nodded and sat down at the end of the table.

Meanwhile...

"Girlfriend?" Sally and Ginger asked.

"Yes, just a few minutes ago," Laura said.

Sally and Ginger looked at each other with a scared look on their faces.

"Don't you think that is a little fast?" Sally asked.

"No. We have been friends for the past two weeks, and he waited till last night to kiss me for the first time," Laura said.

Sally and Ginger nodded.

"Wait. Your first kiss," Sally said.

"The one and only," Laura said.

Sally and Ginger were happy and concerned at the same time.

"I'm hungry. I'll be right back," Laura said.

Laura jumped up to grab her food, realizing the girls had something to eat; yet she had forgotten her lunch.

Meanwhile...

The library was just crowded. Keith studied his notes for each of his classes. He tried to focus mainly on his quiz next period.

But it was hard. His mind kept trailing off to the subject of Laura. He didn't know what to do about the deal he had made.

The deal was harsh, and Laura is too sweet for it.

He thought back to when Corey and him made the deal.

"Hey, new kid," Corey said.

Keith nodded.

"I heard about what you did at your last school. Is it true?" Corey asked.

"Sort of. She had promised she would have sex with me that night, but on prom night, she didn't want to go through with it. I didn't want to hear that, so I just proceeded anyways," Keith said.

"I'm still not sure if I believe you," Corey said.

"That's your decision. I have nothing to prove," Keith said.

"All right. Tough guy. We will accept you as part of the popular crowd if you actually follow through on a deal this time," Corey said.

"What's the deal?" Keith said.

"There is this girl, Laura, who along with her friends destroys the curve in our math class. She has destroyed it for the past three years. I think she should pay. I want you to prove that you are tough guy and break her heart. Wait better yet. Rape her at prom," Corey said.

"I don't know her," Keith replied.

"Are you scared or something? Maybe you aren't so tough," Corey said.

Keith knew he was tough.

"I'm tough, and you have a deal," Keith said.

HIS WRATH

Keith walked off, knowing who he must find.

He wasn't sure if it was worth it. Laura had been nicer and more helpful to him than anyone else since he started school here. Besides Corey was right, he didn't rape his ex-girlfriend, she just says that because he broke up with her later that week. He broke up with her because she cheated on him, but she will never admit to it.

Keith wasn't a virgin by all means. He had just only slept with girls at parties and never girlfriends, because the girlfriends he seem to choose had less experience than the drunk girls at parties. He hadn't been to a party like that since his previous school.

He decided it might help if he made a list of pros and cons.

He took a piece of paper.

Pros:
Being Popular
Respect
Friends and parties
Free answers to tests

Cons:
Hurting her
The possibility of getting caught
Graduation—only two months away
Losing a friend, girlfriend and a study partner

Realizing that both lists had the same number of reasons, he sighed.

He turned the page in his book and went back to studying.

Meanwhile...

Laura, Sally and Ginger continued their meal.

"Tell us about the kiss," Sally said.

Sally and Ginger had yet to have their first kisses. It was a big deal for Laura to be graduating from the true virgin category.

"It was a nice, sweet one on the lips and then as he left he grabbed me gently and kissed me one more time on the lips," Laura described.

She smiled.

"No tongue yet then," Sally asked.

"I bet that's interesting," Ginger commented.

Laura kept smiling.

"I can't wait," Laura said rubbing it in.

Ginger and Sally sighed wishing they had boyfriends, and at the same time, wishing it wasn't Keith.

"Our evening was cut short last night by Keith's mom coming home. She wants to spend some time with him tonight. I'm guessing they are not very close," Laura said.

"Neither are you and your mom," Ginger said.

"That's because she tells her women's group everything I tell her. There are no secrets. I can only trust you two and Nate," Laura said.

Ginger and Sally smiled.

"That's what friends are for. I wish your mother was like mine," Sally said.

"You've got a great mom," Laura said.

The lunch bell rang as the girls rushed to their math class.

Nate ran into lunchroom and then decided to go to the library instead.

Keith ran out of the library dropping his pro and con list on the floor, but he hadn't labeled it. He had left Laura's name off on purpose. He didn't notice he had dropped until it was too late.

Nate picked up the paper as he walked to a table. He noticed Keith had dropped it. He figured he would just hand it to Laura later for her to deliver it back to its owner.

Nate sat down at the table and began to read it.

> Pros:
> Being Popular
> Respect
> Friends and parties
> Free answers to tests
>
> Cons:
> Hurting her
> The possibility of getting caught
> Graduation—only two months away
> Losing a friend, girlfriend and a study partner

Nate thought to himself as he read the paper:

HIS WRATH

What are these pros and cons of? Who is she? Could it be Laura? What is he thinking about doing to hurt her? Would he hurt her? Should I show this to Laura? What would she think? Do Sally and Ginger have any clues about this? Could this be an old note? Is it even Keith's? Should I just discard it and forget I found it? Why did I have to notice him dropping his papers? Why did I pick it up? What should I do with it now?

Nate was torn with his emotions. He just could not make a decision.

Meanwhile...

Keith rushed into his next class. He sat down and skimmed through his notes. He realized he had dropped his list. He was worried about it getting into the wrong hands.

However, he knew that by now, someone had picked it up or it had been thrown away. He just hoped that somehow it didn't get back to Laura.

But...

Nate knew he had to warn Laura out of protection and love. He started thinking about it again.

How do I tell her? What does it mean? What was he going to do?

"I can't let him hurt her," he thought.

Should I tell him I have this? Should I go to Laura first? Should I go to Sally and Ginger first? What am I to do?

Nate began to get a headache from thinking about this matter. He decided he would talk to Laura about it tonight.

Meanwhile...

Laura, Sally and Ginger sat in math class.

Laura was in the greatest mood today. Her mood caused Sally and Ginger to worry about her getting hurt on prom night.

Meanwhile...

Keith's mom worked hard at her job downtown.

Her attention was to work extra hard in order leave early. She wanted to make Keith dinner and spend some valuable time with him.

She wondered why he was distant towards her.

Was it because I was never around? Is it because he is a guy? Is it because we moved for his dad's job?

"Maybe I should have been a housewife, but I would have hated that. I love my job and my past role in our private company. But I love my family too. I feel as if I have missed out on Keith's life," she thought.

"What can I do now? Is it too late? I hope not. I am going to make the best of our last few months before he leaves for college," she thought.

She called home and left a message for Keith telling him that she would be home around 4 p.m. to cook dinner for him.

Keith couldn't focus in his English class. He wondered if anyone had picked up his list. He also wondered what he was going to do. Making that list didn't make his decision any easier.

And now, it might have fallen in the wrong hands.

What do I do? What can I do? What will I do?

I can't hurt Laura. I just don't want to lose her. There that's that. I'm not doing it.

Nate finished studying for his quiz just as the bell rang for the next class period. He dashed out of the library.

They finished the school day and went home.

Nate called Laura and told her to come on over when she was ready.

Laura wondered why Nate was persistent about her coming over. Usually they met at their lockers to talk and then once in a while they would study for a test together. Laura knew prom was just around the corner. She wondered if this visit had anything to do with Keith.

Knock. Knock.

Laura knocked on Nate's door, after being let in by his mom.

"Come in," he said.

Laura opened the door and walked through.

"I already finished all of my homework, because I got the feeling this was important," Laura said.

Nate nodded.

"First, I want to show you what I found in the library today. Keith dropped this," Nate said.

He handed a piece of paper to Laura. Laura glanced at it.

Pros:
Being Popular
Respect
Friends and parties
Free answers to tests

Cons:
Hurting her
The possibility of getting caught
Graduation—only two months away
Losing a friend, girlfriend and a study partner

Laura looked over at Nate.
"Do you have any idea what that is about?" he asked.
Laura shook her head to say "no."
Nate looked over Laura's shoulder at the paper. They both wondered what the list meant.
"I think it is about you," he said.
"Maybe. But this might not even be his," she said.
"What do you mean?" he asked.
"He could have picked it up by accident. It could have been in a book he was reading. It could have been left on the table before he came in. There are so many possibilities," she said.
"I guess," Nate said.
"I guess I can ask Keith about it," she said.
Nate nodded.
Laura just smiled.
"I'll take care of this," she declared.
"Good. I'm worried about another thing, though," Nate said.
Laura nodded.
"Guys have minds of their own when it comes to women. I have been trying to figure this Keith guy out. He has a hidden past and an interest in you. I'm worried," he said.
"I know," she said.
"I fear that you do not," he said.
"I've spent time with Keith. None of you have," Laura said.
"I think you are being a little naïve," Nate said.
"Maybe you, Ginger and Sally should spend some time with him before you go judging him," she said.

Laura stood up to leave. She had enough of Nate's accusations. She didn't want to hear any more doubts about the man she was falling for.

"Please, stop. Calm down. I just want to talk," he pleaded.

Laura sat down to give Nate another chance.

"Just don't act like you know everything," she said.

Nate nodded.

"You're right. We don't know everything, but what we do know frightens me," he said.

Laura nodded.

"In which case, I am just asking you to be careful and to grab me if you need me for anything," he added.

Laura nodded again.

"Laura, you are my best friend, and I don't want you to get hurt," he said.

Nate smiled. Laura smiled back.

"I know. I appreciate your concern," she said.

"I do know guys better than you in general well because I am one. If you have any questions about Keith or guys in general. I'm here for you," he said.

Laura nodded. She felt too awkward to ask anything though.

Nate smiled.

"Thanks, Nate. I have to go now," she said.

She felt uncomfortable.

"Thanks for listening. I'll see you tomorrow at school," he said.

Laura nodded, stood up and opened the door to leave.

Nate smiled as Laura left his room and his house. He had the feeling that what he had said had meant something to her.

Laura walked back home with the paper Nate had found in her pocket.

She opened the door to her house and went to her room.

Chapter 7

Laura sat on her bed thinking about what Nate had found. She glanced at it once again.

> Pros:
> Being Popular
> Respect
> Friends and parties
> Free answers to tests
>
> Cons:
> Hurting her
> The possibility of getting caught
> Graduation—only two months away
> Losing a friend, girlfriend and a study partner

She stared on each of the lines. Reading it slowly to herself. She pondered several questions. These questions danced in her head.
What could this mean? Is this Keith's? Who is he talking about? What is he going to do? Or what was he going to do? Should I tell him I have this? Should I discuss it with him? How do I explain having it? Oh, what could it mean?
Laura buried her head into the pillow and sighed. She was overwhelmed by this news.
Nate picked up the copy he had made of the list. He had made a copy to show to Ginger and Sally when they come over to discuss their plan on Friday night. He figured if he didn't fill them in, no one would.
Meanwhile...
Keith arrived home after school to find his mom home early. She had left work at 2:30 p.m. in order to meet him. Keith sighed to see his mom home. He had no idea how to communicate with her about anything.

"Hi, baby," his mom said.

She was trying really hard to be nice and reach him while there was still time before he went off to college.

Keith just nodded.

His mom smiled.

"How was your day?" she asked.

Keith pretended not to hear her.

"Fine," he answered.

He finally responded realizing that she was not going to leave him alone. He began to go up the stairs to his room.

"Keith, come down those stairs and spend some time with me. I hope you don't have lots of homework, because I want to hear all about your new school and how everyone there is treating you. I want to hear about this Laura girl. I want to know everything," she said.

Keith was surprised at the sudden interest and was not ready to share anything with his mom. He felt so uncomfortable. He turned around.

"Why? Why do you care now?" he asked.

His mom looked shock by his remark.

"What do you mean, honey?" she asked.

"You show up all of sudden the other night and interrupt my evening. You continue to get to know me. Mom, I am 18 years old. I have raised myself for the most part. I will leave for college in the fall, and now you are putting in effort to get to know me. It's too late for me to explain everything to you now. Besides I have homework," he said.

He walked up the rest of the stairs fast hoping she would just let him go.

"Keith. I love you, and I'm sorry. But I'm here now, and I want to talk to you," she said.

He opened the door to his room and shut it hard, paying no attention to her plea.

Keith's mom sat down in the living room and buried head in a pillow. She felt like a failure. Tears began to fall down her face. She thought to herself maybe it was too late; maybe there was no relationship for them to have.

Keith smiled once behind his door. He sat down to look through his bag.

HIS WRATH

As he was digging, he realized once again that he had left his list of pros and cons of raping Laura on the library floor. He was sure it was gone or it had fallen into the wrong hands.

He sighed. He hoped Laura had not found it.

The phone rang.

Keith's mom answered.

"Honey, is that you?" Keith's dad asked.

"Yes," she answered.

"How is it going?" he asked.

"Not that good," she responded.

"Why?" he asked.

She explained to him Keith's reaction to her being home and wanting to spend time with him.

"Give him time. He'll come around. Do you want me to talk to him?" he asked.

"No, that's all right. I'll just try again at dinner," she said.

"Okay. I have to go. I have a committee meeting tonight. Bye, dear. I love you," he said.

"Love you too," she said.

She hung up the phone. She then picked herself up off the couch and walked into the kitchen. She had given the servants the day off, so she could make her son a home cooked meal.

But she had no idea what to cook for Keith. She walked up the stairs and knocked on his door.

Knock. Knock.

He didn't respond.

"What do you want to eat for dinner?" she asked.

"Whatever," he replied.

"Please, help me out here. I know you are mad at me, and you don't want me here, but at least tell me what to cook for dinner," she said.

Keith felt bad for giving her such a hard time.

"Barbecue chicken, pasta and some vegetables. Thanks, mom," he said.

He figured that might make her feel a little better. He turned his attention back to his homework.

"Thanks," she said.

She smiled. She was happy that he called her mom and said thank you. She walked down the stairs and began cooking in the kitchen.

Meanwhile...
Nate thought about the list once more.

Pros:
Being Popular
Respect
Friends and parties
Free answers to tests

Cons:
Hurting her
The possibility of getting caught
Graduation—only two months away
Losing a friend, girlfriend and a study partner

He wondered what it could mean. He knew Sally and Ginger might have an idea.

He grabbed some paper out of his desk and began making list of things they needed in order to plan on Friday night.

He then decided to call them and make sure they were doing their parts.

Nate picked up the phone.

"Hello?" Sally asked.

"It's Nate. I'm just checking in," he said.

"Okay. I spoke to Ginger earlier. We have a map of the place and a phone number for it too. We also know where Keith is taking Laura to dinner. We are ready to plan," she said.

"Great. Where is Keith taking Laura to dinner?" he said.

"She told us at lunch today. It was the Pleasant Pheasant. They have some great food I hear," she said.

"Uh. Huh. Can we meet at your place? What time?" he asked.

"Just come over after school. I'll tell Ginger," she said.

"Great. Bye," he said.

Nate hung up the phone. He had never really liked Sally and Ginger. They acted too much like girls. They wore makeup and gossiped. Laura had always been more of a tomboy. She was easier to get along with. Nate figured this was just business, and he was only doing it out of concern for Laura. He cared about her so much. He hoped she realized that.

HIS WRATH

Meanwhile...
Laura picked her head up out of the pillow. She had no homework to work on, leaving her mind to wonder on this list.

> Pros:
> Being Popular
> Respect
> Friends and parties
> Free answers to tests
>
> Cons:
> Hurting her
> The possibility of getting caught
> Graduation—only two months away
> Losing a friend, girlfriend and a study partner

What could it mean?
She hated that Nate had given it to her. She knew that it was going to bother her until she was able to talk to Keith about it. She didn't want to call, because she knew his mom was in town.
What do I do? She pondered that question for a while.
The phone rang.
Keith had decided he needed to talk to Laura in case she did get that paper. He needed to clear up the issue before prom rolled around.
"Hello?" her mom asked.
"Is Laura there?" he asked.
"Hold please. Laura, it's for you," she yelled.
Laura picked up her phone.
"Yes," she said.
"Hey, girlfriend. How are you doing?" he asked.
"Good and you?" she asked.
"Just fine, but my mom is bothering me," he declared.
"I'm sorry," she said.
"But you seem to be putting a smile on my face. What's up?" he said.
"Keith, Nate found something that I think belongs to you," she said.

"What's that?" he said.

"He said you dropped a list of pros and cons in the library earlier today. He thought it might be important, so he picked it up and passed it to me to give to you," she said.

"Yeah. I thought I might have dropped something. What does it say; maybe I'll recognize it," he said.

"Okay," she said as she began to read it.

Pros:
Being Popular
Respect
Friends and parties
Free answers to tests

Cons:
Hurting her
The possibility of getting caught
Graduation—only two months away
Losing a friend, girlfriend and a study partner

He stopped halfway through.

"Stop. Right there. Can you hold on for just a second? I think I hear my mom," he said.

Keith put down the phone. Could he? Should he tell her the truth? Did it matter?

"Sorry. My mistake. I don't believe that paper is mine. I believe it got stuck in my notebook from whoever left it on the table earlier. You know how careless people can be," he said.

"That's good news. I'll just throw it away then," she said.

"Great," he said.

"Keith! Dinner!" his mom yelled.

"Oops. This time my mom is actually calling me for dinner. I best run. Bye, girl. I'll see you tomorrow in school," he said.

Keith hung up feeling uncomfortable. He didn't want to lie to Laura, but he didn't want to lose her by telling the truth about the list especially when he didn't know what he was going to do yet. Plus, he was running out of time. He was letting his stomach make the next move when he walked out the door and ran down the stairs without realizing how Laura might feel.

HIS WRATH

Laura placed the phone down and threw the paper out even though a voice in her head made question what Keith had just said.

Keith walked into the kitchen and took a seat in front of his dinner plate.

"Hungry?" his mom asked.

Keith nodded.

"Good. Eat up," she said.

She slid out the chair and sat next to him. They dug in.

Time passed as they stuffed their faces.

"So maybe we could talk for a little while. I realize I haven't been there in the past for you, but I want to be here now," she said.

"I wish I could say that's all that matters, but I don't know how to talk to you, since I really never have," he said.

"Just give it a chance. I'll start," she said.

Keith nodded.

She began talking about the recent happenings of her job and what his father was experiencing in Washington D.C. Keith just ate, trying to look interested. At least his stomach was amused.

She stopped mid-sentence realizing Keith's facial expression of boredom.

"Keith, I'm sorry. I got caught up in my story. Why don't you try telling me more about this girl I found you with the other night?" she asked.

Keith nodded.

"Laura is in my history class. We met the first day. She is a really smart girl with straight A's. She agreed to help me catch up since I moved in late into the semester. Ever since then, I have liked her," he said.

His mom nodded.

"She seems to be a sweet girl. How long have you two been going out?" she asked.

"I met her around two weeks ago, but we only kissed and started dating this week. We are going to prom together on Saturday," he said.

His mom nodded again.

"See, I'm not that hard to talk to. I would like for her to come for dinner Friday night," she said.

"I guess. Sure. Can I call her and let her know she is invited?" he asked.

She nodded.

Keith ran off taking the opportunity to escape.

The phone rang. Laura picked it up.

"Laura?" he asked.

"Yes," she said.

"My mom just invited you over for dinner tomorrow. Can you come?" he asked.

"Sure. Let me just check. Hold on," she said.

Laura walked down the hall to get permission from her parents for dinner at Keith's tomorrow night. After receiving it, she walked back with just a curfew, since Saturday night was the prom.

"Keith?" she asked.

"Yes," he said.

"It's fine. I'll ride home with you tomorrow," she said.

"Great. I must get back to my mom," he said.

He sighed.

"Okay, bye," she said.

She hung up the phone and smiled.

Laura laid her head down. It had been long day. It was time for bed.

Keith's mom looked over at him as he hung up the phone. She could see his face well from the kitchen. She could tell he really liked that girl.

"Mom?" he asked.

"Yes, dear," she said.

"She'll be here for dinner tomorrow," he said.

"Great. What should we have made?" she said.

"I don't know," he said.

"I'll figure it out," she said.

"Okay. Thanks for wanting to meet Laura," he said.

"No problem. Do you have homework to finish?" she said.

"Yes. May I be excused?" he asked.

"Yes. It's good to see you wanting to pull up your grades," she said.

"I have to look good next to Laura. She's got a 4.0, you know," he said.

He chuckled and ran off up the stairs.

His mom sat down on the couch. "Not bad," she thought. "Not bad. He is talking to me."

She sat sipping her tea and thinking of when Keith was born. Nate on the other hand, could not get his mind off of the list.

Pros:
Being Popular
Respect
Friends and parties
Free answers to tests

Cons:
Hurting her
The possibility of getting caught
Graduation—only two months away
Losing a friend, girlfriend and a study partner

He knew it was his duty to protect Laura.

People had asked him for the past few years if they were dating. Laura and Nate had never stepped over the line of friendship. Not even once.

But sometimes, each of them had considered it.

Laura and Nate attended the same middle school. Laura was rather quiet for most of those years. They played all sorts of sports together and studied for class.

But Nate thought back to an incident in ninth grade.

Nate had his first girlfriend in ninth grade, Joann Watson. Nate asked Joann out, and they went steady for two months, before Joann dumped him for a more popular guy.

Nate was rather hurt after losing his first girlfriend to popularity.

That night, Laura and Nate were studying for some test, he couldn't remember what test.

They finished studying at around 10:30 p.m. Laura was so tired, when they finished.

Nate let her lay her head in his lap. She closed her eyes.

He could still picture her lying in his lap. She was wearing a yellow top and jeans. It was springtime.

She awoke in his lap 30 minutes later.

"I must go home," she said.

Nate nodded.

He got up and walked her to the door of her house and hugged her good night.

He remembered wanting to kiss her very badly.

He thought to himself, what would it be like now if I had.

He smiled. Keith better treat her right.

He pictured Laura in his lap. He had not dated anyone seriously. All of his relationships had been a few weeks just like with Joann.

He wondered why. He knew he had been attracted to Laura since high school started. She had matured over the summer during camp.

He remembered how pretty she was the day she came back to town.

He sighed. Do I have feelings for Laura?

He had never been sure. He also never attempted to find out.

When others asked about them, he would reply, time will tell. He left himself and others wondering.

He wondered if Laura ever wondered.

He was sure she hadn't since Keith entered her life.

Keith was upstairs in his room, thinking of Laura too.

He was not getting much of his homework done. He was thinking about his decision.

He knew he was not going to make another list. He hated lying to her.

But, could he go through with it?

He didn't know. He just wasn't sure.

He turned over and closed his eyes and thought back to day he drove her home in his car the first time.

Keith fell asleep. He was snoring when his mom walked by on her way to bed.

She opened the door, picked up his papers and piled them together.

She kissed him on the forehead and went on to bed.

Friday morning was here, only 24 hours to prom. Keith had already made his decision.

The kids set off to school and piled into their morning classes.

Sally and Ginger were busy making copies of maps.

Keith has overlooking notes before a quiz.

Nate was busy studying Laura's face as their first class of the day began.

Laura was rather excited as the prom was approaching. She loved new experiences, and since being in a relationship was a brand new to her, every moment excited her.

Keith's mom arrived at work early, in order to leave early for dinner. She spent most of her lunch hour searching for a special recipe.

At the end of the first class, the bell rang.

Keith ran out of his class and down the back to one of the middle halls. He proceeded to run down the hall to find Laura standing at her locker.

"Hi there," he said.

Laura just nodded.

"What's wrong?" he asked.

Laura sighed. Corey had been in her last class, and she had received a note that was not signed.

Laura handed the note to Keith.

> Laura—
> Don't be too excited about tomorrow, smart girl. You are going down.

Keith had a look of shock on his face. He knew it had to be Corey, and he had gone too far. He had no right to scare Laura.

"I'll take care of it," he said.

"Do you know what it is about?" she asked.

"Well. Some of the popular guys don't like that I'm dating you. They are jealous, but I don't care what they think. I'm dating you, because I like you. I won't let them hurt you," he said.

Laura nodded.

Keith leaned in and hugged her.

The second class bell rang, and they broke off to their classes.

Laura just sighed and walked off to class. She felt so confused about the note.

Who did come from? Why? What is going to happen?

Keith rushed off to his next class in order to plan on what he was going to say to Corey at lunch.

The rest of the morning continued for each student.

The lunch bell finally rang.

Keith rushed off to the "popular students" table.
Keith was furious.
He walked up to Corey and tapped him on the shoulder.
"Excuse me," he said. "Can I have a word with you alone, outside?"
Corey shrugged.
Keith and Corey walked outside.
"What is this?" Keith asked.
He held the note in front of Corey's face.

> Laura—
> Don't be too excited about tomorrow, smart girl. You are going down.

Corey just stared at the note, trying to look surprised.
"It is just a warning," Corey said.
"Don't you think that this ruins my plan?" he said.
"No. You might have to try harder, but I think she is an easy target," he said.
"No. Now she might not go to prom with me, nor talk to me. Don't you think that will make it harder for me to hold up my end of the deal?" he said.
Sally had gone outside to get a breath of fresh air before walking into the lunchroom. She overheard Keith and some guy talking. She moved behind a tree.
"What deal?" she thought to herself.
"She has to go to the prom with me. That is how the deal works," Keith said.
"Well, that's your problem, then," Corey said.
Corey walked off really fast.
"Wait," Keith cried out.
Keith began walking after Corey, then thought what difference does this make, it doesn't change my decision.
He walked off and went into the lunchroom. He located Laura's table and headed that way.
Sally dashed off to the ladies room knowing Ginger would be there waiting for her.
Ginger patiently waited Sally's arrival.

Sally pushed open the door to the ladies room.

"Ginger," Sally said.

"Yes. Let's talk as we walk to the lunchroom. I'm hungry," Ginger said.

"Okay. But you are not going to believe this," Sally said.

Sally took a deep breath.

"Keith is evil," she declared.

"What do you mean?" Ginger asked.

"He made some deal with that kid, Corey. The deal concerns prom night," Sally said.

"Do you know what the deal is?" Ginger asked.

Sally shook her head.

"I overheard the two of them talking in the courtyard about five minutes ago. Corey left Keith speechless after telling him he better follow through with the deal, but I got the feeling Keith didn't want to complete the deal," Sally explained.

"Then, maybe we have nothing to worry about, but I think you should check with your sister on this Corey," Ginger said.

"I will. This is between us until then," Sally said.

Meanwhile…

Keith had taken a seat next to Laura.

"Don't you worry about that note. I will protect you tomorrow night," he said.

Laura smiled.

"You're sweet. Thank you," he said.

Keith nodded.

"You are not allowed to worry about stuff like that, when your boyfriend is as strong as I am," he said.

Laura chuckled and smiled.

Keith leaned over and kissed her on the cheek.

Sally and Ginger were walking towards the door of the lunchroom when they noticed Keith was sitting next to Laura.

Sally turned and looked at Ginger. She was in a state of shock.

"I figured he would be sitting with his 'popular' friends," Sally said.

"Maybe, he decided to switch sides," Ginger suggested.

Ginger wanted Keith to be a decent guy for Laura's sake. She smiled at Sally.

"Come on. I'm hungry," Ginger said.
Sally nodded.
The two girls walked over to their usual table and took a seat. They smiled at Keith.
"Keith, nice of you to join us, today," Sally said.
She said hiding her feelings.
Ginger nodded.
"Thank you. I always enjoy eating lunch with you, ladies," he said.
Meanwhile...
Across the lunchroom, Corey was planning.
"I don't think that kid is up to this challenge," Corey said to his best friend, Bobby.
"Do it yourself. Bang that hot honey. Hurt her yourself then," Bobby said.
Corey just nodded.
"Are you chicken? I bet you would like it. Just think about it," he said.
Corey nodded once again.
"If you want it done, you have to do it yourself," he continued.
He chuckled.
Bobby was a built football player like Corey. Both of them had trouble in school and had always wanted to teach those who screwed up the curve a lesson.
"Maybe, I will," Corey said.
Bobby smiled.
"Score!" Bobby exclaimed.
Corey thought to himself about the idea. "It would be easy," he thought. "I just have to get her alone and show her who is boss."
Corey smiled back at Bobby.
The two of them knew a plan was set, and it was on for tomorrow night.
But across the lunchroom, Laura and Keith had no idea what Corey and Bobby had just decided.
The two of them, Sally and Ginger were just eating their lunch as plans were being made. Keith had also made up his mind on prom night already.
Prom was a night set for danger. Maybe Laura should stay home. Stay tuned.

Chapter 8

Nate walked into the lunchroom for his lunch hour after the second lunch bell rang.

He was hungry and ready to meet with Sally and Ginger tonight.

While the kids went through their school day, Keith's mom was planning a meal for her guest.

She had found a recipe for an appetizer, a main course as well as a dessert. She emailed all of them to the servant for her to begin cooking. She knew she would not have enough time to prepare a three-course meal.

She smiled thinking how well tonight would go. She was anxious to meet the girl Keith liked so much. She knew little about Laura. She intended on leaving work early to beat traffic and be home in time for dinner.

She was so excited that she was having trouble concentrating on her work that she sped out the door at around 3:30 p.m.

Meanwhile…

Laura, Sally and Ginger sat in math class taking notes.

Sally's mind began to wander.

What deal were they talking about? How did Corey scare Laura? What did that note say? Where is the note now? What does this mean? What will happen tomorrow night? Will we be able to protect her?

The questions whirled in her head. She was worried about Laura's safety.

She looked over at Ginger.

Ginger nodded. She knew what that look meant. Sally was concerned about tomorrow night. She wasn't alone in neither her thoughts nor feelings.

Ginger herself was trying to be more positive about the event. She hoped Keith truly cared for Laura.

Ginger smiled over at Laura.

Laura's mind was on the note she received earlier today. She could remember it clearly in her mind.

Laura—
Don't be too excited about tomorrow, smart girl. You are going down.

She felt threatened by the note.

She knew the note could have nothing to do with Keith, but then who?

Who wants to get me? How does he want to get me? Is he threatened by my grades? Is that what smart girl remark means? Does it concern Keith? Someone else?

Laura smiled back at Ginger. She didn't want them to worry about her.

Sally noticed the smile and smiled back.

I wonder if Laura got that note today. I wonder what it said. She thought to herself.

The girls continued to think while they were trying to take notes in class.

Keith sat in English class. He wondered if Corey was going to break any rules tomorrow night.

What is that kid going to do? Maybe, Laura and I shouldn't go? What does this mean for the deal? How does this affect my decision?

Keith wanted to take Laura to the prom since this would be her first prom. He also wanted her to have a memorable night.

He hoped everything would go all right tomorrow night.

Meanwhile…

Keith's mom rushed home.

The school day began to near the end of the day.

The kids attended their last class.

Keith's mom rounded her last minutes of traffic.

Keith and Laura piled into his car to drive over to his house for dinner.

Sally, Ginger and Nate rode over to Sally's house in her car to prepare for tomorrow night.

Keith's mom finally arrived home just after Laura and Keith arrived.

Smells filled the kitchen. Everything smelled absolutely delicious.

The servant smiled as the three of them entered the house. She knew her work was done.

Laura and Keith wondered what was for dinner as they sat talking on the couch in the living room. They were waiting for Keith's mom's arrival.

The door swung open as Keith's mom dropped her bags and yelled out a greeting. She was excited to be home.

"Kids, doesn't that smell good?" she asked.

Keith and Laura just nodded.

Keith wasn't in a talkative mood after his day at school. Laura was nervous about spending time with Keith's mom.

Keith's mom walked into the living room and sat down. Since it was only 4:30 p.m., they had some time to talk before dinnertime rolled around.

Meanwhile...

Corey was busy thinking about his plan. He had been imagining how it would happen in his mind.

Laura is standing off in the corner in line waiting for the ladies room. He grabs her.

The prom was to be held at the Fox Theatre. Corey knew where all of the back rooms were located, since his mom participated in the women's theatre club.

He pulled her harshly around corners and into a side room. He locked the door behind him.

He approached her slowly with an intense look of authority in his eyes.

Laura was scared. You could see a frightened look written all over her face.

She ran for the door. It was locked. Corey imagined himself pouncing on Laura.

In his first daydream, Laura begins to enjoy what he was doing. She agrees to become his girlfriend and help him to pull up his grades. She then publicly dumps Keith causing him to breakdown in tears in front of everyone.

Corey smiled.

But he thought, "I want a challenge."

He then imagined Laura kicking and screaming for Corey to stop. He continued until he was content with the damage and pain that he had caused her.

He got up and smiled.

"Now, you better not tell a single soul, otherwise I will sue, and you know I will win," he said.

Corey left and locked her in the room behind him. He had stolen his mother's keys the night before.

He knew he had done the right thing.

He smiled after his daydream and walked into his mom's room. He picked up the keys and walked back to his room.

He felt a sense of power now.

Corey had a love/hate relationship with Laura. He hated her because she was smart, poor and not popular, but he had always had a huge crush on her because of her black beauty. Those two things combined can only be dangerous...

Sally, Ginger and Nate arrived at Sally's house.

Sally ushered all of them down to her room, so their get-together didn't seem like such a big deal.

Once down the hall, Sally and Ginger set out a map of the Fox Theatre in Downtown Atlanta.

"We can't leave Laura alone at any time," Sally said.

"Good idea," Ginger said.

Sally began highlighting the danger zones. Nate watched as his mind drifted.

Nate was so worried about Laura that he was having problems concentrating.

Sally had highlighted the bathrooms, hallways and private rooms.

Nate turned his attention back to the map realizing that most of it had been colored yellow.

"Sally, you do realize there are only three of us," he said.

Sally nodded.

"I know. I figured if we keep our eyes open and wear these, then we can cover all of the problem areas," she said.

Sally was holding up walkie-talkies while she was talking. She had purchased them for this event.

"I think we can do this, but we need to concentrate and plan really well," she said.

Ginger nodded.

"We also need to consider it could be Keith, or it could be someone else that is after Laura," Ginger said.

"Exactly," Sally said.

Nate nodded.

"It's too bad. This is Laura's first and last prom, and that is the reason she wants to go so badly. If she has a bad experience, it could brand her for life. She is such a wonderful person. I don't want her to get hurt," he said.

Sally and Ginger shook their heads.

"Neither do we," they said.

Each of them picked up a walkie-talkie off the floor.

Sally looked around at her crew and smiled.

"Laura is lucky to have us looking out for her," Sally said.

Ginger nodded.

"Let's get started," Sally said.

Keith's mom, Keith and Laura sat down for dinner after several moments of awkward silence. Keith's mom had tried rather hard to find out several details about Laura and Keith's feelings for each other.

"Doesn't this look delicious?" she asked.

Keith and Laura just nodded.

Keith's mom thought, this girl is awful quiet.

"Laura, tell me about your dress for tomorrow night," she asked.

Laura looked up and began to describe the dress to Keith's mom.

"The dress is red. It has spaghetti straps and then it crisscrosses back and forth with the material making the dress rather form fitting. I also bought red-strapped shoes to go with it," she said.

Keith's mom nodded.

"That sounds beautiful. I bet you look great in red," she said.

"Thanks. I hope so," she said.

Keith smiled.

"You'll look great tomorrow. I can't wait to see you in that dress," he said.

Keith had always thought of Laura as a beautiful girl.

He smiled once again, knowing he had made Laura feel pretty.

"That's a nice thing to say, Keith. My son, the charmer," his mom said.

She chuckled trying to lighten the mood.

Laura still feeling uncomfortable just smiled.

"Tough crowd. I know you two feel weird with me here, but I don't bite," she said.

"I'm just nervous. You are the first parent of Keith's I've met," Laura said.

"I know," his mom said.

"Mom, lay off all right. Just because you swing in now, doesn't mean you will become instant friends with my girlfriend or any of my friends for that matter," Keith said.

Keith was sick of his mom's persistence.

"I tried, but this is just too hard for me. Laura, would you like to go upstairs and finish this in my room," he added.

He pointed to the dinner plates. He picked up his and hers and began walking out of the kitchen.

Laura didn't want to choose sides. She just sat there motionless.

"Go ahead, Laura. I have upset Keith, and I'm sorry," his mom said.

Laura picked up their glasses and followed Keith up the stairs.

They sat down at the table on the left side of Keith's room.

Laura smiled at Keith.

"She tries so hard to get into everyone's business. I'm sorry," he said.

"She wasn't that bad. I just have trouble when I first meet new people," she said.

Keith nodded.

"She gets me so frustrated. She doesn't understand kids our age. She hasn't acted like a mother to me for years, and now all of sudden she is trying to be my best friend," he said.

"She probably is trying to hold on to you as you grow up and get ready to go off to college," she said.

Keith nodded. He knew she was right.

"Keith, where are you going to college?" she asked.

"I applied to a few places, but with my low grades over the past years, my options are rather slim. I did do well on my SAT's though," he said.

Laura nodded.

"I leave in August for Georgia Peach University in Middle Georgia. I'm sure with high SAT scores you will get to go somewhere, besides you are working rather hard to bring up your grades this semester," she said.

Keith nodded.

"I guess," he said.

Even with her words of encouragement, he doubted the odds.

"This is delicious," she said.
"Our servant made it. She is a great cook," he said.
Laura and Keith continued talking rather easily. She had a talent for making Keith feel more comfortable.
Laura smiled.
After dinner, the two sat on Keith's bed.
Keith smiled at Laura and leaned in for a kiss.
It happened.
It was Laura's first make-out session.
Knock. Knock.
Keith's mom stood outside the door.
"I just came upstairs to grab the dirty plates," she said.
Keith gently moved back from Laura's lips to get the door. He jumped up and opened the door to let his mom in.
"I'm just going to grab your plates," she said.
"Thank you," he said.
"Yes, thank you," Laura said.
Mom nodded and walked out the door.
Keith closed the door behind and looked at Laura once again.
"I'm sorry, things are so weird between my mom and me. She was just never here for me, and I don't know how to handle this change," he said.
Laura nodded.
"You should probably give her a chance before you leave for college, otherwise you may never get this chance again. However, if it makes you feel better, I don't have the best relationship with my mom either," she said.
Keith nodded.
"Why?" he asked.
Laura sighed.
"My mom and I had our chance. We were good friends when I was younger, but once I entered high school, it became harder for me to share things with her. I was growing up and talking to your mom about things just wasn't cool. She just didn't understand being that she was a teenager a long time ago. And then, when I did tell her news, she would share it with her ladies group. After that, we grew apart, and she grew closer to her ladies group. They meet at our house three nights a week now," she answered.

Keith nodded.

"That sucks. I bet those ladies are annoying and say you are cute. They probably grab your cheeks," he said.

Laura smiled and laughed.

"You bet they do," she said.

Keith laughed.

"But enough about parents. Where were we?" he asked.

He leaned back in and kissed her.

The kiss turned into another make-out session.

Meanwhile...

Sally, Ginger and Nate were mapping out their plan, in order to protect Laura.

Sally had shared with everyone the map of the theatre.

They had started formulating assignments.

"We need to keep our eyes open," Sally said.

Ginger and Nate nodded.

"You and I especially, because if Laura runs to the bathroom, we have to be next to her in line," Ginger said.

"Good point. That would be an easy place for someone to grab her," Sally said.

Sally looked over at Nate.

"The drink and food table is going to be here," Sally said.

She pointed to a large rectangle in the middle of the ballroom.

"You should get a good view of our dancing couple from here," Sally said.

Nate nodded.

Sally looked over at Ginger.

"You and I need to man the doorways that way we are closer to the bathrooms," Sally said.

Ginger nodded.

"We are going to wear these," Sally added.

She was holding up the walkie-talkies.

"We need to keep up each other and check in," Sally added.

Ginger and Nate nodded.

"You got it," he said.

He smiled.

"I think we should have code names," Sally said.

"Can I be snaps after Ginger snaps?" Ginger asked.

Sally nodded.

"Sally, you should be director or something like that," Nate said.

"I was hoping for chief," she replied.

Nate nodded.

Sally turned her head to Nate.

"That leaves you. I think since you are the only of us that will have to fight if things get out of hand, you should be the protector," she said.

Nate nodded, expressing approval of his code name.

"I'm going to borrow my mom's cell phone, just in case we need to call the police," Sally said.

"Good idea," Ginger said.

The crew was almost done planning. They smiled at each other, knowing this was a productive way to get together.

Not much later, Nate and Ginger left Sally's house, in order to get some sleep before the plan went into action tomorrow night.

Meanwhile...

Laura gently pushed back from Keith before their kissing moved too far.

"Laura, we have grown close over the past few weeks, and I want to share something with you," Keith said.

Laura just nodded. She was uneasy about where this discussion was going.

"I have feelings for you like I have never had for a girl before, so I have decided to apply to Georgia Peach University, so our relationship may last even longer," he added.

Laura smiled.

"I hope you get in. I'll help you with the application, if you would like," she said.

Keith smiled back.

He knew he had conveyed his plans sincerely.

"Sure. I'll get a copy on Monday, and we can work on it next week," he said.

He hoped they were still dating next week, as tomorrow neared.

Laura nodded.

She then noticed it was nearing 11 p.m. Laura's parents were rather protective of her. She figured she should go ahead and take the option of leaving.

"Keith, it's almost 11 p.m. I should be getting home," she said.
Keith was caught off guard by that remark.
"Sure. I'll give you a ride," he said.
"Thank you," she said.
They walked down the stairs and through the kitchen to the garage. Keith's mom heard their footsteps.
"Is everything all right?" his mom asked.
"I'm just going to take Laura home," he said.
Keith's mom smiled noticing the time.
"Be careful," she said.
Keith and Laura climbed into this car and drove off to her house. They arrived not too much later at her house.
Nate drew the blinds open from his window to get a better view.
Keith walked Laura to the door and gave her kiss good night.
Nate sighed out of jealously. He feared he was going to lose Laura to Keith, especially since he had a scholarship for the University of Georgia.
Laura opened the door and walked rather fast to her room, in order to avoid her parents being nosy about her date.
Nate closed the blinds before Keith could notice him watching.
Keith walked back to the car with the weight of the world on his shoulders. He knew tomorrow he might have to let go of Laura, and he also knew that his plan could help them to grow closer.
As he climbed into the car, he felt like someone was watching him. He looked around and found no one.
He turned on the engine and drove home. That feeling unnerved him as he drove. He knew that Laura's friend, Nate, lived across the street. He had always wondered how their relationship worked. He had never heard of many girls having guy friends. He figured Nate was interested, but too chicken to admit it, and then when he entered the picture, Nate figured he had no chance, so rather he just marvels from afar.
Keith smiled assuming that Nate was no threat to his relationship with Laura.
He arrived at his house and opened the garage door remembering that his mom was probably there awaiting his arrival.
Nate lay down on his bed as Keith left the scene.
He was tired and anxious about tomorrow at the same time. He was curious about Keith's look as he walked to his car.

HIS WRATH

He appeared as if he had a lot on his mind.

What did that look mean?

He pondered that question until his eyes closed, and he ventured off into dreamland.

Keith opened the door to the house slowly, trying not to catch his mom's attention.

The door shut behind him.

Keith's mom smiled knowing she had heard the door close behind her son.

She jumped up to go to the kitchen.

At the same time, Sally finished putting away the supplies for the mission tomorrow.

She smiled knowing the crew was ready for tomorrow.

She lay down and picked up the phone so she could hear her sister's phone call.

You know "gossip queens."

For Sally's benefit though, what she overheard was usually accurate.

Chapter 9

That Saturday morning each of the children awoke early. The sun was shining on a bright April morning.

Laura jumped out of bed to go to breakfast. She was very excited about tonight.

Keith rolled around dreading what tonight could bring.

Sally and Ginger awoke anxious and ready to put their plan to work.

Nate feared the possibility of Laura getting hurt. He couldn't bear to see her heart break.

Corey stuffed his face with pancakes as he smiled thinking about taking a young girl's virginity.

Keith's mom was busy in the kitchen making pancakes, since she had given the servants the weekend off. She was living by her philosophy of if at first you don't succeed, try and try again.

Laura's mom was cooking French toast. She knew it was Laura's big night, and she wanted her to prepare for it.

Laura walked down the hall to the kitchen.

"Hi. Dear. Take a seat," her mom said.

Laura nodded and sat down.

Laura's mom placed a plate of French toast in front of her to eat.

Laura began to cut the toast into pieces. She hid her smile about later from her mom.

Laura's mom continued to cook another batch for her brother.

Meanwhile…

Corey finished his pancakes, left his plate on the table for the family's servant and strolled off down the hall.

He was ready for what the night may bring.

Sally ate her breakfast while she thought the plan for later that day. Sally also thought about how uninteresting her sister's phone call was last night.

HIS WRATH

Her sister had spent most of the call talking about her dress and makeup, which caused Sally to fall asleep, so she hung up early. Maybe Sally had missed some news. She hoped not.

Sally and Ginger were rather excited about the plan and hoped it went well.

Nate lay in his bed until his mom screamed for him to come out to the kitchen. Since he was going to the prom that night, he was spending Sunday with his dad.

He slowly got up and walked down the hall to the kitchen.

Keith on the other hand, got up eventually because he could smell the sweetness of the blueberry pancakes, his mom was making.

He walked down the stairs following the scent.

Keith's mom smiled as Keith entered the room.

"Would you like strawberries and whipped cream on yours?" Keith's mom asked.

Keith just nodded allowing his hunger to speak for him.

Keith's mom placed a set of blueberry pancakes topped with strawberries and whipped cream.

He smiled and dug in.

Keith's mom sat down next to him with her own plate.

"Is everything all right? You look like something is on your mind," she asked.

Keith knew his mom would notice him being deep in thought. Mothers always notice.

"I'm just hungry," he answered.

He attempted to avoid the subject all together, being it was not something he wanted to discuss with his mother.

He had an important matter to handle tonight. He had to keep an eye on Corey.

He also had to make sure his plan went well without any complications. He was worried about Laura's friends getting in his way.

He wanted tonight to be a night for Laura to remember. A Magical Night, he thought to himself.

He knew he had a big task ahead of him as he continued to eat.

Keith's mom smiled noticing Keith seemed to be enjoying his breakfast.

While, everyone ate their breakfasts, the workers at the Fox Theatre applied the finishing touches to the ballroom.

Stepping back from their masterpiece, they smiled.

They knew their overtime had been worth it. The ballroom looked absolutely beautiful.

Prom day was beginning.

Girls were piling on makeup, wearing expensive dresses and shoes and paying over $100 to style their hair.

Guys were throwing on suits and ties and grabbing limos to pick up the girls.

The dance floor awaited hundreds of feet, while the food was placed out, and students began to prepare for the night ahead.

Each of the students finished their breakfasts and allowed the afternoon to dawn as they began to get ready for the prom.

Prom hour was approaching…

Laura's face was beaming as Keith's car pulled into her driveway. The top was down, and Keith was decked out in his suit.

He parked the car in her driveway and strolled up to her front door.

Knock. Knock.

Laura's mom opened the door. Keith stepped in holding a red rose corsage for Laura.

Laura took one more look in the mirror before she walked down the hall to her prince.

Keith stood there staring as the black beauty entered the hallway.

Laura's red dress tightly accented her good points while being stylish. Her smile caused her to look absolutely amazing.

She stood in directly in front of him and began to put the boutonnière on his jacket even before Keith opened his mouth.

He could only express one word to describe her beauty.

"WOW," Keith said.

That is the best compliment a girl could ever receive.

Laura smiled from ear to ear.

"Thank you," she said.

She positioned his boutonnière and held out her hand for him to decorate. Keith slipped the corsage over her hand.

Laura's mom was so touched by the couple tears began to gather in her eyes.

"Ready?" he asked.

Laura nodded. She was too excited to answer.

They posed for pictures, and Laura gave her parents a hug good bye.
Keith walked her down the front stairs and to his car.
Nate watched from his window as the couple drove away.
He picked up his phone to call Sally.
"Hello," Sally's mom said.
"Is Sally there?" Nate asked.
"She's getting ready for the prom. Hold on," she said.
Nate waited about a minute.
"Protector?" she asked.
"Yes. Ready?" he asked.
"You bet. Snaps is here with me," she said.
"Good. I'll be over to pick you girls up in about an hour," he said.
"Great," she said.
"Over and out, chief," he said.
Sally hung up the phone and chuckled.
It was the crew's big night. All of their planning was going to be tested tonight.
Sally and Ginger continued to apply makeup while Sally's mom added the finishing touches to their hairdos.
Sally was wearing a sky blue sparkling dress with spaghetti straps and black-strapped shoes. Ginger was wearing a black dress with a white slash and black shoes.
They were excited and pleased with the outfits they had chosen.
Time passed quickly as they finished getting ready and gathered all of the equipment for Project Laura.
Nate arrived on time. They had agreed to go Dutch for dinner.
Knock. Knock.
Sally's mom opened the door as Ginger and Sally walked up behind her.
"Aren't I lucky?" Nate said.
Sally and Ginger smirked.
"One girl for each arm," he added.
He placed his arms on his hips so the girls could insert their arms inside.
Sally's mom just laughed.
The girls took the hint and locked arms with Nate.
"I'll have them home on time," he said.

Sally's mom nodded.

"Have a good time," she said.

She yelled as Nate escorted the girls to his mom's car.

He had borrowed the car for the night.

The three of them piled into his car and drove off.

Meanwhile...

Keith's mom had just noticed that Keith had already left for the prom. She had been cleaning the upstairs when he left.

Noticing that he had left without saying good-bye, she felt forgotten.

She grabbed a carton of ice cream and a movie, *Sleepless in Seattle*.

Dinnertime.

Laura and Keith arrived at Pleasant Pheasant about an hour after leaving her house, due to downtown traffic.

Keith had been to the restaurant several times with his dad when he was senator for the state of Georgia, but Laura, on the other hand, had never been to this fancy of a restaurant.

Keith had been a perfect gentleman so far by opening car doors and the door to the restaurant. He even pulled out her chair.

Laura smiled as she sat down.

The waitress came over and filled their water glasses. She proceeded to take their drink orders of two Cokes.

Laura studied the menu carefully overwhelmed by the number of choices.

"What are you looking for? You can order whatever you want," Keith said.

Laura nodded.

"Thanks, but I just have no idea," she said.

"I'm getting the steak, and I recommend the duck," he said.

Laura nodded.

"I have never had duck before," she said.

Keith gasped.

"Then you should try it. It's dark meat and rather juicy," he said.

Laura nodded, deciding to take the risk.

The waitress appeared with their drinks about a minute later.

"Are you two ready to order?" she asked.

Keith nodded. He looked at Laura in order to let her go first.

"I'll have the duck, please," she ordered.

HIS WRATH

The waitress wrote down her order, nodded and turned to Keith for his turn.

"I'll take the steak, medium well. Thank you," he said.

The waitress wrote down his order and looked up.

"Those will be out soon. Is there anything I can get you in the meantime?" she asked.

Keith and Laura said "no, thank you."

The waitress walked off.

Laura smiled at Keith. She felt like a princess.

Meanwhile…

Nate had taken the girls to a much less pricey restaurant.

They arrived while Laura and Keith were still sitting in traffic.

Nate and the girls were ushered to a booth inside of Chili's. The three of them sat down to eat.

The waitress appeared to greet them and take their drink orders. She received the order of three waters.

The three of them studied the menu, calculating the amount they could spend.

"Does anyone want to split something?" Sally asked.

"You two can since you two are on the same side," Nate suggested.

Sally and Ginger nodded.

They shared a menu and began to choose items together.

Sally and Ginger discussed certain items based on each of their likes and dislikes. They finally settled on one.

The waitress arrived with three waters and took their orders.

Sally laid out the map.

"All right, chief. Let's review," Nate said.

The crew reviewed their plan for that night.

As dinner arrived, they knew they were prepared.

Meanwhile…

Keith and Laura's meals arrived. Being rather hungry, they dug in.

"Wow. This is good," she said.

Keith smiled, knowing he had made a good recommendation.

"I told you," he said.

He laughed. Laura smiled.

Keith also enjoyed his steak.

The two of them enjoyed small talk as they munched on their food.

The prom hour neared.

The crew was nervous, yet ready for the task on hand.
But so was Corey...
Stay tuned.
Prom hour had arrived.

The doors to the Empress Ballroom opened allowing its visitors to enter. Keith and Laura wrapped up their meals, as Keith paid the bill. Keith decided to lay his message on thick tonight. He opened the door for Laura as the couple left the restaurant. Continuing to be a gentleman, he also opened the car door for her.

"Your coach waits," he said.

Laura nodded and smiled.

"I feel like a princess." She blushed.

Keith just smiled knowing his actions were effective.

He started the car and drove them over to the Fox Theatre.

Meanwhile...

The crew had finished their meals.

Ginger and Sally were enjoying the sandwich they had chosen to split, while Nate had finished the last few bits of his dinner.

The waitress dropped off the check.

Each of them grabbed their wallets and figured out the amount they each owed. The crew paid and left the restaurant.

They were ready to embark on their journey.

Almost no one arrives on time and especially not early to a prom. Therefore, the ballroom awaited its guests as cars began to head that direction.

The crew drove down highways towards downtown. They knew they had to get there around the same time Keith and Laura arrived, for every minute was precious.

Nate focused on his driving and tried his best to reach the theatre in time.

But...

Corey was determined to give himself an ample amount of time to accomplish his evil plan.

He was rounding corners and speeding up in order to grab Laura with fewer witnesses around.

But the police would not allow him to get away with his reckless driving.

The sirens went off a couple of cars behind him.

He quickly turned off the road in order to lose them, fearing that it might be him they were after.

Corey didn't really care if he was caught. He only ran because if they caught him, he might lose his window of opportunity.

He made a couple of more sharp turns until he could no longer hear the sirens. Realizing that he had reached a parking lot close enough to the theatre, he parked his car.

Corey had no date for the prom, but he didn't want one. He knew that a date would require a lot of his attention, and he was on a mission.

He was focused on that mission and only that mission.

Meanwhile...

Laura and Keith arrived at the theatre. Keith parked the car and walked around to open Laura's door. He spotted Corey in the distance. He had no idea what Corey was up to, which scared him.

He ushered Laura inside the theatre and up the stairs to the ballroom.

Laura's eyes lit up as she walked into the ballroom. The decorations were absolutely beautiful.

The couple was one of the first 20 people to arrive. The ballroom appeared rather empty.

Keith grabbed Laura's hand ushering her to the tables of food in order to offer her some punch. He figured this way; they would be near parent volunteers in case Corey were to try something.

Keith could see Corey walking up the stairs. He didn't trust him, and he was unsure how to react in any situation that Corey could be planning.

Meanwhile...

Nate had just exited off the highway.

Sally picked up the map and directed him down streets to the theatre.

Only 15 minutes later, Nate parked the car and ushered the ladies into the ballroom.

The crew took their positions and checked their walkie-talkies.

Code names were used.

It was time for Project Laura to begin.

Corey was standing in the corner staring over at Keith and Laura as they enjoyed small talk by the punch bowl.

Each of the crewmembers kept an eye on the doorways as well as Laura's whereabouts.

Laura smiled knowing the moment that she had waited a long while to enjoy had begun.

Keith looked into her eyes seeing her happiness.

The music played in the background as couples began to dance.

Keith extended his hand to usher Laura to the dance floor.

Laura accepted. Her night of magic had begun.

Chapter 10

Couples twirled around the dance floor.

The crew stood in their places watching Keith and Laura as they joined the other couples on the dance floor.

Corey eyed his prey. He was prepared to strike as soon as Laura was alone.

Keith ushered Laura onto the dance floor. The couple began to dance.

Laura smiled. She was enjoying herself as Keith swung her in circles. She was pleased that her partner was just as good of a dancer as she was.

Chief Sally smiled, even though she was a bit jealous of Laura's luck of finding such a gentleman. She only hoped that his actions tonight would not change that.

Nate watched with a suspicious eye. He didn't trust Keith. He focused his attention on Keith. He was not about to let anything happen to Laura.

The couples continued to gracefully twirl. The music played in the background.

Laura and Keith continued to dance. They didn't speak much rather they just enjoyed the atmosphere.

After several dances, the two took a break.

Laura walked off to the ladies room.

Sally and Ginger moved towards the ladies room. The three stood in line not too far behind each other.

Laura was first of the three girls. Sally was third behind her, while Ginger was sixth.

Corey saw Laura leave for the ladies' room. He moved closer in order to get a better view.

Nate was hot on his tail.

He hid himself not far from Corey, making sure Corey could not see him.

Keith sipped his punch while waiting for Laura to return.

The line began to move at the ladies room.

Finally around 10 minutes later, Laura took her turn.

Sally and Ginger watched waiting for her to come out.

Sally moved inside and took her turn, but Laura had not exited yet.

Ginger removed herself from the line to find Nate. She was having trouble reaching him on the walkie-talkie.

Laura exited the bathroom only a couple of seconds later.

While Ginger's back was turned, Corey grabbed Laura's arm.

Laura turned her head to realize who had latched on to her arm, only to find herself several feet from the ladies room.

She was in a state of shock.

Corey pulled her down a long hallway.

Nate followed making sure he was not seen by Corey.

Keith had grown impatient. He left the table to make his way to the restrooms.

Sally exited the ladies as Ginger approached her in a panic.

"She she she she is gone," Ginger said.

Sally look confused.

"What do you mean?" Sally asked.

"I don't see Laura or Nate anywhere," Ginger replied.

Sally gasped.

"Nate is not answering his walkie-talkie," Ginger added.

Sally could not believe her ears.

"When did you last see her?" Sally asked.

Ginger glanced down at her watch.

"About 10 minutes ago, when she went into the bathroom, before you came out. I spoke with Nate about 10 minutes before that," Ginger said.

Sally pulled Ginger over to the side.

"We have to find Laura and Nate. They could be in trouble," Sally said.

Fear was overcoming them.

Keith noticed Sally and Ginger by the ladies room. He walked up to them.

"Hi, ladies," he said.

Sally and Ginger turned to recognize his presence.

"Have you two seen Laura? She left me to go to the bathroom a while ago and has not returned yet," he asked.

Sally looked over at Keith.

"We saw her go into the bathroom. We did not see her leave, and she is not in there now," she said.

Keith just stared back.

A name entered his mind.

Corey. Corey. Corey.

"You mean she is missing and has been for at least 10 minutes.," he said.

Sally and Ginger nodded. They were too afraid of the possibilities.

Keith nodded and took off running.

He ran down the hall. Sally and Ginger followed, thinking he might know something about Laura's whereabouts.

Meanwhile...

Corey dragged Laura down the hall. He had knocked her out by pushing her into a wall earlier.

Nate wanted to attack Corey, but he didn't think he could take him on by himself.

He moved away into a side room, allowing himself to have a view of Corey, but far enough away to be out of earshot.

Nate picked up his walkie-talkie. He began to whisper into it.

"Chief, snaps, hello?" Nate asked.

Ginger pulled Sally over letting Keith run off alone.

"Listen," she said to Sally.

She held her walkie-talkie so they could both hear better.

"I'm on Corey's tail. He's got Laura. I need back up. I'm down in room 313, follow down the 300s. Corey has taken Laura into room 316. Hurry," Nate said.

Ginger looked up at the numbers on the doorways. The girls were standing under the doorway of 203.

"Where's your map?" Ginger asked.

Sally held up the map, while the girls looked for 316.

They split up. Ginger ran off to room 316, while Sally ran back to the ballroom.

Sally grabbed the first male chaperone she saw and explained to him the situation.

Sally ushered him down to room 316.

Laura regained consciousness. Corey looked at her. He had just locked the door behind him.

Laura realized who had grabbed her now.

She let out a loud scream hoping someone would hear.

Nate heard her. He moved and outside 316. He turned the doorknob; hoping help was on the way.

The door was locked.

Nate was scared. He was supposed to protect Laura and now he couldn't rescue her.

He could hear footsteps.

He smiled, knowing help was on the way.

Corey walked towards Laura.

"Shut up," he yelled.

He pulled out a knife.

Laura stood still in fear.

Corey walked closer.

"What do you want from me?" she asked.

Corey stared at her.

"You are going to get what you deserve," he declared.

Laura stepped back.

"Don't you move! I'm not afraid to hurt you," he ordered

Laura screamed again.

"Shut up. I don't know what you are worried about. You will like it," he said proudly.

Laura stood in confusion.

Footsteps became louder.

Ginger ran past room 307 getting closer to her destination.

Sally and the chaperone approached the 300 hallway.

Meanwhile...

Keith found himself lost.

He glanced at the doorways surrounding him. He had no idea where he was or how to get back to the ballroom.

He was lost.

Keith began to backtrack his steps.

He turned around and ran back down the hall.

Every hall looked the same.

Time was running out.

He knew he had to get to Laura.

He turned a corner.

One name was rushing through his head.

HIS WRATH

LAURA LAURA LAURA

He began to scream her name, hoping someone would hear him.

LAURA LAURA LAURA

Keith felt as if he was running in circles. All of the hallways looked the same.

Meanwhile…

Ginger tapped Nate on the shoulder.

Nate nodded.

They awaited Sally's arrival.

About a minute later, Sally and her new friend stood beside them.

The four of them went to work on the door.

On the other side, Corey was hearing his time growing short.

He turned his focus to Laura. He had already strapped her down on the floor.

He placed the knife back into this pocket and reached one of his hands down the top of her dress.

"Get your hands off of me," she screamed.

She raised her knee to try to nail him in the groin. She was unable to succeed.

"Watch it," he said.

He reached his other hand into his pocket and took back out the knife.

"I'm not afraid of hurting you," he said.

Laura was scared. She could hear people on the other side of the door. She hoped they would rescue her soon.

Corey was enjoying himself though. He continued to caress her boob.

He then removed his hand from her breast and bent down on one knee. He had the knife in one hand, while the other moved up her leg.

Outside Sally was looking through her purse for the screwdriver, she had brought.

She handed it to her math teacher, Mr. Moore.

Mr. Moore went to work on the doorknob.

He had to work fast. Corey's hand was moving fast.

Corey reached up under her dress and touched her panties. He began to remove them with one hand.

But Laura was not going to let him violate her.

She shook back and forth.

The knife flew out of his left hand. The knife had slide its way underneath a desk.

She looked at the desk, as Corey punched her.

Laura's head then hit the floor. She was knocked out once again.

Corey shook his head. He wanted her awake for his next move. He wanted her to feel pain.

The doorknob of the door began to rattle.

Mr. Moore had removed the knob and was now able to unlock the door from the outside.

Corey knew he had to buy himself more time. He pushed the large desk against the door as Mr. Moore began to open it.

The door was pushed closed.

Corey picked up Laura and moved her to the corner of the room.

Her laid his body down on top of her.

The crew along with Mr. Moore began to push the door. It would not budge.

Corey removed Laura's panties once again.

He then proceeded to pull off his boxer shorts.

He lay down on top of her body half-naked, but the desk behind him began to move just slightly.

Corey jumped up and pushed the desk back into position, but the pushing of the door continued.

He used all of his muscle to push the desk into the door.

Laura opened her eyes regaining consciousness. She tried to sit up and loosen the bands. She looked up at Corey.

"Did you?" she asked.

"Not yet. I will though," he said.

She was able to undo the bands, while Corey fixed the position of the desk.

Laura kicked up her leg and hit Corey in the head really hard. He fell backwards. She pulled back up her panties.

The desk came loose, as the door opened enough for one person to come in or to leave.

Laura smoothed out her dress and slid out of the room. The door shut behind her as she collapsed into Nate's arms.

Nate smiled, knowing Laura was now safe.

He just held her tight as Sally and Ginger stood beside them.

Mr. Moore slid into the room.

HIS WRATH

Corey was awake, but lying on the floor with his pants pulled down. As he saw a man enter the room, he quickly pulled up his pants and stood up.

"Corey, you're in trouble. Just wait until the principal hears what you attempted to do to that poor girl," Mr. Moore warned.

Corey just stared. He never thought he would get caught.

Mr. Moore paged the school's principal.

The crew escorted Laura off to the nearest restroom, so she could compose herself.

The principal arrived about a few minutes later.

She walked into the room to find Corey standing with his pants only half buttoned and Mr. Moore standing across from him just staring at Corey in shock.

"What happened?" she asked.

Mr. Moore turned his head to acknowledge her presence.

"Corey, here, attempted to rape Laura Lynn Timberwood. He locked her in this room and assaulted her. Luckily, her friends and I caught him before he was able to actually force her into sex," he said.

The principal looked over at Corey, who looked rather guilty.

"I see. Well, Corey, it looks like you are now suspended for the rest of the semester and will be forced to spend another semester in high school. I'll let the police handle the rest," she said.

She proceeded to page the policeman on duty.

Corey watched her as she paged the policeman in fear.

"I can't be suspended or arrested. I was only giving her what she deserves," he claimed.

He was devious. The evil boy truly felt as if he had done the right thing and that these two had interfered in him finishing his project.

The principal, on the other hand, wanted to ring his neck for trying to rape one of her students.

"I can't believe you. Inflicting pain on someone is never right. The police are on their way and believe me you are in trouble," she said.

Corey just glared at them. He realized there was no way out. The window was at least four levels off the ground, and the doorway was blocked by Mr. Moore. He could hear the policeman's footsteps coming down the hall. He was moving rather fast.

Meanwhile...

Laura cried in the ladies' room with Ginger and Sally at her side. Nate stood outside the doorway.

Keith was running so fast. He ran right past Nate and didn't even notice him.

"Keith!" Nate yelled.

Keith was shocked to hear his name. He had been lost for awhile. He turned around to see Nate standing outside of a restroom, and he walked over to Nate.

"Have you seen Laura?" Keith asked.

Nate nodded.

"She's inside cleaning up with Ginger and Sally," he said.

Keith looked confused.

"I lost her around an hour ago. What happened?" Keith asked.

"Sally, Ginger and I found her locked in a room with Corey. He was planning on raping her as justice for her good grades. We stopped him with Mr. Moore's help," Nate said.

Keith breathed a sigh of relief.

"Phew. Where is that Corey now?" Keith asked.

Nate pointed down the hall.

"In room 316 with the principal and Mr. Moore," he said.

Keith nodded and walked off in the direction that Nate pointed. He stood outside the open door where he could hear the policeman, Mr. Moore, the principal and Corey discussing his punishment.

He wanted to kill Corey with his bare hands. Raping Laura was his end of the deal not Corey's. Whether he was going to through with it or not was now irrelevant. Instead of Laura having a night to remember because of her time with Keith, she will have one because of Corey's decision to mess up the deal.

He was so angry with Corey that he let his feelings get the better of him as he pushed opened the door.

"What the hell is your problem?" Keith screamed.

"Keith, watch your language, and this does not concern you. I would appreciate it if you would leave," the principal said.

Keith's face turned red with anger.

"Laura is my girlfriend, and Corey has ruined her prom night," he declared.

The principal nodded.

"I understand. I'll excuse you for your outburst, but I think you should leave and let us handle this. Trust me. Corey will be punished," she said.

Keith nodded. He quietly turned away and walked back to Nate.

Corey was suspended for the rest of the year. He also sat in jail that night and would go to court for aggravated assault with intent to rape in the summer.

Keith and Nate just stood next to each other as they awaited Laura's recovery.

Meanwhile...

Inside the ladies room...

Laura was falling apart inside.

She had locked the door to the bathroom and shut herself out even from Ginger and Sally.

Ginger and Sally seemed hurt, but had no idea about what Laura had just gone through.

With the door locked, Laura's mind was spinning with questions.

Why would someone do that? Why me? Why me?

She held her head in her hands and stared down at the floor.

She was trying not to focus on the events that just happened, because she didn't want them to control her night.

Her body felt dirty. Corey had lain on top of her and gotten rather close to entering inside of her body.

What if he had? What if my friends didn't rescue me?

Laura didn't want to know the answers to those questions. She was hurt.

She had grown up in a rather loving environment. Her mother was her best friend throughout elementary and middle school. She was also blessed with a loving extended family.

Laura was a rather lucky child.

She had never been treated like she just was. Corey blamed her for everything grade related.

He made her feel as if somehow she actually deserved this punishment. She would also have a constant reminder of this night for a long time. There was already a bruise forming on the inside of her right leg from Corey and his persistent use of his strength to gain control of the situation.

She wondered if it was premeditated.

Laura was crushed and embarrassed.

Ginger and Sally stood outside her door, hoping she would let them in.

They were trying to offer a sense of comfort.

But it made no difference. Nothing could change what just happened.

The almost rape would have a large effect on Laura.

She was entering college in just a few short months to start a life of her own.

Her trust in people had been crushed. She would enter her new life by cutting herself off from the world.

She wondered how she could continue to face even her friends.

How could they understand? How did they get there so fast? Where was Keith? Did he have anything to do with this?

She knew that Corey and Keith had sat near each other at lunch before the two of them began dating.

Keith had also read the note and told Laura that he would take care of it.

That dreadful note...

> LAURA—
>
> Don't be too excited about tomorrow, smart girl. You are going down.

Laura pictured it her head.
And there was the paper that Nate found...

> Pros:
> Being Popular
> Respect
> Friends and parties
> Free answers to tests
>
> Cons:
> Hurting her
> The possibility of getting caught
> Graduation—only two months away
> Losing a friend, girlfriend and a study partner

One question stared her in the face.

Did they have anything to do with each other?

She realized she knew too little about Keith, but her feelings for him were too strong for her to believe that he had anything to do with the events of tonight.

She quickly dismissed the idea and allowed tears to stream down her face.

Laura was hurt.

She didn't know to express her pain in words.

She buried her head down in her lap.

Sally and Ginger pleaded for Laura to come out and let them care for her.

Laura was also in a state of denial.

Did this just happen? Am I here? Was I just attacked? Did it all really happen?

She picked up her head and stared at the door of the stall.

IT DID ALL HAPPEN!

She was just attacked.

She began to read the written markings on the bathroom walls.

Jenny was here.

Jenny is gay.

Call 897-3348, for a good time.

She wasn't sure if that was the number. The last four digits were written over by another comment.

I did. It was good.

It read.

That almost happened to me. It hit her.

Laura let out a large scream and started crying really hard.

Ginger and Sally stood outside the door repeating, "Let us in."

They banged on the door.

They even considered crawling underneath, but they figured that would be an invasion of Laura's privacy.

They wanted to end Laura's pain and to be supermen and rewind time.

IT WAS TOO LATE. THE DEED WAS DONE.

Sally and Ginger held each other as they waited patiently for Laura to give them a chance.

But Laura was not ready.

She had to get out and run away.
She stood up and began to mess with the door.
She pulled it open and ran out past Ginger and Sally.
She felt as if she was running from her past. She ran faster and faster with each minute passing.
Sally and Ginger grabbed Nate and Keith as Laura ran down the hall.
"Any idea where she is headed?" she asked.
All of them shook their heads and took off running after her.
Laura was running bare foot with her shoes in one hand and her purse in the other.
Nate was not far behind her.
Ginger and Sally were a few feet back.
Keith had exited to the parking lot and climbed in his car.
He rounded to the front of the building, hoping Laura would run out the front door.
Laura did not want to go home, rather she wanted to run until all of it disappeared.
Footsteps echoed down the halls of the theatre.
Chaperones worked hard to keep the students dancing and enjoying the prom, while Corey was escorted out and taken to a jail.
Meanwhile...
Keith's mom sat in the living room with a bucket of ice cream.
She felt as if she had failed him. She had failed her only son.
It was rocky road that she drowned her sorrows in.
Meanwhile...
Other parents waited for their children to return home as Laura's speed increased.
She only slowed down to enter an elevator.
She pushed the button for the top floor.
Ginger, Sally and Nate entered the next elevator and pushed every button. They landed on each floor and poked out their heads to see a trace of Laura, but by the time they reached the floor, Laura had already begun her journey back down.
Keith waited her arrival outside. He turned up the radio hoping that she would hear it.
Laura rode back down an elevator with tears gliding down her cheeks. She landed on the first floor and ran off down the first hall.

Ginger exited off at the top level and began searching for Laura, while Nate and Sally rode back down.

They had lost her.

They had no idea where she went.

Laura was scared and running from her past all by herself.

She felt as if no one could understand the emotions she was tackling.

Sally and Ginger didn't understand how Laura was reacting to this.

Neither of them had ever had any physical contact with a guy.

They had expected Laura to run into their open arms and let them take her home.

Laura had done no such thing.

Therefore, the girls felt crushed.

Nate had been in several relationships some of which had been rather physical. He had always been the one shelling out the pain at the end rather than receiving it. He had broken up with over 10 girls over the past two years.

His break-up talks used the phrases of: It's not you, it's me. I need some space. I just don't think we should date any more. We should see other people. He could only imagine what each of his former girlfriends felt after hearing those.

He didn't know what to say to Laura.

Rather he wanted to hurt Corey. To pick him up with his bare hands and choke him to death.

That was the extent of anger rushing through Nate's body.

But his anger was pointless.

Corey was sitting in the back of a police car on his way to the local jail.

Corey was disappointed and pissed on the inside.

He had been unable to finish his job, and he blamed Laura's friends. They had been added to his list of his victims.

He figured he had all night to ponder how to get them back for cutting his time short with Laura.

He imagined what he could have done if he had time.

He closed his eyes and replayed the events in this head.

Corey had laid his body on top of Laura's half-naked body.

He reached his right hand up.

BOOM.
The police car rode over a speed bump, and Corey's thoughts were jolted.

He opened his eyes realizing he was still in a police car.

"My parents are going to kill me," he commented to himself.

The sirens roared above his head.

Meanwhile...

Keith sat outside the front of the building blocking a portion of the front entrance.

Keith continued to hope Laura would hop into the car.

But Laura turned another corner.

She collapsed as she walked into the box office area.

She collapsed onto a couch and buried her head into the cushions.

She sat up and realized where she was. She saw Keith waiting outside in his car.

She fought all of her unanswered questions and jumped in Keith's car.

Keith leaned over and tried to hug Laura. He was overjoyed to see her.

Laura pushed Keith away and turned her head to look away from him.

"I'll take you home," he said.

"I don't want to go home," she whined.

Keith seemed confused.

"I'll take you anywhere you want to go," he said.

Laura just shook head.

"That place does not exist," she said.

Keith pulled out of the parking lot.

Laura placed her shoes and purse on the floor.

She just shook her head and as tears continued to fall down her cheeks.

Keith pulled onto the highway as Laura continued to shut him out.

Meanwhile...

Ginger, Sally and Nate had met back up at the box office on the first floor.

Each of them disappointed in losing Laura.

They sat on the same couch Laura had buried her head in only a little while ago.

They were dismayed, overwhelmed and without a plan.
The crew sat with their equipment piled to the side.
They wished they could've only gotten to the crime scene earlier.
BUT IT WAS TOO LATE! LAURA WAS SUFFERING FROM THE WRATH OF COREY.
    Corey had accomplished his mission even if he was disappointed.
He had hurt Laura.
He had hurt her enough to cause her to lose her trust in others.
That was one of the features of her wholesome personality.
Corey had destroyed that.
Part of her identity was now missing.
Laura was not herself.
She just sat in Keith's car unable to face the truth.
She stared out at the highway watching cars pass by.
The music roared on the radio.
Keith focused on his driving as he tried to think of a quiet place to take Laura too.
Corey had stolen the night with his actions.
Keith's mission didn't matter anymore.
The night was already a night Laura would remember, but not for the reasons Keith wanted.
He had dropped his original plans and decided to just figure out how to bring a smile back to Laura's face.
Laura would never know what Keith had planned for her that night.
She would only see some clues much later in life.
At that time she would know the difference.
It was too late for Keith and too late for Laura.
Their lives have already been changed by Corey and his actions.

Chapter 11

Sally, Ginger and Nate were about to abort the mission, when Sally turned to Ginger and looked at her in fear.

"I wonder if this all leads back to Keith. Where is he?" Sally asked.

Ginger and Nate just stared back.

They had no idea where he was.

"Let's see if his car is still parked outside," Nate said.

The crew picked up their equipment and dropped it off in their car.

They walked over to where they had seen Keith park his car earlier.

IT WAS GONE.

Sally shook her head.

"Where is he?" she asked.

"Does he have Laura?" Ginger asked.

Nate stared at the empty parking spot.

The crew was rather worried about Laura's whereabouts.

"If he has her, they are long gone now," Sally said.

Ginger just nodded.

Nate kept staring, hoping the car would reappear with Laura in it, but no Keith.

THIS WAS BAD.

The crew knew it.

Laura was hurting inside while she was driven off somewhere by Keith.

Sally wondered what would happen to her.

She looked over at Ginger and Nate and motioned for them to follow her.

She walked back to her car.

They each climbed in.

Sally turned on the car and pulled out of the theatre.

She didn't know where she was driving to.

HIS WRATH

She just knew Laura needed them.

And she needed them now.

Sally was driving as fast as the speed limit would allow her. She had no idea where she was going.

Nate and Ginger sat in the car worried about Laura's safety, hoping Ginger had a good idea.

Meanwhile...

Keith turned in a local county park. He parked his car in the front parking lot.

Laura realized the car had stopped a few seconds later. Keith had already exited the car and was walking around to her door.

He stood in front of her door.

She just turned her head and stared at him.

Her head was spinning: What does this kid want from me? Can he turn back time? Could all of this be his fault? Why won't he just leave me alone?

"Laura," Keith said.

He extended out his left hand and held the door open with his right hand. He welcomed her to the park.

"I brought you here to relax. I go here to think sometimes, when the world becomes too hard to handle. I just come here and think. It's peaceful," he said.

Laura just nodded. She was not in the mood to think. She ran from her thoughts only around 30 minutes ago.

"I know you want to run from your past, but you can't. You are a strong girl, and I'm here for you," he said.

Laura just nodded.

"Come on. Let's go for a walk," he pleaded.

Laura accepted and placed her hand on top of Keith's. He squeezed it and helped her out of the vehicle. He continued to hold her hand as he spoke.

"Let me show you where I go, okay," he said.

Laura nodded once again. She had no will to speak.

Meanwhile...

Sally on other hand exited off the highway. She had no idea where she was going. She just kept thinking: If I were Keith, where would I go? Home? No. To a quiet place? Maybe. To Laura's house? No. But where?

She pulled into the first gas station on her right. She needed to think. The car came to a halt.

Ginger turned to look at Sally. She had been thinking too. She wondered why Sally had stopped.

Nate was just worried and was trying not to think. His only thoughts were on if Keith was trying to take advantage of Laura's vulnerable state.

"We need to think," Sally said.

Ginger nodded.

"Keith might take Laura to a quiet place where they can be alone. Where would that be?" Sally said.

Ginger stared outside of her window.

Nate looked down at the floor, hoping that one of them would have a brainstorm.

"What's quiet around here? Nature, maybe?" Ginger said.

"That's it. Ginger! A park!" Sally screamed.

Ginger didn't even realize that her idea made a lot of sense. Laura is disturbed and of course nature is a good cure for that.

"Now where is a good park in this city?" Sally asked.

Ginger shook her head. None of them had ever been to a park in the city.

"Who would know where all the parks are? How do we choose which one?" Sally wondered.

The crew had a dilemma.

They needed to get to Laura, but too many details were missing.

Will they make it in time? Will Keith try anything? Will Keith continue being a gentleman towards Laura?

Meanwhile...

Keith's mom wondered the same question.

She continued to chow down on her ice cream. She knew her boy was a typical teenager.

She wondered how involved he has been with his girlfriends and Laura. She was only thinking like a protective mother. Being that she did not have a daughter, she considered Laura as one.

She didn't want anything to happen to her, especially with her boy Keith.

She was watching a movie on Lifetime. *Sleepless in Seattle* had ended.

These movies always made her wish she had chosen to be a full-time mom.

Did she make wrong decision? Is Keith suffering from not growing up with a mother?

Tears fell down her face.

She began to sob.

She knew she had worked, so that Keith could grow up being able to have whatever he needed or wanted.

But did she spoil him?

Other mothers might say she did. However, she just wanted her son to have the privileges she didn't have growing up.

After all, that is part of a mother's duty, but was the cost too high? Had she missed out on her son's life and maybe his future?

She continued to drown herself in tears.

Her son Keith was down at a local park.

He had escorted Laura over to the nearest swing set.

Laura sat down on a swing.

"Would you like me to push you?" he asked.

She shook her head, "no."

Keith frowned. He wanted her to be happy again, but it was too late. She was already hurt.

Keith sat down on a swing next to her.

"Do you want to talk about it?" he asked.

Laura just sat still and didn't reply.

Keith was trying rather hard to be there for her, but he got the idea that she just wanted to be alone.

"Do you want to be alone? I can take you home," he said.

Laura just nodded.

Keith nodded and reached out his hand.

He escorted her back to the car, and he drove off to her house.

He arrived not too much later and walked her to the door. He hugged her.

Laura just smiled and walked inside the house.

She ran down to her room, darting her parents' attention. She certainly didn't want to talk to them.

She locked her door behind her and turned on some music. She then tore off her dress and threw on a big t-shirt.

She laid her head into her pillow and cried a million tears.

Her one and only high school prom night had been ruined.

Keith arrived home a few moments later to find his mom in tears.

Feeling sorry and already having had a ruined night, he figured he would give her a chance.

"Mom, are you all right?" he asked.

He being home so early surprised her. She ran over and wrapped her arms around him.

Keith just let her hug him.

"Would you please let me in?" she asked.

Keith had little strength left, so he just nodded.

Keith's mom smiled and backed up.

"Want to watch a movie? Want a snack?" she asked.

Keith smiled. His mom was trying so hard to be a mom before he went off to college.

The two moved into the kitchen and put ice cream sundaes together. They then threw in more of an action movie than her lifetime movie.

The doors had been opened. The two of them could reunite...

BUT Sally, Ginger and Nate were still looking for a nearby park.

The crew had gained a list of parks, but none of them had any idea of where they were.

Sally started driving the car back to her house from the gas station.

She drove for a good 15 minutes, finding herself still 10 minutes from her house.

The crew was about to give up when they saw Keith's car was sitting in a parking lot across the street. The parking lot belonged to a park.

Sally sped up and made a u-turn at the next light.

She pulled in and parked near the end of parking lot almost out of view from Keith's car.

Out of the corner of her eye, she could see a female and a male enter Keith's car and drove off.

Sally backed up and followed far behind the car.

Keith's car turned towards Laura's home; about three cars behind them, Sally turned too.

Little talk occurred in the crew's car, since Keith's car was their focus.

Keith was so focused on getting Laura home that he didn't even notice that a car was following him.

HIS WRATH

He turned into Laura's subdivision.
Sally followed him.
"I think he is taking her home," she said.
Sally continued driving through the subdivision and pulled into Nate's driveway as Keith sped out of the subdivision, and Laura walked down the hallway of her home.
Sally breathed a sigh of relief, knowing Laura was home safe. She turned around and drove to her house. Ginger was spending the night at Sally's.
Nate climbed out of the car and walked around to the front door of the car.
"Thanks for the night ladies," he said.
He walked them to the door.
Sally and Ginger nodded.
"Since, Laura is home safe; it looks like our job is done," he said.
Sally and Ginger nodded.
"Good night," he said.
The girls smiled.
Nate drove off to go home.
Sally and Ginger were home safely.
Nate arrived home and looked outside his window.
He couldn't see anything, so he picked up the phone.
"Hello," Laura's mom said.
"Is Laura home?" he asked.
"I think I saw her run in. Hold on," she said.
Laura's mom walked down the hall and knocked on Laura's door.
"Go away," Laura said.
"But Nate's on the phone," her mom said.
"I'll get it," Laura said.
Laura's mom walked back up the hall.
Laura sat up and wiped her cheeks with her hand.
"Hello," she said.
She spoke softly not having the will to talk.
"I just called to let you know I'm here for you, and if I could I would kill that Corey for what he attempted to do to you," he said.
Laura nodded. She knew Nate was a true friend.
"Thanks," she said.
She took a long breath.

"But I'm not in the mood to talk," she added.
"I understand, but I'm here if you need me," he added.
Laura nodded.
"Okay. Good night, then," Laura said.
She hung up and threw her head back in the middle of the pillow.
Nate put the phone down, hoping his gesture was understood.
But neither of them knew that Laura's mom had listened in on their conversation.
Laura's mom stormed down the hall and pounded on Laura's door.
KNOCK. KNOCK.
"Come out here and talk to me young lady," her mom begged.
Laura tried to ignore her.
"I know you can hear me," her mom continued.
Laura threw on some pants and pulled up her screen on her window and shined a flash light over at Nate's window.
The two of them used to do this often as a call for help.
Laura had no way out of her room, but Nate did shine a light back on her light.
He wasn't sure what to do. He quickly changed into jeans and t-shirt and walked across the street.
Laura's mom was rather angry still knocking on Laura's door and yelling for her to come out when Nate rang the doorbell.
Laura's mom walked down the hall and opened the door for Nate.
"Hi. Laura asked for me to come over," he said.
Laura's mom nodded.
"Go ahead down the hall," she said.
She walked off with her face red with anger. She wanted to find out how her daughter's only prom went.
Nate knocked on Laura's door.
Laura walked slowly to the door with little energy.
She let Nate in.
"Are you all right?" he asked.
Laura just nodded.
Nate could see that she was trying to get out of having to talk to her mother about her night.
Nate sat on the bed next to Laura.
Nate was waiting patiently for Laura to feel comfortable enough to share her inner turmoil with him.

HIS WRATH

Meanwhile...

Keith and his mom continued watching the movie together.

They have not spent more than an hour with each other in a long time. Keith's mom was rather enjoying spending time with her son.

Keith enjoyed having a mother again. When he was younger, he looked to his mother for comfort and approval, but the lack of her availability had caused him to shut her out. Letting her in was a large accomplishment for him.

Keith still held grudges, but he was giving her chance.

Keith's mom smiled over at her son, letting him know that she cared about him.

Her smile caused him to feel special, especially after how wrong the day had gone.

He didn't share the events of the night with his mom. Sharing his feelings and events in his life with a person that basically just reentered his life would take a while.

Right now, just being civil to his mom was hard enough.

Keith had grown up in a parentless environment therefore he grew up on his own with little guidance.

That's tough in a generation where his or her fellow students judge a student each day. A child needs the love and attention of his or her parents.

Keith sighed as he remembered how he missed out on boy scouts and father/mother-son trips.

Rather he spent his time with other kids who had been abandoned. They were raised by the dollar sign.

The popular crowd took him. He envied children, who had parents who spent time with them, but he ostracized them and members of the middle class just like rest of the popular crowd.

When he met Corey, he wanted so badly to earn his and others' approval as he started at a new school.

But Laura just accepted him for who he was. That was the first time anyone had opened his or her heart to Keith.

He didn't know how to respond. He had shared pieces of himself with her, but opening up his heart as well as she did was hard for him.

He had sealed off feelings of love. That's why the idea of hurting and raping someone didn't even phase him until he had really gotten to know Laura.

She trusted him and shared her feelings on several issues with him. She also shared her future goals and aspirations in life with him.

Keith could recognize the emotions she shared with him. He could see the pain that Corey caused in her eyes earlier.

The anger he felt towards Corey was one of the few emotions he had felt in a while.

He knew that he enjoyed every minute of his time with Laura, and he wanted to be able to return the attention.

He had actually fallen for a girl, instead of treating one like an object.

But Keith's lack of feeling was holding him back from getting the full experience of a first love relationship.

Keith knew in order for him to continue dating Laura, he would have to respond and begin to open up. That task would take a lot of growth.

This was truly a developing stage for Keith.

Meanwhile...

Sally and Ginger were tucked in their beds.

Laura's mom was waiting impatiently for an update from her daughter.

Nate on the other hand was acting like a true best friend.

He hugged Laura and comforted her.

"I'm here for you. You take your time," he said.

Laura just nodded. The state of shock was still settling in.

Corey had destroyed Laura's innocent outlook on the world.

Nate knew that Laura would be able to share her feelings with him in her own time.

"Nate, I appreciate you being here for me. The events tonight really shook me. I still feel like I'm running from the past," she said.

Nate nodded.

"Laura, you have a beautiful heart and a great personality. I hope as your friend that you don't let Corey's actions change any of that. You don't deserve this," he said.

Laura just nodded.

Laura was grateful for Nate's friendship and Ginger and Sally's also. After all, they did rescue her from the wrath of Corey.

She just wished that she would have reconsidered her decision to attend prom in the first place. She hated that her only prom had been tainted.

Chapter 12

Laura laid her head down on Nate's lap. He stroked her hair as she fell asleep.

Nate knew it was time for him to leave. He had accomplished his mission by keeping her mother from bothering her.

He kissed Laura on the forehead, moved her head to the pillow and slid out her door, closing it tightly behind him.

"Nate," Laura's mom said.

Nate turned around to find Laura's mom standing next to him. He had been unsuccessful on leaving without being seen.

"Laura's asleep," he said.

Laura's mom nodded.

"I wanted to talk to her. She came home earlier than we expected, and I wondered why," she said.

Nate nodded.

"Laura had an interesting night, but I'll let her talk to you about it in the morning. Good night," he said.

Laura's mom sighed. She didn't want to wait until morning.

"Good night," she said.

Nate turned and walked down the hall and left the house.

Laura slept a wonderful night's sleep.

Her mind drifted to a far off place from the inner turmoil.

Keith, on the other hand, was just beginning to let his mom in, in an effort to end his inner turmoil.

The movie had ended and the two had parted for bedtime.

Keith was looking forward to the next morning. He felt a little kid who had just gotten his mother back.

His mom was glad he had decided to give her a chance.

She was on the phone with the senator.

"Hello. Honey," Keith's dad said.

Keith's mom smiled.

"He opened up to me. He watched a movie with me," she said.

Keith's dad chuckled.

"I guess our Keith can forgive us, well at least you," he said.

"He will forgive you in time, if you spend the summer here with him," she added.

Keith's dad nodded.

"I plan on it," he said.

Keith's mom smiled.

"Wonderful. It's a surprise!" she said.

Keith's dad chuckled.

"Sure is. I don't think the three of us have spent a summer together in a while. I was hoping we could go on a family trip," he said.

Keith's mom was glad that her family was reuniting.

"That sounds lovely. I'll ask Keith where he would like to go," she said.

Keith's dad nodded.

"I only wish that he had shared more with me about his prom night," she said.

Keith's dad nodded.

"Give him time. He needs to know that he can trust you before he opens up," he said.

He paused.

"Maybe, tomorrow. He might need the night to sort through things," he said.

The couple continued on with their conversations and later said good night.

Nate called the police to assure them that everyone had gotten home all right after the night's occurrences.

"Hello. This is Nate. May I have the police officer on duty when Mr. Corey Dawson was brought in?" Nate asked.

The secretary asked him to hold.

"Yes. Nate, Corey is locked up for the night," Officer Fuller said.

Nate nodded and smiled.

"I just wanted to inform you that the girl he attacked got home all right," he said.

Officer Fuller nodded.

"Good. I was just about to check in on her. I just found a phone number for her family," he said.

Nate smiled, knowing that he had stopped him from calling Laura's house and scaring her mother.

HIS WRATH

"Well, I have done my job. Good night," he said.

"Nate, I appreciate your help in catching Corey tonight. I also appreciate you making sure the girl got home all right. I usually check in on the family the day after a case like this. I plan on calling them in the morning," the officer said.

"I don't think that's necessary," Nate said.

"It's part of my job. It would be great, if you could be there too. I'll call you tomorrow," the officer said.

Nate gave the officer his phone number.

"Thank you and good night," the officer said.

Nate hung up.

He logged onto his computer.

Laura and he had set up an online message system when they were younger.

The system could only be accessed by a password that only Nate and Laura knew.

Nate opened the system with their password.

Laura's message stated: "At the prom dancing away the night."

Nate sent her a message.

"The officer that arrested Corey plans on calling you in the morning. He wants to come over to see how you are doing. I hope you get this in time. I didn't want to wake you with a phone call or leave a message with your mom."

He signed off and climbed into bed.

"Sunday is another day," he thought.

Sunday morning's sun appeared high in the sky as Laura sat and rubbed her eyes.

She had slept well.

She noticed that Nate had left the flashlight showing his window, which meant he had sent her a message.

Laura couldn't remember the last time he sent a message. The system had been neglected due to her new relationship.

It must be important she thought.

She rushed over to her computer, turned it on and logged on to the message system.

Eventually her message inbox popped up, saying "one new message."

Laura pressed the button and waited for the message to appear.

It read: "The officer that arrested Corey plans on calling you in the morning. He wants to come over to see how you are doing. I hope you get this in time. I didn't want to wake you with a phone call or leave a message with your mom."

Laura was surprised by the message.

Laura closed her message box and dashed out the door of her room to the kitchen. She arrived in the kitchen to find her mom cooking pancakes.

"Has anyone called this morning?" she asked.

Laura's mom shook her head. She motioned for Laura to have a seat at the table. Laura followed her direction.

"Do you want to explain why you came home early and Nate came over here to see you?" her mom asked.

Laura just wanted her mom to leave the subject alone and let what happened last night be none of her business, but she new that she would not drop it. She also knew that an officer was going to call and come over. Laura figured it would be better for her mom to hear it from her than the officer.

"I was attacked last night," Laura replied.

Laura's mom turned around with a cooking utensil still in her hand.

"You were what?" her mom gasped.

She couldn't believe her ears.

"Corey, a student, attacked and attempted to rape me," Laura continued.

Laura's mom turned off the pan and angrily threw the pancakes on a plate and placed in front of Laura's face. She then brushed off her apron and sat down across from Laura.

"Are you all right?" her mom asked.

Laura nodded just staring at the large pile of pancakes sitting in front of her. She was starving.

"Corey grabbed me, pulled me into another room and proceeded to threaten me with a knife, and he attempted to rape me. However, I was rescued by a teacher, Sally, Ginger and Nate," Laura said.

Laura's mom looked confused and angry.

"Where was Keith?" her mom asked.

"He was trying to find me," Laura said.

Laura's mom nodded, but she was suspicious of his actual whereabouts.

"After the police arrived and took Corey off, I ran out of the building, and Keith was outside in his car waiting for me. He took me home early," Laura said.

Laura's mom nodded.

"The officer on duty wants to come over here today, in order to check on me and talk to you and dad. He should be calling some time soon," Laura said.

Laura's mom nodded once again. She was too angry to speak. How dare someone attack her little girl?

Laura stood up after sharing the story with her mom and grabbed herself a plate, some utensils, and glass of orange juice and pancake syrup. She was done with talking for the day. She just wanted to eat and then hate the world for what had happened last night.

Her mother just sat their at the kitchen table with her jaw dropped. She was in a state of shock.

The phone rang.

Neither one of them moved.

Someone must have picked up the phone, because it did not ring a second time.

"Hey, pick up, it's for you," her brother yelled.

He yelled down the hall.

Laura was speechless. She slowly walked over to the phone picked it up.

"Laura?" the officer asked.

"Yes," she said.

She said it so softly.

"Are you all right today? You went through a lot last night," he asked.

She repeated, "yes," in the same way.

"We have taken Corey in, and I want to assure you he will receive a severe punishment. You are pressing charges right?" he asked.

She repeated, "yes," once more.

"Good. Some girls blame themselves after something like this," he added.

Laura just nodded.

"Listen, I want to come over and make sure you are okay. I also want to talk to your parents. You should also go see a doctor as soon as possible," he said.

Laura repeated, "yes," once again.

"I will," she said.

"Good, I'll be over in an hour," he said.

Laura nodded.

She hung up knowing that it was over, but she would have to face an officer in person soon.

"Mom," she said.

Her mom just turned her head. She was too focused on what Laura had just shared with her.

"The police officer will be here in an hour," Laura said.

"Oh my. I'm not ready," her mom said.

That wasn't exactly what she should be worried about, but she ran down the hall to make herself more presentable.

She also shared Laura's news with Laura's dad.

Not to mention her brother who always overheard too much for his own good.

Laura just sat at the kitchen table and ate her food slowly. She was in no hurry.

Not too much later, her brother tapped her on the shoulder.

"So someone tried to get you for being smart?" her brother said.

Laura waited a second. She didn't expect for her brother to find out. This was private and none of his business.

"Who told you?" she asked.

"I overheard. You know where my hiding place is," he said.

Laura just nodded she was embarrassed.

She picked up her plate, threw away what was left and then placed it in the sink. She stormed off down the hall and shut her door behind her.

She proceeded to lock it. That's it.

The world had really done it. Corey had taken a nice, smart and pretty girl and turned her into a depressed, confused and angry teenager.

She signed herself back onto the message system and sent Nate a message. He was the closest friend she had right now.

"NATE, GET OVER HERE NOW!"

It read.

She jumped on the bed and buried her head in her pillow. Her life had been turned upside down.

Meanwhile…

Nate was just getting out of bed when his computer dinged letting him know that he had a message.

He jumped out of bed, grabbing a pair of jeans in the process.

He put them on as he pulled up his message from Laura.

He sat down in front of the computer, wearing no shirt and pants without socks.

The message opened on the screen.

"NATE, GET OVER HERE NOW!"

Nate knew what that meant—the police officer was on his way.

He shut off his computer, rushed over to his dresser and grabbed a shirt, socks and went then in the closet for shoes.

Nate threw his outfit on and grabbed his house keys and ran out the door.

"Bye. I'm going to Laura's," he yelled.

"Okay," his mom said.

She was in the kitchen making herself some eggs. She thought nothing of it. She knew they were close friends.

Nate dashed across the street and banged on the front door.

Laura's mom was dressed now. Thinking it was the officer, she walked casually to the door.

She opened it.

"Nate?" she looked surprised.

Nate nodded.

"I'm here to see Laura," he replied.

Laura's mom nodded. She was disappointed that Laura had not told her that Nate was coming over.

"Well, you can go find her. She's here somewhere," she said.

She walked back down the hall to apply more makeup, since she had more time.

Nate knew Laura was in her room.

He walked down the hall and knocked on the door.

Laura used all strength left and walked over to the door. She opened it and shut it behind him.

"When is the officer supposed to be here?" he asked.

"In 30 minutes or so," she answered.

Nate nodded.

"I'll do all of the talking. We will get you through this," he said.

Laura nodded and lay back down on the bed.

"I'm so angry, and I feel so dirty. He wants me to go see a doctor," she said.

Laura and Nate had a friendship where they both felt so comfortable that sharing anything didn't bother Laura.

She knew that on some level he understood.

She buried her head back in the pillow.

The world had done her wrong.

Laura was not the type of person to blame GOD for the events of last night. She attended church, but she had not felt a passion for religion nor had a personal relationship with him for years.

She blamed Corey. Nate blamed Corey.

Nate sat down next to her and stroked her hair. There was nothing he could say to make her feel any better. Rather he knew what was done was done.

Time flew by.

For Laura, hours could pass, days could pass, but all she wanted to do was to rewind time.

BUT what was done was done.

Meanwhile...

Keith woke up and walked downstairs to find his mom cooking, since she had given the servants the weekend off.

"Good morning. I need to call Laura," he said.

His mom just nodded.

Keith picked up the phone.

Laura's brother answered it once again.

"Hold on," he said. "Hey, it's for you again," he yelled.

Laura and Nate barely heard him with her door closed.

Laura spoke into the pillows.

"Would you get that?" she said to Nate.

Nate picked up the phone.

"Hello," he said.

"Is Laura there?" Keith asked.

"She's next to me. This is Nate. She's not really in the mood for chatting," Nate said.

Keith nodded.

"It's Keith. I was calling to see how she was doing and to see if she needed me to come over," he said.

"It was nice of you to check in on her. I'm here for her, but I'll have her call you later," Nate said.

Keith nodded with disappointment.

"Okay," he said.

They hung up the phone as the doorbell rang.

Officer Fuller was standing at the front door.

Laura's mom opened the door and let the officer in on the third or fourth ring.

"Officer Fuller, ma'am," he said to Laura's mom.

He shook her hand.

"Nice to meet you. I'm Laura's mother. Would you like something to drink?" she asked him.

He nodded and the two of them walked towards the kitchen.

Nate and Laura looked over at each other knowing it was time to face the officer's questions.

They left Laura's room and walked to the kitchen out of obligation.

"Thank you for the coffee," he said.

He paused to take a sip.

"Hello there, Laura," he said.

Laura just nodded, and they sat down at the kitchen table.

"And Nate, right?" he added.

Nate nodded.

"Laura, how are you doing after last night?" he asked.

Laura was not in the mood to be questioned.

"I'm fine," she said.

The officer knew that the conservation would be light after an attack like last night.

"What you went through last night must be hard on you," he said.

Laura nodded.

"We have a counselor on staff, if you would like to talk to her. I will also keep you updated on Corey's situation. He is being charged, since we caught him red-handed. He spent the night in jail, and since it was a school-sponsored event, he has already been expelled from your school," he continued.

Laura nodded. She was glad he was being punished, but it didn't fix the past.

Officer Fuller had realized by now that he wasn't going to get much out of Laura. He felt for her. He had seen several ladies raped or attacked during his years as an officer. This is a visit he certainly did not enjoy nor ever want to do, but he did enjoy meeting new people.

Laura just listened to all the officer had to say and stored it in her memory, rather than responding. It was too soon.

Nate rubbed Laura's back to show support during the officer's visit.

The officer turned his attention to her mother.

"Mrs. Timberwood, do you know the full story?" he asked.

She nodded, standing over the counter.

"Laura filled me in this morning. Of course, I'm not sure who Corey is or how his reasoning led to threatening my baby," she said.

He could hear the anger in her voice.

"He felt that it was Laura's fault that he was failing his senior year. People with that little hope tend to blame others and then lash out at others," the officer said.

Laura's mom just nodded with a stern face.

"Nevertheless, it gives him no right to hurt my baby, and he better pay," she said.

Officer Fuller understood her anger.

"Believe me, being that he was caught red-handed, thanks to Laura's friends, he will," he said.

All of them nodded on that account.

"Nate, I appreciate you, as I am sure Laura does looking out for her. If it wasn't for you and those two other ladies, something even more devastating could have happened to our Laura. That would have been a travesty," he added.

Nate nodded.

"Well, Laura received a note from Corey earlier that week," Nate said.

He read it aloud.

> Laura—
> Don't be too excited about tomorrow, smart girl. You are going down.

Officer Fuller nodded listening attentively to the new information.

"Once Laura notified me, Sally and Ginger about that note, we became worried about her safety for the prom. We formed a plan to protect her. Laura has also been dating a guy, who is new to the school and has a questionable past according to some sources. He has been wonderful to Laura, but nevertheless, we figured it was necessary for us to be prepared," he said.

Officer Fuller took notes on the new information.

"I'm going to add this new information to the record, if you don't mind. Additional threats could cause a harsher sentence for Corey especially since he is just over 18. I appreciate you looking out for Laura's safety. Is there anything else I should include in my report?" he said.

Nate shook his head. Being that Keith had nothing to do with the attack, he left out the paper he had found on the library floor. He still personally pondered Keith's involvement in the attack, but there was no evidence, and he knew Laura would disagree with him.

Officer Fuller knew his visit was over.

Officer Fuller said thank you and left the family, while Laura and Nate took their chance to exit to Laura's room.

Meanwhile...

Keith's mom had cooked French toast, his favorite. She was excited that Keith was giving her a chance.

Keith on the other hand was having trouble grasping what Laura was going through. He wanted to help her and be there for her. He felt as if Nate had taken his spot, and moved on in.

He wondered what that meant.

Nah. He discarded that thought as quickly as it had entered. He knew that they had a friendly history, and he did live closer.

Therefore, it means she called him for comfort. Besides she might not feel comfortable around her boyfriend right now.

But he missed her and wanted to do his part.

He just listened to the dial tone as he thought. He hadn't realized that he was still holding the phone.

"Keith? Are you hungry?" his mom asked.

Keith snapped back into reality. He finally hung up the phone.

Keith's mom waited patiently for his response.

"Oh yeah. I'm very hungry," he answered.

Keith's mom turned her head.

"Is everything all right? You look confused," she said.

Keith sat down at the kitchen table before replying.

"It's just Laura," he said.

Keith's mom nodded with hopes that he would continue.

Keith all of a sudden felt inclined to continue.

"She was attacked last night," he continued.

Keith's mom turned around really fast shifting her attention to him.

"What?" she asked.

"This guy attempted to rape Laura last night," he continued.

Keith's mom didn't respond. She just wanted to hear more.

"The officer got to her in time before he did anything. Her friends and I tried to comfort her after it happened. I even took her home last night, but she is suffering," he said.

Keith's mom nodded encouraging him to continue.

He took a deep breath.

His mom walked over to the pan lifted out his toast and placed it on a plate.

She served him the toast with a fork, juice and syrup on the side.

"I just called Laura to check on her. Her friend, Nate, is there comforting her. Therefore I'm not needed," he said.

She took a seat next to him with her own glass of juice. She had eaten before Keith awoke.

"I'm sure you are needed, but she might need to be alone right now. Nate is probably just there," she said.

He looked over at his mom He didn't expect an answer like that.

"What do you mean?" he asked.

"Well. Does Laura get along with her family?" she asked.

Keith thought for a minute.

"They are rather overprotective, and her mom is rather nosy," he said.

Keith's mom understood.

"Keith, I'm going to share something with you okay," she said.

Keith began eating slowly in order to pay attention. He also nodded.

"When I was a teenager, I was raped and became pregnant. I had a miscarriage though," she said.

Keith just stared at her.

"What? Mom?" he asked.

She nodded.

"I grew up in a broken home and a poor neighborhood. Several girls my age in our city were attacked or raped while I was in high school," she said.

Keith just nodded.

"So you have been in Laura's position," he said.

Keith's mom nodded.

"Actually I was worse off, since I was not only raped, but I was pregnant for two weeks before I lost the baby," she said.

Keith was silent as he finished his food.

"Maybe, it would help Laura if she knew that she wasn't alone," she said.

Keith just continued eating.

"I'll talk to her the next time she comes over," she said.

Meanwhile…

Laura and Nate sat in her room.

Laura was attempting to cope with her feelings of anger, depression and fear.

She just lay on her bed falling in and out of consciousness.

But it was time for everyone else to check in on her.

The phone began to ring again.

Ring.

Laura's brother picked up the phone.

"Hey. Pick up," he screamed at his sister.

"Nate, would you?" she responded.

Nate nodded.

"Hello?" he said.

Ginger had gone over to Sally's about an hour earlier.

"Who is this? Is Laura there?" Sally asked.

Nate smirked.

"It's Nate, Sally," he said.

Sally sighed.

"How's Laura? Ginger's here, and we are worried about her," she said.

Nate nodded.

"She's resting. The officer came over a little while ago and talked to everyone," he said.

Sally nodded.

"You mean Laura had to tell her mom?" she asked.

"Yep," he said.

Sally shook her head. She was on speakerphone so Ginger could hear too.

"Oh no," Ginger said.

Nate realized that he was on speakerphone.

"Yep," he said.

Laura turned her head.

"Who is it?" she mumbled.

"It's Sally and Ginger. They are checking in on you," Nate said.

They both yelled into the phone.

"Hi. Laura," they said.

Laura turned over. She was not in the mood to talk.

"She's okay. Her mom, however, is still in shock," Nate said.

Sally and Ginger nodded.

"I bet," Sally said.

Nate reached over and stroked Laura's hair.

"Should we come over? Laura probably needs her friends right now," Sally asked.

Nate shook his head. He looked over at Laura.

She was looking out the window wishing she was somewhere else and someone else.

"I think she just wants to be alone. I'm only here to keep her mom away if you know what I mean," he said.

The girls nodded. They understood.

"Call us if you need us," Sally said.

Nate nodded.

"I will," he said.

He hung up the phone.

Laura turned back over.

"Can we go somewhere? It's so pretty outside," she asked.

Nate nodded.

"Let's get you out of this house," he said.

Laura stood up to follow Nate.

He opened the door and Laura followed him out.

They managed to make it to the front door without being heard. But as soon as they opened the front door.

"Laura?" her mom asked.

Laura and Nate turned around to find her mom standing next to her.

Her mom wanted a moment of her time.

Laura wanted to talk to no one at the time.

"Laura, you went through a tough time last night, but I would like you to know you have a concerned mother that is here for you," her mom said.

Laura nodded.

"I just need to go for a walk," she said.

Laura's mom nodded.

Laura and Nate left.

Laura's mom frowned knowing that Laura was not ready to talk just yet.

Laura had been attacked. Her mom didn't know how often or how an incident like this affects someone, but she figured it would take a while for her daughter to return to herself.

Meanwhile...

Keith had gone upstairs to finish his homework before school started back on Monday.

His mom had dropped a rather large bomb on him, and it is one of the few facts he knew about his mom's past.

Since, his parents were mainly absent in his upbringing, he knew little about his parents' childhoods.

This story was the only information he had about his mom's past, and it was rather disturbing.

His mind was racing.

What if that had happened to Laura? How would that have affected her? How did my mom get through this?

It was hard for him to focus on his work.

Keith had no idea what either of them had gone through and the emotions that Laura was currently going through.

He knew finding out what was going on in Laura's head would take a large investment of his time.

He wanted to be there for Laura, but all of this was new to him.

Remember this was Keith's first relationship where he has actually had feelings for his girlfriend.

Keith didn't know how to handle this.

Part of him, wanted to face it and go visit Laura and part of him wanted to run from the relationship. He was torn between running and staying.

One side of him would win eventually, but instead he tried to concentrate on his homework and the music playing on his radio.

Sally and Ginger did just the same—try to focus on something else. They were worried about Laura and how she was getting through her day.

But there was person, who was not worried about Laura and rather about himself.

Corey woke up that morning in a jail cell. He focused in on the bars in front of him.

Where am I? He thought for a second before he remembered what had happened last night and how he got here.

Angrily he just stared at the bars. Let me out, he thought.

It was too late, he had been caught red-handed.

"That darn girl. I should have at least gotten laid out of this," he thought. He stomped around trying to get someone's attention.

The cell next to him held two guys, who looked as if they were suffering from hangovers. He figured that the two of them had been picked up for DUIs.

Corey knew he would have to go to trial soon. Corey continued to stomp and pace back and forth.

One of the guys in the cell next to him joined him in the stomping motion. All of them wanted out.

Finally, an officer walked down the hall and into the holding cells area.

"What is all of this noise? Do you realize it is like 8:00 a.m.? And I should be mad, because I have no donuts," the officer asked.

Corey rolled his eyes.

"Don't we get some phone calls?" he asked.

The officer nodded.

"Each of you gets one, but after I find some food first," he said.

He walked off.

Corey became angrier.

"Wait a minute. Why do you get food, and we don't?" Corey asked.

The officer turned around.

"I didn't break the law," he said.

He continued to walk to the break room. Corey grumbled.

He continued to stomp. He mumbled under his breath: "Unfair. Unfair."

The two in cell next to him turned their attention to him. Small talk was their only chance of staying awake.

"What's your name?" one of them asked.

Corey turned around.

"Corey," he answered.

They nodded.

"I'm Todd, and this is Matt," he said pointing to his friend.

Todd looked over at Corey.

"What are you in for?" Todd asked.

Corey was not in the mood for small talk.

"Listen, it's none of your business," Corey said.

Todd turned to Matt.

"Excuse me," Todd said.

Corey had managed to cause Matt and Todd to focus on themselves as he continued to pace back and forth.

Around an hour later, the officer came back.

"All right. Who wants their phone call first?" the officer asked.

Corey looked over the officer trying to get his attention.

"You have been making an awful lot of noise; so I'll let one of these guys go first," the officer said.

He let out Todd and then Matt. Each of them made their phone calls separately.

After he locked them up, he walked off once more. The officer sat at his desk and filled out some paperwork on the two DUI offenders.

"Hey," Corey screamed down the hall.

He felt forgotten. About 30 minutes later the officer returned.

"Right. You get a phone call too," the officer said.

He let Corey out, and Corey picked up the phone. The officer stood right there, while he dialed the numbers.

Corey dialed his dad.

"Dad?" Corey said.

His dad nodded.

"Where are you? Where have you been?" his dad asked.

"I'm in jail. I got arrested last night," Corey said.

His dad did not reply. He was rather angry and shocked.

"I need you to prepare to plea my case," Corey said.

Corey's dad was a lawyer.

"What are you guilty of?" his dad asked.

Corey would rather tell him in person.

"Just get down here so we can talk. I know my rights," he said.

His dad nodded.

"I'll be there in around an hour," his dad said.

Corey hung up the phone. The officer locked him back in his cell.

Corey knew his rights since he had grown up as a lawyer's son. Corey sat down on the bench and moved his feet up and down against the ground.

The officer walked off to his desk to fill out more paperwork.

Minutes passed by slowly as Corey awaited his father. Todd and Matt waited for their parents. The cells were rather quiet as late morning naps began.

Corey's dad arrived one hour later. He pulled out his identification as the officer approached him at the door.

Chapter 13

The officer allowed Corey's dad to proceed. Officer Fuller arrived at the office and walked back to check on Corey. Officer Fuller, Corey and his dad went into a bulletproof room to discuss Corey's sentence.

The door was locked behind Corey's dad. Corey of course was in handcuffs.

Officer Fuller turned to look at Corey's dad, William.

"Your son attacked a young lady with a knife and intended to rape her, last night. I caught him red-handed," the officer said.

William nodded. This was not the first time that Corey had broken the law, but this was the worst crime he had committed. William turned to his son.

"Corey, why the hell would you attack an innocent girl?" he asked his son.

Corey did not reply.

"His reason after I found him was that this girl was known for ruining the curve, if you know what I mean," the officer continued.

William nodded. He continued to stare at his son with disappointment.

"The principal has already suspended him for the rest of the year. I held him overnight here and the rest is up to a judge," the officer continued.

William nodded, taking notes.

"He will be considered on the accounts of aggravated assault with intent to rape," the officer continued.

William nodded and continued to take notes.

"Can I speak to my son and client alone?" he asked.

Officer Fuller nodded.

"I'll be outside if you need me," the officer said.

He walked outside of the door and closed it behind him.

William turned to his son.

"Corey, do you realize that since he caught you red-handed the best we can hope for is a settlement?" his dad asked.

Corey just nodded. He felt as if he had been backed into a corner.

"Corey, how many witnesses were there at the scene of the crime?" his dad asked.

Corey counted them in his head.

"Laura, her three friends, the principal, a teacher and then the officer," Corey said.

William nodded and continued to take notes.

"Do you think Laura would testify?" his dad asked.

Corey thought about it for a second.

"Maybe," he said.

William nodded.

"Corey, this is a losing case. I'm just being honest with you, son. I'll try to figure out something, but it's doubtful," he said.

Corey nodded.

"It hurts even more that you have already turned 18," his dad said.

Corey nodded once again.

"Can I speak as your father now?" his dad said.

Corey turned his full attention to his father's next comment.

"What the hell is wrong with you? Attempting to rape a female? You should be locked up for life," his father continued.

Corey did not expect that harsh of a reaction.

"I don't want to even claim you as my son let alone defend your case. I would rather beat the crap out of you," he continued.

He paused.

"Do you understand me? You have gotten yourself into a big mess," he declared to his son.

He paused again.

"I'm not even sure if I want to get you a settlement," he said.

He shook his head. He was ashamed of his only son.

Corey just sat there. He didn't think that he could do or say anything to make a difference.

"I hope you are satisfied with your decision and how you made this poor girl feel, because that satisfaction might be all that will keep you company in jail," his dad said.

Corey felt overwhelmed by his father's honesty.

"What do you mean? Are you going to represent me?" Corey asked.

His father paused.

"I'll think about it. In the meantime you can stay here and think about what you have done," he said.

He knocked on the door. Officer Fuller proceeded to guide Corey's father out of the station and then Corey to his cell.

Corey sat in his cell in a state of shock.

Not only was he in jail, but also in order to get a lesser degree of a sentence he would probably need an impartial lawyer instead of his dad.

Corey did not know any lawyers outside of his dad.

He knew if his dad even recommended another lawyer, the lawyer would still know his dad. He hung his head down and placed it in his hands. He had never expected to get caught.

The cell next to him was empty. The two boys had been dismissed.

He sat in complete silence. The only noise in the station was the officers filing papers.

His father, however, sat in the parking lot trying to make sure he wasn't imagining anything. He had turned the music down to think while he drove home.

William eventually arrived home that Sunday morning. He pulled in the garage and walked up the stairs of his house. He found his wife sipping some coffee in the kitchen.

"Coffee?" Corey's mom asked.

William nodded and made himself a cup.

"Natalie, guess where your son is now, and what he did last night?" he asked.

She knew that since he said your son, it must be bad.

"With Corey, our troublemaker, I have no idea," she replied.

He sat down at the table next to her and sipped his coffee.

"Well he's currently in jail for attempting to rape a girl last night," he said.

Natalie placed her cup on the table and turned her head to look at her husband.

"That's not funny," she said.

"I'm serious," he said.

Natalie sat upright in her chair.

"You're serious? Then, our troublemaker has stepped over the line," she said.

William nodded.

"He chose to attack a girl with a knife and the intent to rape her on her senior prom night," he said.

Natalie nodded.

"I'm just thankful that he didn't succeed," she said.

William nodded.

"Me too. I'm not sure if he is though. He was caught red-handed meaning he basically has no case," he said.

Natalie nodded.

"You're not defending him, are you?" she asked.

William shook his head.

"Well aside from not having a case for him to use, I can't. As his father, I think he should be punished for this," he said.

Natalie nodded rather hard.

"You bet. Did he even have a reason for attacking this girl?" she said.

"That's the best part. She is known as a 'curve breaker,' according to the officer on duty. Therefore, he was mad about his own grades and decided to take it out on a girl," he said.

Natalie's jaw had dropped.

"That's one of the worst reasons I have ever heard. Not that any reason would have made this situation any better but," she said.

She didn't finish her sentence instead she took a rather large gulp of her coffee.

William nodded. He felt her anger.

Natalie set down the cup and looked over at William.

"That poor girl. I wonder how she is doing," she said.

William nodded.

How is Laura doing? You ask...

Meanwhile...

Laura and Nate had arrived at a local park.

The sun was shining on a beautiful spring day. The flowers around them were blooming. The park was peaceful and quiet as if all of city had gone on vacation.

The swings rocked back and forth with no visitors. The playground sat empty awaiting a child's arrival.

It seemed peaceful yet almost boring. The silence almost seemed to increase Laura's depressed and confused state.

Nate looked over at Laura after noticing the peaceful state of the park.

"Want to walk?" he asked.

Laura didn't answer she just sat down on a swing and began to push herself back and forth. Nate eventually sat down next to her.

The two swung back and forth with no words spoken for quite some time.

The silence was at the point where it was beginning to drive Nate nuts.

Laura had not noticed the difference; she was rather busy focusing on swinging.

Swinging was good for that. It had managed to calm her mind and allow her to just focus on her height and how hard she pushed her legs—in and out went her legs and up and down went her body.

Swinging could always brighten her day, even a day this bad. She was practically smiling on the outside. Too bad she was in pieces on the inside.

Her insides were featuring a combination of feelings including anger, fear, confusion and anxiety. All of which she did not want to face nor deal with.

Laura continued to swing faster and higher each time.

Laura's mom, on the other hand, was losing her mind. She was worried about her daughter and didn't know who to call.

None of her friends had ever experienced anything like this. Nor had anyone in her family.

Rather she picked up a phone book and began to turn the pages. A few seconds later her finger reached P for psychologists.

She reached over and grabbed a pen off of her nightstand. She started underlining the ones that were located near their home.

She figured this was expensive but possibly worth it for Laura's recovery.

Several minutes later she had 15 names underlined.

She planned to call them on Monday for appointments and prices.

She then turned the phonebook over still open on the pages and placed it on her nightstand.

She walked down the hall to find her husband munching on a snack.

Laura had been gone for almost two hours now, if she stayed out much longer she would miss church. Church was one of Laura's mother's favorite family times.

But her mother was sure that even Laura understood that it was Sunday, the day of the Sabbath.

She sat down next to her husband at the kitchen table.

"Are you okay?" Laura's dad asked.

She just nodded.

"I'm worried about Laura," she said.

Laura's father moved his chair closer to his wife and gently placed his arm around her.

"All of us are," he said.

She nodded once more. He rubbed his hand up and down and then in a circular motion on her back.

He was trying very hard to be compassionate, but his rubbing didn't really change her mood.

The only thing that would would be talking to Laura and trying to be a comfort to her.

That may never happen...

Chapter 14

But Laura's mom was sure that Laura would need her, so she was going to do all that she could.

She looked over at her husband.

"What do you think we can do for her?" she asked.

Laura's dad placed his sandwich down and turned his neck to look at her.

"Just be her compassionate and caring family that would be the best thing," he said.

She nodded. Not quite the answer she wanted.

"I thought it might help for her to talk to a psychologist. I picked up the phone book and underlined some of them," she said.

Laura's dad nodded as he listened to her.

"I thought I might call them and check on prices and appointments," she said.

He nodded once more and swallowed his food.

"That might help, but you might want to talk to Laura about it before you schedule anything," he said.

She nodded.

"Plus, there is a school counselor that she could talk to, right?" he asked.

She nodded.

Laura's mom had not considered any of that; she was too worried to even think clearly.

Laura's dad continued to eat his snack.

Laura was gone the entire time they talked.

Laura's brother was downstairs playing video games, his favorite past time.

He was playing them without a care in the world, which reflected the lack of friendship between Laura and her younger brother.

They had never been close; rather he was too occupied with sports and video games to even give any member of his family the time of day.

Laura had sometimes wished that she had had somewhat of a relationship with her brother, but then she had Nate who attempted to protect her like an older brother.

Meanwhile...

Keith was torn between running from his relationship and becoming more committed.

He had planned to apply to Georgia Peach University on Monday.

He also planned to apply to other colleges that summer.

She had helped him achieve better grades this semester, which was going to bring up his grade point average.

He sat down at his desk and placed a blank piece of paper in front of him. He picked up a pen and drew a line down the middle. He wrote:

Pros
Being single again
More free time

Cons
Less time with Laura
The loss of a friend and a girlfriend
The possibility of running into her again
The pain he could cause her that he might not be able to deal with

After listing the pros and cons of their breakup, he turned over the paper and listed the pros and cons of staying with her.

Pros
More time to spend with Laura
The possibility of growing closer

Cons
Less time on my own
More emotional commitment

He was absolutely torn. He stopped there, not knowing what to do or to write anymore. Keith cared about Laura, but he had no idea how to be there for her in her time of need.

He might have fallen for Laura, but his fear of the unknown was holding him back. Can he overcome that fear? Will Laura turn to him in her time of need?

Those questions concerned him.

He placed his head down on top of his hands.

Silence filled the room.

A few minutes passed as Keith's head did not move. Keith finally picked up his head when he heard a knock on his door.

Knock. Knock.

Meanwhile...

Laura's legs began to become tired, so she slowed down on her swinging.

She eventually came to a stop and allowed the wind to move her back and forth gently.

Nate noticed Laura's change in movement.

"Laura," he said.

She cut him off.

"I need something to eat. I'm starving," she said.

It was obvious that she did not want to talk; rather she wanted to pretend like nothing happened.

Nate had noticed that. He wanted to help her work through it, but she wasn't letting anyone in. Therefore, he could only show support.

He nodded.

"Where would you like to go?" he asked.

Laura smiled as she thought about her food choices.

"Arby's," she said.

Nate nodded and came to a stop in his swinging. So did Laura.

They left the park in Nate's car, which he had borrowed from his mom.

He drove them towards a shopping center. A few minutes later, they arrived at the restaurant.

Nate and Laura exited the car and entered the restaurant.

Each of them made their orders, picked them up and sat down in a booth.

Laura had ordered a market fresh ham sandwich while Nate ordered roast beef cheddar. Each came with fries and a soda.

At the booth, they unwrapped their sandwiches and began eating.

The two ate mostly in silence.

Laura was so hungry that she was taking bigger bites than usual.

Nate, on the other hand, was taking his time, hoping that Laura would slow down and talk to him.

Eventually, Laura took a deep breath and a sip of her Coke.

She looked up at Nate. She thought to herself how good of a friend he was.

He had always been there for her even when he was dating someone else. He had always made time for her.

She felt comforted that he was spending so much time with her this weekend. It helped to have a friend, even if she wasn't ready to talk.

Nate sipped his Sprite.

"Laura. I realize you are still grieving, and well, do you need to talk?" he asked.

She shook her head.

Talking was the last thing she wanted to do.

"I'm not ready yet, but let's talk about something else," she said.

Nate nodded.

Laura figured this might take her mind off of last night.

"What are you doing for the summer?" she asked.

Nate finished his bite.

"I'm going on a trip to visit my dad for two weeks, but otherwise I'll be here. This time, I'm going to California instead of him coming here for a weekend," he said.

Usually, his dad spent the weekend in a hotel and visited Nate at the same time, but in the summer, he tried to spend more time together.

Laura nodded.

"I hope he follows through this time. Last time, he lost my tickets, and he ended up paying double. The time before that he forgot to pick me up," he said.

Nate shook his head.

"He is just horrible," he added.

Laura nodded. Nate had a father that just didn't quite care enough. His dad had let him and his mom down several times in the past.

She never understood why Nate kept believing eventually he would get it right.

Nate needed a father like all children do. He needed one that cared.

HIS WRATH

"We are visiting my grandparents and cousins this year," she said.
Nate nodded.

Laura's family attended a family reunion in middle Georgia every other year. Her mom was one of five children, while her father was one of three. Both of their families grew up there.

Laura had over 10 cousins in the state of Georgia. The families got together for games, soul food and time to catch up with each other.

"You'll have fun. You always do," he said.

Nate was right. Laura usually came back with some pretty crazy stories from the reunions.

"I'm sure the stories will be crazy like they always are," she said.

She took another bite of her sandwich.

It felt good to be talking out loud and thinking about nothing.

"How is yours?" he asked.

Laura finished chewing her bite of the sandwich.

"Satisfying my craving," she said.

Nate chuckled and smiled.

"Good," he laughed.

Nate thought to himself how good it was to see Laura happy and talking about anything.

Nate jumped up from the table to grab himself and Laura refills.

At the same time, not only did Ginger and Sally arrive, but Erica came in behind them. Erica was with three other members of the popular crowd.

Ginger and Sally dashed over to talk to Nate.

"Hi there. We thought you and Laura might have gotten hungry and gone to her favorite fast food place," Ginger said.

Nate nodded.

"Why don't you join us?" he asked.

Ginger and Sally nodded.

"We'll order and find you," Sally said.

Nate walked back to the table with drink refills. He placed Laura's in front of her. He sat down in the booth.

Laura looked up and thanked Nate.

"Sally and Ginger are here," he said.

Laura nodded.

"They want to join us. Is that okay?" he asked.

Laura nodded once again. She figured this way she could stop everyone's worrying at once.

Erica tapped Laura on the shoulder.

Laura turned her head around. Laura did not know Erica.

"Looks like he didn't even scar you," Erica said.

Laura looked confused.

"What are you talking about?" Laura snapped back.

Nate looked up from his sandwich, realizing that Erica was bothering Laura. He knew who she was.

"Erica, leave us alone," he said.

Erica ignored Nate's request.

"You know Corey. He attacked you, right," Erica said.

"That's none of your business. Leave us alone," he said.

Erica gave Nate a look.

"I'm talking to her, not you," she said pointing at Laura.

Nate stood up.

"I'll ask you one more time nicely, leave us alone," he said.

"Fine," she said.

She walked off disgruntled.

Laura turned to look at Nate.

"Thanks. Who was that?" she asked.

Nate sat back down as Sally and Ginger came over to join them.

"A friend of Corey's is all that I know about her," he said.

Laura nodded.

Sally and Ginger sat down beside them.

"Is everything okay?" Sally asked.

Nate turned his head to answer her question.

"Erica was bothering Laura, and I had to get her to leave," he said.

Sally nodded, thinking about whom he was referring to.

"Erica, the girl who worships Corey?" she asked.

Nate nodded.

Erica…

Erica has had the biggest crush on Corey for years. He could do no wrong in her eyes; therefore, she thought Laura had made the entire story up.

She didn't believe for one second that her dream man could attack a girl.

Erica had sacrificed a lot to get into the popular crowd, and she did it to get Corey to look her way.

She used all of her allowance to buy the "hip" clothes. She sucked up to the members of the popular crowd for months before they even offered her a seat at the lunch table.

At a party a few months ago, she got Corey's attention. He was rather drunk, and she was rather sober.

But when you worship someone and want to do everything to please them, you sometimes make bad decisions.

Erica lost her virginity that night to Corey, he may have never called her, nor talked to her after that, but in her eyes it was still a great night.

Corey, on the other hand, probably doesn't even remember that night.

Poor Erica. She just wouldn't know what do to with a good guy.

Why doesn't she think she deserves any better?

Her dad skipped out on the family when she was baby, therefore she doesn't even remember him.

Her mother is a hardworking executive and was never home.

Erica was forced to raise herself. She even took on a job at the age of 16 at a retail store.

Minus her low self-esteem, she has come a long way.

Meanwhile...

Sally and Ginger had begun to eat their meals.

No small talk had been made.

Laura decided out of effort to keep her mind off of things to begin a conservation.

"Sally, Ginger what have you two been up to today?" Laura asked.

It took them a second to realize that Laura was actually talking yet alone talking to them.

"You must be feeling better?" Sally said.

Laura did not reply.

"I think she is trying to keep her mind on other things," Nate said. Sally nodded.

"I understand, but sometime soon you will need to face the pain. I have no idea what you went through or what you are currently going through, but you do need to face the pain soon," Sally said.

Laura just nodded. She was not in the mood for a lecture.

Sally noticed Laura's response and just continued talking.

"Anyways, Ginger and I have spent all of today together, and we were actually busy on homework and thinking about you," Sally said.

Ginger nodded in agreement.

"Which is why we came out to eat; you know we thought you might be here," Ginger said.

Sally nodded.

Laura smiled. It was nice to know she had friends that cared.

She just wished that someone among them had had secret powers and saved her earlier last night or that she had listened to them in the first place and stayed home.

They continued their lunch, while Keith had finally decided he needed to see Laura.

He left the house and climbed in his car. He drove over to Laura's house and knocked on the door.

No one answered. Laura's family had gone to church and Laura was still out with Nate.

Keith walked across the street and knocked on Nate's door.

"Yes and you are?" Nate's mom asked.

Nate's mom had never met Keith so she talked to him through the door.

"I'm Keith. I took Laura to the prom. I am trying to find her. I need to talk to her," he answered.

Nate's mom opened the door slightly.

"Yes. I remember you. Nate took her to the park quite some time ago. But that's all I know," she said.

Keith nodded.

"Thank you," he said.

Nate's mom nodded, shut the door, locked it and went back down the hall.

Keith turned around and climbed back into his car.

He drove over to the park. He had no idea what Nate's car looked like. So, he just walked around.

He walked around for a good 15 minutes, before he climbed back in his car.

Nate and Laura had already left for lunch by the time Keith had arrived.

He sat in his car for a while just thinking…

Is this a sign? Where is she? Maybe I should run? What would my life be like without her? Maybe, she is around town somewhere.

He nodded on that question and began driving slowly around the area.

He was hoping he would find someone or something that would lead him to Laura.

He drove with the music on low, paying more attention to the world around him.

Considering how much he was paying attention to the shopping centers and the sidewalks, it's a wonder he didn't get in a wreck.

He pulled off in each shopping center and drove around.

He even parked the car and walked in and out of some stores.

After awhile, Keith stopped for some food.

He walked into the local Wendy's, which happened to be across the street from Arby's.

He ordered a combo and sat down to eat.

He kept his eyes on the windows, which faced the street.

He watched cars go by and people walk past restaurants.

He continued to take large bites out of his sandwich when a teenage African-American girl and three friends walked out of the Arby's across the street.

He noticed them out of the corner of his eye.

"Could it be?" he wondered.

He dropped his sandwich, wrapped it up, dropped it back in his bag and dashed outside.

He meandered his way across the street like a game of Frogger, avoiding all of the cars.

Once he reached the other side, he attempted to duck behind a car to make sure she was Laura.

He ducked beside a blue Taurus as the girl walked next to a guy and two other girls over to a car.

He stared at the back of an African-American girl, as she walked away from him and towards a car.

She walked around to the passenger's side and turned her head to receive a hug from one of the girls.

Keith could now make out her profile.

He bent down and leaned forward just enough to see the girl's face.

He could make her eyes, nose and mouth.
He could even make out her hairline and hairdo.
He saw the outfit she was wearing.
"Now she is pretty," he thought to himself.
But was she Laura? Was she his girl? Was he prepared for her to be Laura? What would he do? What would he say?
Questions were whirling around in his head.
Keith leaned a little more forward.
He now knew who it was.

Chapter 15

The girl hugged each of her female friends. The two girls backed up from her.

It was time for Keith to make his move towards Laura.

Keith moved forward towards Laura. He was soon standing behind her, and he tapped her on the shoulder.

Tap. Tap. Tap.

Laura spun around to see Keith standing there.

"Laura, we need to talk," Keith said.

Laura nodded.

"I'm not really in the mood," Laura said.

Keith nodded. He knew she was hurt.

"Okay. I'll just get right to the point then. My mom has been through a similar event as you, and she said she would be available to talk to you about it. I also have something to tell you about us, but that can wait until you are ready, because I want to do this right," he said.

Laura nodded.

"Thanks, Keith. I'll call you," she said.

Keith nodded, knowing Laura would need time. He turned and walked back to his car.

Laura held the car door open as she sat down in her seat.

Nate turned his attention to her once she sat down, and the door was closed.

"Laura, you okay?" he said.

She had this expression of shock on her face.

"Keith said his mom has been raped, and he has made a decision about us, but he wants to tell me it in the right way," she said.

Nate nodded.

"What's the right way?" he asked.

"He didn't say, but we didn't talk long. I'm not sure I trust him. You know that Corey was his friend," she said.

Nate nodded.

"I don't blame you," he said.

Sally and Ginger had already left the parking lot in their own car. Nate turned on the radio and pulled out of the parking lot.

"Laura, where would you like to go now?" Nate asked.

Laura checked her watch. 7:30 p.m. Time had come and gone.

"Home. I guess," she said.

Nate nodded and steered the car home.

Laura sat quietly as Nate drove them home. She wasn't sure if any of this had helped her at all. She still felt dirty and confused. She also felt alone.

She sighed because she knew she would have to call Keith.

But maybe she should let him explain. After all, he could be completely innocent.

Laura just hummed along with the song on the ride home.

Nate turned into their neighborhood.

Not too much later, he parked the car in Laura's driveway.

Nate turned to look at Laura.

"You have been awful quiet on the way home. You know I'm here for you, but I understand you may not be ready to share any of your feelings, so here you are," he said.

Laura just nodded.

Nate opened his door and walked around the car to meet Laura as she exited out of her door.

He hugged her and then walked back to the driver's seat.

Laura stood on the steps of her house and watched Nate drive across the street.

She was not ready to face the inevitable, being home.

She heard the door open behind her.

Her mom peaked her head out.

"Laura, dear, come on in. Are you hungry?" she asked.

Laura turned around walked the stairs and entered the house.

She followed her mom to the kitchen.

"I already ate, and if you don't mind, I need to finish some homework before tomorrow," she said.

Her mom nodded. She was a little hurt, but she understood that Laura needed time.

Laura turned around and walked down the hall.

Meanwhile…

HIS WRATH

Keith drove home disappointed.

He could sense the tension in Laura's voice when they talked. He feared that she blamed him for the incident. He also feared that she might not understand.

He also feared it could get worse. He hoped Laura would talk to his mom.

It was only one day after the incident, but Keith knew there was little time left before college started and everyone split off in his or her own direction.

Keith wasn't the only one worried about Laura.

Nate, Ginger and Sally were among him.

Ginger and Sally had arrived at Sally's house.

They attempted to finish their homework, which was rather hard to concentrate on.

Nate parked his mom's car in their driveway and walked up the stairs.

He didn't eat dinner, but he helped his mom clean up.

Tomorrow was another day, a school day, he thought.

He wondered how it would go, since it was the first day back after prom.

He knew Laura would have to face school. She wouldn't stay home and hide under her covers. Her attitude was too strong for that.

That's one reason why he was so worried. Another was that he knew Laura would keep most of her feelings inside.

She was a quiet girl, who kept to herself. She had always been that way.

She was an independent and strong lady.

Nate could recall several conversations they had had throughout their friendship.

Nate had always been the more talkative one, yet the weaker and more dependent one in the relationship.

They complimented each other well.

He finished cleaning the kitchen and moved on to his homework.

Nate went to bed not too much later, as did Ginger and Sally.

It had been a long day for all of them.

Laura fell asleep in the middle of her homework.

Yes. A long day.

Meanwhile...

Corey sat alone in his cell.
His dad had left to think about what he had done.
Corey had no guilt, just anger.
He was angry for being caught and because he wanted to finish what he started.
That anger could be his doom.
He needed a lawyer that would defend him, not be ashamed of him.
He yelled out to the policeman on duty.
"You think I could have a phonebook?" Corey asked.
Policeman turned around.
"For what?" he said.
Corey raised his voice once more.
"To find me a lawyer," he said.
"If you do not want your dad, ask him to find you one, when he visits again or one will be provided for you. Now. Hush. I'm eating my dinner," the policeman said.
Corey stared at the policeman.
"When do I eat?" he asked.
Policeman turned back to his meal. He never answered Corey's question.
Corey needed a plan, and he knew it. He needed a way to receive a lesser punishment.
Think. Think. Think, Corey. Think.
He thought to himself.
He stared at the cell walls, trying to formulate a plan.
Time passed slowly inside his cell.
Monday seemed so far away.
The policeman finished his meal and started on his dessert. He was awaiting the night shift worker.
He would arrive in about an hour, and then a new shift would start.
He was looking forward to going home. His day had been rather quiet compared to last night.
Corey laid his head down on his pillow and bare bed, still thinking.
He knew he would have to be creative.
Monday morning, the sun rose.

HIS WRATH

Monday meant back to school for everyone.

Laura awoke in fear.

Her mind had wandered off into a nightmare, one where Corey had finished the job. She awoke feeling dirty and violated.

She jumped out of bed and ran into the shower.

As she washed, she attempted to wash away the deed. It wasn't until later she realized that only part of her nightmare was true.

She was thankful that Corey did not succeed, because he would have taken her virginity. But she still has to live with the violation she did suffer.

Corey had seen her vulnerable and parts of her no other man had seen before.

Laura had only kissed guys before that day. Now one had gotten her past second base. He had almost run a home run.

Laura had been rather innocent for most girls her age. Too many girls have gotten pregnant or contracted a disease at her age. Rather her mother pushed her to pursue school and not boys.

She was thankful for that too. That had kept her focused on college and allowed her to endure less emotional pain.

Laura thought about talking to Keith's mom. She figured it might help.

Enduring emotional pain due to a man for the first time in her life was rather hard.

She kept thinking...Why me?

There was no answer to that question.

Meanwhile...

Keith hit his alarm on snooze and turned over for "five more minutes."

He didn't want to face Monday morning.

He had failed in the bet, and that would mean that he would still have to pay up. He knew someone would be covering for Corey.

Keith's mom had already left for work. His dad was due back in town this weekend for a visit.

Not that he was looking forward to that. He barely knew his father, due to the amount of time he spent in Washington.

He finally finished getting ready for school, pulled out of his driveway and drove off.

Not too much later, he arrived at the high school. The day had just begun.

The bell rang for the first class of the day.

Nate, Sally, Ginger, Keith and Laura split off to their classes for the day.

Laura had no motivation today. She felt so lost. Nothing seemed to matter.

The incident had taught that she could not protect herself from being hurt as easily as she thought she could. She was less naïve now.

She just wasn't ready to handle the truth.

History class rolled around, and Laura saw Keith.

"How are you doing?" Keith said.

Laura just nodded. Her fellow students just looked at her as if she was a freak, instead of being friendly and offering support.

They almost seemed to blame her for what happened. They also made it seem like she didn't fit in. She had never really wanted to be part of the popular crowd, but some days it would have been nice to be invited. However, knowing some of them convinced Corey to do his deed caused her to wonder what really was going on.

She figured she was better off not knowing, but that didn't mean she wanted to be looked at differently.

"Did you think about what I said yesterday?" he asked.

Laura nodded once more. Keith had realized by now that he would have to do all of the talking.

"Would you like to talk to my mom?" he asked.

Laura nodded once again.

"You could ride home with me today, if you want," he said.

Laura actually responded this time.

"I'll have my mom bring me over later," she said.

Keith nodded. He could only guess why Laura was not too keen on being alone with him.

He knew that would make telling her his feelings even harder.

Laura was unsure about her feelings for Keith. She remembered how much she liked his company and how close they were before Saturday night.

BUT

His involvement in the event worried her. The small events that occurred right before bothered her too.

HIS WRATH

That made her worried about trusting him...

But she knew with the end of school coming, she needed to focus and cope with her feelings.

Maybe talking to Keith's mom would help; she hoped so.

The school day went slow for everyone.

Laura took the bus home, and later asked her mom if she could visit Keith. She explained that his mother had apparently suffered a similar event. Her mom understood and dropped her off that night for around an hour.

Laura knocked on the door.

Knock. Knock.

Keith's mom opened the door.

"Hi. Laura. It's nice to see you again. Keith told me you might drop by. He's upstairs," she said.

Laura nodded.

"I actually came to talk to you," Laura said.

Keith's mom nodded, as they walked to the kitchen.

"Would you like some tea?" Keith's mom asked.

Laura nodded.

"Keith told me I should talk to you," Laura said.

Keith's mom nodded as she turned the tea kettle on.

"I'm glad you came here. That shows courage," Keith's mom said.

Laura nodded.

"Have a seat, and I'll share my story with you," Keith's mom said.

Laura sat down at the kitchen table. She smiled up at Keith's mom. She was a sweet lady, different from how Keith described, but then he is bitter towards her for putting her work first, which Laura understood.

"Laura. When I was a teenager, I was raped and became pregnant. I had a miscarriage though," Keith's mom said.

Laura nodded.

"I grew up in a broken home and poor neighborhood. Several girls my age in our city were attacked or raped while I was in high school," she continued.

Laura just nodded.

"I was pregnant for two weeks before I lost the baby," Keith's mom continued.

She looked over at Laura; both of them were sipping their teas.

"So, Laura. You are not alone on this road," she said.

Laura nodded. "So there is hope yet," she thought to herself.

She looked up from her tea at Keith's mom. She was smiling. Laura respected her for moving so far past what she had experienced as a teenager.

Keith's mom grew as an inner city kid.

"Laura, you know my experience actually inspired me. I didn't want my kids to grow up in that kind of neighborhood. That's why I went to college, got my degree and started working hard," she said.

Laura nodded.

"In a way, this could be a positive for you. But you know you did get lucky in a way," his mom continued.

She chuckled.

Laura nodded. She knew that was true.

COREY WAS CAUGHT!

"I appreciate you sharing your story with me," Laura said.

Keith's mom nodded.

"I just wanted you to know, you are not alone," she said.

Laura nodded.

"If you are not ready to talk yet, at least you know," she continued.

Laura nodded.

"When I was going through this experience, I was quiet, withdrawn and didn't share my story with anyone for about two years," his mom said.

Laura looked surprised.

"Two years?" Laura asked.

Keith's mom nodded.

"My trust in others was gone. It took a while to build it back up, besides I thought it was my fault. I figured I had some sort of disease, and if I talked to anyone they would catch it," she said.

Laura nodded. She felt like it was her fault too.

"That's the hard part. You first have to learn that it was not your fault," his mom said.

Laura nodded.

She did blame herself in a way. She did that because of what Corey said to her that night.

HIS WRATH

HE TOLD HER:
This deed was to get back at her, to teach her a lesson for screwing up the curve and having good grades.

He committed the sin out of jealously and anger, which he made sure she knew.

Those words hurt her and had caused her to believe it was her fault.

Laura felt like sharing this with Keith's mom, since she had shared so much with her.

"But it partly was," she said.

Keith's mom raised her head as if to make sure she had actually heard someone speak.

"What do you mean?" she asked.

Laura took a deep breath.

She then explained to Keith's mom what Corey told her.

Keith's mom shook her head.

"Now. Corey blames you. That's his fault. It was his decision, his fault," she continued.

She shook her head again.

"There is nothing there that makes his reaction rational. It is not your fault," she said.

She paused.

"You may not understand that for a little while. Take your time, but let it out okay," his mom said.

Laura nodded.

"All of us are here for you," his mom added.

Keith was walking down the stairs at that moment.

He nodded as heard his mom say that.

Laura smiled. She knew it was true.

Keith's mom and Laura both stood up as Keith appeared in the doorway.

Keith's mom smiled at him. As did Laura.

"Feeling better?" Keith asked.

Laura nodded.

"I'm glad," he said.

He smiled, knowing he had good news for her.

"Laura, could I talk to you for a second," he said.

Laura nodded.

She smiled at his mom as she walked up the stairs to Keith's room.

"I need to tell you something. It's best that you hear this from me," he added.

Laura nodded as she sat down on a chair.

"Laura. What Corey did to you well that was supposed to be me," he said.

Laura look confused.

"I was the new kid in school, so in order to be accepted into the 'popular crowd,' I had to perform a deed. Raping you was my deed. As you can see though, I told Corey, no. I fell for you and didn't want to hurt you. He then took it upon himself to do it," he said.

Laura nodded.

"I should have told you, but I didn't know he was going to try to rape you, since I told him that being popular was not worth losing you," he said.

Laura nodded.

"I tried to find you that night. I didn't know he was going to do that to you. I wish I had, and then I could have protected you. Laura. I'm so sorry," he said.

Laura could feel the tears coming.

"I wish I could change the past, but I can't. Laura, I care about you. I applied to Georgia Peach, among others today. We might go to college together," he said.

Laura didn't know what to say.

"That's my good news," he said.

Laura nodded.

"Thanks for being honest for me. It is a little late you know. I need to think about what you just shared with me," she said.

Keith nodded as Laura left his room.

She called her mom and was picked up. She arrived home and picked up the phone.

She needed a friend.

As Nate answered, she felt relieved to hear his voice. She couldn't believe what she was going through; weeks ago she was just another teenager going to high school.

BUT NOW.

She was preparing to go off to college, yet she had almost been raped. For the first time in her life, she was groped and felt up. Her head was spinning as someone answered the phone.

"Hello?" his mom asked.

"Umm. Oh. I. Umm. Is Nate there?" Laura asked.

"Hold on," Nate's mom said.

She screamed down the hall at Nate to pick up the phone.

"Hello," he said.

"Hey," she said.

Nate didn't expect Laura to call.

"I thought you were going to Keith's," he said.

"I did. His mom was raped in high school," she said.

Nate nodded.

"I guess that means you were lucky," he said.

"This is not funny. She also had a miscarriage. That could have been me," she said.

"But it's not. Laura, Corey failed. All he did was touch you," he said.

She nodded.

"Did he? I mean he hurt me. Plus, I don't remember what happened right before finding him half-naked and on top of me. He might as well have succeeded; I still don't think I could ever trust a man again," she added.

Nate was confused.

"All men are not like Corey," he said.

"Nate, I'm not finished. Keith told me something too. Want to go for a walk?" she asked.

"I guess. I'll meet you in the middle," he said.

Each hung up their phones and walked to the middle of the street. The two of them began to walk together down the sidewalk.

"What did you mean you are not finished?" he asked.

Laura turned her head to look at Nate.

"Keith told me this quote unquote. What Corey did to me was supposed to be him," she said.

Nate look confused.

"He was the new kid in school, so in order to be accepted into the 'popular crowd,' he had to perform a deed. Raping me was his deed, and he told Corey, no. He fell for me and didn't want to hurt me, which is why Corey came after me," she said.

Nate nodded.

"I knew he was bad. I didn't trust him," he said.

Laura nodded. She expected that reaction.

"He didn't rape me. Instead, he loves me and wants to go to the same college I am going to in the fall," she said.

Nate stepped in front of Laura.

"Don't you think his deed came from what he did to his ex?" he asked.

Laura shook her head. She was still naïve.

"We don't know the whole story there," she said.

Nate nodded.

"I guess," he said.

They waited quietly for awhile.

"We should get back. There's more school tomorrow," she said.

Meanwhile...

Corey had woken up Monday morning still in the same jail cell. He hit his head as he realized where he was.

His dad was looking right at him.

"Corey?" his dad asked.

Corey sat up. It was shortly after 7 a.m. His dad had come to visit before work.

"Morning," he said.

He said rubbing his eyes.

"I'm not going to represent you. Someone will be appointed to you or you can choose someone else from my law firm," his dad said.

Corey just nodded. It was too early.

"I have to go now. I am very disappointed in you, son. Your mother and I did not raise you to be this way," he continued.

Corey screamed out as his dad walked away.

"Whatever, Dad. Just go to work. That's what matters to you," Corey screamed back.

Corey's dad began to turn around and walk back to his son's cell. But as he did the clock on the wall caught his eye, he was late for an early morning meeting.

He walked out of the jail and drove off to work.

Corey lay back down. It was pointless to be awake this early. He had nowhere to be.

Monday ended as Corey went to sleep another night in a jail cell.

HIS WRATH

Meanwhile…
Tuesday morning arrived for everyone.
Laura awoke Tuesday morning from a nightmare.
In the nightmare that she had dreamt, Corey had succeeded.
Laura rolled over and hit the snooze button as her mother yelled down the hall.
"Laura, get up for school," her mom said.
Laura had around a month of school left before summer break, which meant three and half months before college began.
Laura sat up in her bed, turned over and buried her head in her pillow.
She knew she had to face the world again.

Chapter 16

With a few weeks of school left, Laura just focused on schoolwork, trying not to think about what she had been through.

Her friends were rather worried about her. It wasn't until a week later when she got up the nerve to tell Ginger and Sally what Keith and his mother had shared with her.

It was a Wednesday lunch.

"Girl, I need to fill you two in on something," Laura said.

Ginger and Sally nodded hoping for good news.

"Keith's mom was raped in high school. She had a miscarriage," she continued.

Ginger and Sally were shocked as they continued to listen to Laura.

"Keith told me something too," Laura added.

Both girls nodded awaiting the news.

"Keith was the new kid in school, so in order to be accepted into the 'popular crowd,' he had to perform a deed. Raping me was his deed, and he told Corey, no. He fell for me and didn't want to hurt me, which is why Corey came after me," she said.

They nodded, and then their jaws dropped.

"What? He was supposed to what?" Sally asked.

Laura nodded. She expected that reaction, so she just continued.

"He didn't rape me. Instead, he loves me and wants to go to the same college I that am going to in the fall," Laura said.

Ginger turned her head and looked at Sally and back at Laura.

"So where was he when Corey was raping you?" Ginger asked.

Laura paused.

"He was trying to find me and got lost. He didn't have a map," she said.

They nodded.

"Good thing, we did," Sally said.

Laura nodded.

"I am thankful for what you three did for me that night," she said.
Sally and Ginger nodded.
"That's what friends are for," Sally said.
Ginger took a deep breath.
"Of course, we wish we didn't have to protect you that night, but some people are just evil," Ginger said.
Sally nodded.
"I guess we saw Corey's true colors. I hope he gets punished," Sally said.
Sally looked up from her lunch to see Erica walking over. Erica had been eavesdropping on their conversation.
"Excuse me," Erica said.
She took a seat at the table near Laura.
"You don't know Corey like I do," she added.
The girls tried to ignore her, but she continued.
"You egged him on. You made him mad. He was just showing you who is boss," she said.
Sally was mad now.
"Who made him boss? He had no right to touch Laura. You need to realize how twisted he is," Sally said.
She paused.
"Now leave us alone," Sally added.
Erica looked over at Laura.
"Let's hear you talk for yourself," she said to Laura.
Laura turned her head and stared at Erica.
"You and your thoughts about Corey are not worth our time," Laura said.
Realizing Erica was not going to leave. Laura picked up her stuff.
Sally and Ginger followed her lead to the library.
Erica yelled after them.
"Chicken. It would have been better if you had just given him what he wanted," she said.
She got up and walked back to her table. She finished her lunch.
The girls proceeded to the library and sat down at a table together.
They had escaped Erica.
BUT Laura could not escape the truth. She was hurting inside.

ERIN MICHELLE KATHERINE

She may never be able to look at the world in the same way.

Her friendships with Nate, Ginger and Sally were rather one-sided. Laura didn't say much rather she just listened. They were there for her, but she was not ready to move past the event yet.

Chapter 17

In June, after school got out, and they graduated from high school, Keith decided he had given Laura enough space.
He knocked on the door to her house.
Laura's mom answered the knocking.
"Hello, Keith," she said.
He just nodded. He had been patient enough.
"Is Laura home?" he asked.
Laura's mom nodded.
"She's home, but she usually doesn't take visitors," she said.
Keith sighed.
"I have important news," he said.
Laura's mom pointed down the hall.
"Go see if she will let you in," she said.
Keith walked down the hall to Laura's door. He knocked on it.
The knocking awoke her from her nap.
"Come in," she said.
She thought it was her mom.
Keith walked through the doorway.
Laura sat up and rubbed her eyes.
"Keith, what are you doing here?" she asked.
Keith handed her a letter.
Laura read the letter to herself.
"This is an acceptance letter to Georgia Peach," she said.
Keith nodded.
"I thought you should be the first to know," he said.
Laura smiled.
"That's sweet. I guess we are going to college together after all," she said.
Keith smiled back.
"Laura, I must know how are you doing with what I told you," he said.

Laura paused, gathering her thoughts.

"Keith, I don't know how I feel about us, or about our relationship," she said.

Keith nodded and sat down next to her.

"After what I went through, I need some time to figure things out," she said.

He nodded again.

"What you told me was shocking. It affected my trust towards you," she said.

He just stared at her, thinking about her beauty.

"I know at one time I did feel the same way. But now, I don't know how I feel," she said.

Keith just nodded. He wished he had never made that deal.

"I understand. You need some time," he said.

Laura nodded.

"Do you think we could still hang out and start our relationship over slowly?" he asked.

Laura didn't know what to say. She wasn't ready for that either.

"I'll think about it," she said.

Keith nodded.

"Don't let the whole summer pass us by, okay," he said.

He stood up and walked out the door. He was hoping Laura would yell after him.

She just rolled over and went back to sleep.

Keith left the house and drove himself home.

That weekend his family went on a vacation.

His dad came down on Friday and took him camping.

This was the first trip out for Keith and his dad.

Keith wondered what it would be like and what Laura would decide.

As Keith went off on a trip, one member of the group took a large risk.

Chapter 18

Ginger knocked on Sally's front door one day in June.
Sally's mom answered the door.
"Ginger, how is your summer going?" her mom said.
Ginger smiled.
"Good. Is Sally home?" Ginger said.
Her mom nodded and pointed down the hall.
Ginger said "thank you" and walked down the hall.
She proceeded to knock on Sally's door. Sally answered the door.
"Ginger?" she said.
She wasn't expecting any visitors. She had just come back from the neighborhood pool and was still wearing a bathing suit.
Ginger shut the door behind her, making sure it was locked.
Ginger was ready to share her secret with her dear friend, and she only hoped Sally would respond well.
Sally backed away from Ginger and sat down on her bed. Ginger followed her and sat down next to her.
The two girls sat next to each other on Sally's bed.
Ginger leaned in and planted a kiss on Sally's lips. She smiled as Sally reacted to her news.
"Ginger, what are you doing?" Sally said.
She had a hard time speaking, since she was in a state of shock.
Ginger placed her hand on Sally's shoulder and looked into her eyes.
"Sally, I'm sharing my true feelings with you. I'm gay," Ginger said.
Sally just stared at her with her jaw dropped. A few seconds later, she was able to speak.
"Is that why you wanted us to go to the prom together?" she asked.
Ginger nodded.
"How long have you had feelings for me?" Sally said.
Ginger paused to count the months in her head.

"Almost a year. Only I knew though. I thought telling you, might help me have the courage to tell my parents," Ginger said.

Sally nodded.

"Ginger, I am not sure I feel the same way," Sally said.

Ginger nodded.

"I'm sure my news took you by shock, so you have plenty of time to think it over. My family is going to Niagara Falls next week," she said.

Sally nodded.

"Are you going to tell them then?" Sally asked.

Ginger nodded.

"It is time. I wanted to tell them before college. I also wanted to tell you, since we are going to be roommates in the fall," she said.

Sally nodded. "Roommates," she thought to herself.

"Sally," Ginger said.

She ran her fingers through Sally's blonde hair.

"I want us to be more than just roommates. Think about it," she added.

And with that she was gone.

Sally heard her footsteps, as she left the house.

Sally sat on her bed in a state of shock for a while.

Soon, she moved and decided to visit her only other friend in this world, Laura.

Meanwhile…

Nate had gone to visit his father, and Laura was preparing to pack for a reunion.

Her family reunion was in one week.

Sally got dressed and hopped in her car to drive to Laura's. A few minutes later, Sally parked her car outside of Laura's house.

She walked down the driveway and through the flowerbed to the front door. She knocked on the door.

Knock. Knock.

The house seemed quiet. Maybe I should had called first she thought as Laura's brother answered the door.

Laura's parents were out on a date.

"Laura's in her room, whatever your name is," her brother said.

Sally just nodded and walked down the hall.

She needed a friend.

She knocked on Laura's door.

Laura sat up on her bed. She was reading a magazine article about other girls her age that had been attacked. Their strength to come forward seemed to helping her work through her pain.

Laura heard the knocking and responded by opening the door for Sally.

"Hi. How are you?" Laura said.

Sally shut the door behind her and sat down on Laura's bed.

"I don't know," Sally said.

Laura looked over at her. She was concerned. Laura sat down in her chair.

"What do you mean?" Laura said.

Sally paused for a moment.

"Ginger is gay, and she likes me," Sally said.

Laura just stared at Sally. She wasn't ready for this type of news.

"So she wants to date you?" Laura asked.

Sally nodded.

"How long has this been going on?" Laura asked.

"Well..." Sally said.

She paused.

"This whole year," Sally said.

Laura nodded.

"She hid it well. Has she told anyone else?" Laura said.

Sally shook her head.

"She plans on telling her parents this weekend, but she wanted me to be the first to know," Sally said.

Laura nodded.

"Does she know that you are telling me?" Laura asked.

Sally shook her head once more.

"But I had to talk to someone about it," Sally said.

Laura nodded.

"Don't worry about it. You can trust me. This doesn't leave this room," Laura said.

Sally nodded.

"Thanks," Sally said.

Laura walked over to Sally and proceeded to give her a hug.

Sally smiled.

Laura then walked back to her seat and sat back down.

"I needed one of those," Sally said.
Laura nodded.
"I could tell," Laura said.
Sally decided it was time to change the subject.
"So what are you reading?" Sally asked.
Laura held up the magazine cover.
"There is an article on rape. These girls are speaking out against their attackers, warning others," she said.
Sally nodded.
"Reading about others seems to be helping me to move forward," she added.
Sally nodded.
"When I return from my reunion, I plan to sit down with Keith's mom again," Laura said.
Over the summer, Keith's mom and Laura will become close friends.
Sally smiled.
"That sounds like a good idea. I'm glad to see that you are getting back to your old self," Sally said.
Laura smiled back.
"Well, that's the thing I'll never be my old self again. I have learned a valuable lesson. The world is a different place to me now," Laura said.
Sally nodded.
"I know the truth that evil is within our midst, and I know that I'm not out of its reach. Living here, does not mean we are safe, you know," Laura said.
Sally nodded.
"This experience has given me wisdom. Wisdom that will help me in college," Laura said.
Sally nodded once more.
"Good point," Sally said.
Laura nodded.
"Well, would you like to help me pack?" Laura said.
Sally nodded.
The two of them began packing.

Chapter 19

Keith and his dad arrived at Ruby Waterfalls for their father/son hiking trip.

This place features beautiful flowing waterfalls along with a large variety of hiking trails.

Keith enjoyed nature, because it allowed him to think and relax.

His dad, on the other hand, felt differently. Nature was pretty from afar, but close up it meant bugs, rocks and dirt.

Keith knew that his dad had chosen this type of adventure, so that Keith would go.

Keith and his dad did not have a lot in common. Therefore this was going to be an interesting adventure.

They hopped in the car and drove off on their adventure. Keith's dad was driving, and Keith sat in the passenger seat.

"So tell me about what's going in your life, son," his dad said.

He was trying to be Keith's friend. Keith, on the other hand, was not happy about attending this trip or having to put up with small talk.

"Not much," Keith said.

Keith's dad nodded.

"Not much of a talker, are you?" he asked.

Keith did not reply. He was not in the mood.

Keith leaned his chair back and began to doze off. His father got the hint and turned the radio on.

The drive passed by rather slowly.

Meanwhile...

Laura had finished packing. Her parents had also begun packing for the trip. The family planned to leave tomorrow morning.

Sally had gone home to continue taking in Ginger's news.

Nate was on his way to the airport. His father was going to meet him at the airport in California. His dad usually would stay in town, and they would spend a weekend in a hotel room, but since it was summer, Nate was performing his annual trip out there. His dad had moved out there just a few years ago after being transferred for his job.

Nate and his mom arrived at the airport. She hugged him as he entered the first line.

A little while later, he boarded the plane and soon landed in California, and his dad was of course an hour late picking him up.

"Well. How are you doing, buddy?" his dad said.

His dad had called him, "buddy," for as long as Nate could remember. It was his dad's way of trying to be cool.

"You're late," Nate said.

He was annoyed and sick of his father not following through with his duties.

"I'm sorry. I'll make it up to you," he said.

Nate just nodded. He knew that was an empty promise.

Nate handed his father one of this bags, and the two left the airport. They climbed into his father's car. Nate and his father eventually arrived at his downtown home, after spending the car ride almost completely in silence.

"Home sweet home," his dad said.

Nate nodded.

His dad parked the car and helped Nate carry his luggage into the house.

Once inside, Nate settled in the guest bedroom like always. It was almost lunchtime.

"Are you hungry?" his dad asked.

Nate yelled, "yes" down the hall.

Nate's dad made some sandwiches and grabbed a bag of chips, and the two of them sat down in front of the television.

Nate walked out to the living room. He sat down and started eating.

"I realize I was late, but I took off the whole week so we could spend it together," his dad said.

Nate nodded.

"Your mom and I had a conversation about how you are getting older, and if I don't shape up, I'll miss out getting to know my son. Plus, she was almost not going to send you out this year," his dad added.

Nate nodded. He wished she hadn't.

"So I decided to give you a week, before you start college in the fall," he continued.

Nate nodded. "How generous," he thought. He was rather bitter because of all of his father's broken promises.

Nate's dad was in the mood to talk though. The television was not even on.

"Tell me about school," he asked his son.

Nate sighed. He thought, "I guess I have talk to this guy."

"Fine," Nate said.

Nate's dad nodded.

"You know your mom, and I still talk around once a week," he said.

Nate nodded.

"She mentioned that your best friend got raped or something on prom night, and you helped catch the guilty party," his dad said.

He looked over at Nate, hoping for a reply.

"Not exactly," Nate said.

Nate's dad continued to look his way.

"First, the guy failed in his attempt to rape Laura, and then I was one of the people that caught him red-handed. He was about to rape her when we arrived," he corrected his dad.

Nate's dad nodded.

"Wow. I guess your school is just as unsafe as everywhere else," his dad said.

Nate nodded.

"This guy is part of the popular crowd, and he was jealous of Laura's good grades," Nate said.

Nate's dad nodded.

"Laura is the girl you've been friends with since elementary school," his dad said.

Nate nodded.

"How is your school reacting to this?" his dad asked.

Nate placed his sandwich down. This was going to be a long conversation.

"They expelled the kid, but since it didn't happen on school property, they have not increased security or anything like that," Nate said.

Nate's dad nodded.

"So what do you want to do this week?" his dad asked.

Nate had picked his sandwich back up and continued eating.

He shrugged his shoulders in response.

Nate's dad nodded.

"Well, I'll let you think about that," he said.

He picked up the remote and turned the television on.

Nate was glad his dad was the first one to give up on the conversation.

The next morning, Nate woke up in California hours after Laura's family had left for their trip.

Meanwhile...

Laura's family arrived in middle Georgia. They had set up their sleeping arrangements and drove off in their car to the first family get-together.

The first get-together was a brunch. This brunch was outside and featured several tables with all the southern fixings.

Laura's eyes widened as she stared at the food. This was a typical amount of food for this type of meeting.

Laura had made her mom promise not to tell any family members about what had happened at prom. Therefore, she was looking forward to a two-week vacation from reality.

As always the families were first split up into groups, based on their ages.

Laura sat at a table with a group of her cousins. They ranged from the ages of 13 to 21 and filled about two tables. This group had almost as many members as the adult tables. While the younger kids filled almost twice as many tables.

Laura was definitely a member of a large family.

The adults put together plates for youngest kids first. Next, the rest of the kids took their turns, followed by Laura's group, and the adults went last. But, there was plenty of food left over for seconds and maybe even thirds.

She placed her plate on the table and sat down. The reunion had begun.

Her cousin, Keisha, sat down next to her. Keisha was a junior in a high school.

"Hey, cousin," Keisha said.

Laura smiled.

"How's life treating you?" Laura asked.

Keisha placed her fork down.

"Good," she said.

Keisha's family lived in Florida, so her family was one of the few that had flown in. Her mom's job transferred them down there about a year ago.

Most of Laura's relatives still lived in the middle and south Georgia area.

"Are you starting college in the fall?" Keisha asked.

Laura nodded.

She was surprised some fight or argument had not started yet.

"At Georgia Peach University," Laura said.

Keisha nodded.

Laura had spoken too soon. Her family was not only big, but also loud and usually had a lot of fun. Sometimes there were fights though.

Two young boys had begun to fight over the last chicken wing. Of course, their mothers were able to break up that fight pretty easily.

But when her family was not fighting, they were partying, putting together some large plan or just chilling out.

Laura was sure some of the adults were busy planning right now. She hoped so. That would make her vacation even better.

She smiled as she looked back at Keisha. This might just be the vacation she needed, she thought.

Chapter 20

Corey had been assigned a defense lawyer, and the trial was to start in a few weeks.

His parents had taken him home, but were required to place him under house arrest even if it wasn't normal practice.

Corey had been home around one week now. His mom had called in sick with a fever.

"Take care of your momma. I'm off to work," his dad said.

His dad was not only still mad, but also disappointed in Corey.

Corey rolled over. He was disappointed with his punishment.

Corey sighed. He wanted to leave the house. "This is as bad as jail," he thought.

His mom was eating breakfast in the kitchen, when he finally walked down the hallway.

"Hi there," she said.

Corey nodded.

"You really got yourself into some trouble," she said.

Corey didn't look at his mom as he grabbed some cereal.

"Are you sorry?" she asked.

Corey still didn't look at her.

"You know feeling some guilt might help your case," she said.

She just continued even though he wasn't listening.

"You know what you did was a horrible thing. In a way, I'm glad you got caught," she said.

Corey was done with the lecture.

"I'm not in the mood for a lecture," he said.

He screamed and walked out of the kitchen and into the living room, and he clicked the television on.

She followed him.

"You are going to have face what you did and take responsibility for it," she said.

He pushed the volume button, turning the TV up louder.

She turned around and wandered off. Over her shoulder, she yelled one more thing.

"Your lawyer will be meeting with you sometime this afternoon," she said.

Corey nodded.

That was only important thing she had said as far as he cared.

He reached over and grabbed a piece of paper and pen off of a nearby table.

He began to make a list of things he needed to tell the lawyer. This was their first meeting.

After about 30 minutes, his list included:

> My side of the story
> How it was her fault and not mine
> No knife
> How to get out of this
> Lighter punishment

Corey was so stubborn about winning this.

He picked up one of his dad's law books and walked down hall. He closed the door to his room behind him.

He was determined to find a way out.

Meanwhile...

Ginger had arrived in Niagara Falls with her family.

The entire plane ride there she had been thinking about what she told Sally and what she would tell her parents.

How do I say it? What will they think? How will they respond? Have I let them down?

Taking this step was a big one.

"Am I ready for it?" she thought. "How do I start?"

Thinking about this for the past few hours didn't make the task any easier.

They climbed out of the taxi and checked into their hotel room.

The family unpacked their luggage and made dinner plans.

Ginger was also unsure if this was the right time to share her news.

Will this ruin the vacation? Do I say something now or at the end? What do I do?

Her head was spinning.

"I could wait," she thought. "I could tell my mom by myself first."

Sally took it so well, maybe my parents will do the same. She dismissed that thought quickly.

Ginger had no sisters, and she knew that her mom had always fantasized about her wedding and grandchildren.

How do I disappoint her? How do I tell her?

They arrived at the restaurant.

Do I tell them tonight?

Meanwhile...

The reunion was getting louder.

It was mid-afternoon now. Laura was sure the adults were up to something.

And Laura was right, but she wouldn't find out what they were planning until later.

The families split up and came back together for a late dinner party that night.

The adults had rented out a community center. Everyone took seats at the tables.

The first event on the agenda was story time.

Laura's cousin, Billy, got up and stood at the front of the room.

"May I please have everyone's attention?" Billy requested.

They just nodded. Laura enjoyed the stories that her cousins had to tell.

"As most of you know, I live in the Fort Valley, the Peach County area, and the story I am about to tell you happened only a few summers ago," he said.

The group quieted as he began.

"It was a hot, summer day. My friend, Michael, was down visiting for the summer. We decided we would go canoeing," he said.

He paused.

"The river was high and above the water mark, making the rapids rather rough that day. We continued with our plans anyway. We placed the canoe into the water and hopped in. We had our cooler with drinks, some snacks and Mike's backpack in the back," he said.

He paused to allow the audience to form a mental image.

"Let me explain something to you before I continue. Mike was rather connected to this backpack. If you know what I mean. And this backpack wasn't like one that you would find at Wal-mart rather it was a hiking bag," he said.

Laura had heard this story before. He had told it the past couple years, but it was always requested again and again, since it was an exciting story.

Billy continued.

"Since the water was rough, it changed the direction of our canoe, and we began to lose control as we hit rapids. These rapids tossed and turned our boat," he said.

He paused.

"Tossing and turning, eventually we lost some drinks and snacks. But Mike had managed to save his backpack from being thrown out. Picture this: me in the front of the canoe looking out at rocks and rapids heading our way and Mike in the back holding on to his dear backpack," he said.

Some of them knew Mike from past reunions and pictures, but Laura had no idea who he was, so she always pictured some random guy.

Billy continued.

"Eventually, we were both thrown out of the boat into the rapids. The canoe sunk to the bottom. It landed upside down. Mike was floating holding onto his backpack," he said.

He paused.

"He was a good storyteller," Laura thought as he continued. "He was dynamic."

"I placed one of my feet on a nearby stone. At least I thought it was a rock. For all I know it could have been an alligator's head," he said.

He paused for the sound effect.

Some of the kids made an appropriate scream.

"I placed my other food on something hard, maybe a rock. Then with the force of my arms, I dead lifted the canoe off the bottom of the river and brought it up to its original position. Now, this canoe was wooden and rather heavy," he said.

He then flexed his muscles. Billy was one of Laura's better-looking cousins. He was a junior in college. As his muscles bulged, Laura could tell that he had worked out this past year. "He is a nice looking piece of white chocolate," she thought. For her cousin, she meant, of course. He stood about 6' 1" on that stage in front of everyone and probably weighed over 200 pounds, mostly muscle.

"As Michael and I climbed back into the canoe, we saw something swim through the water and to this day, we still wonder if it was an," he said.

He paused as some kids yelled out "alligator."

With that, he bowed and walked off the stage.

He had started the night off well, but it was just getting started as dinner was passed out.

Each of them received a plate and dug in.

Meanwhile...

Keith and his dad finally arrived at the falls.

His dad parked the car outside the lot and piled the camping supplies on his and Keith's backs. They entered the park and began their hike.

"So you got into a college I hear," his dad said.

He figured he would give the conversation another try.

Keith nodded in response.

"Georgia Peach," Keith said.

They began to hike up a large, rocky hill.

"Down in Middle Georgia," his dad said.

Keith nodded. He was focused on the hill in front of him.

This hill was rather rocky and steep.

Keith's dad continued on with his conversation.

"What do you plan on majoring in?" he asked.

Keith shrugged his shoulders.

"I don't know," Keith said.

Keith's dad nodded.

"You have time to decide. My major was business management," his dad said.

The words stumbled out of his mouth, as he lost his balance and fell face first onto the ground in front of him.

Keith's dad had been paying little attention to the hill that he didn't even realize he had fallen until his lips were touching dirt.

Keith had reached the top of the hill and turned to notice that no one was following him. He wondered where his annoying father was.

His father was trying to crawl up the hill. He picked his head up off the ground and tried to yell for Keith's attention.

HIS WRATH

Keith, hearing his name, stepped back towards hill and looked down. He saw his dad struggling to move up the hill.

As Keith proceeded to help his dad, he tripped on a rock, fell and rolled down the hill right past his father. Keith rolled all the way to the bottom of the hill, hitting his head on a tree trunk, knocking him out cold.

His father watched Keith roll down beside him in shock. He could feel that part of his lower body was caught on a root or something, causing to be unable to move easily.

He picked up his head and screamed for help.

No one came. Since they had gone to hike on a weekend, Keith's dad expected someone to walk by soon.

Meanwhile…

The dinner at the reunion had ended. Then cousin Billy walked to the stage to tell his famous hog story.

"Everybody doing all right?" Billy asked.

Laura smiled. She enjoyed this story too.

"My friend Clint, and I wanted to roast a hog one summer. Now Clint was a large muscular guy," he said.

He paused.

"We visited my neighbor's hog farm, in order to get a hog. He told us that we could have any pick of the litter we wanted, and while we were in there, he also told us to kill the weakling. So we opened the doors to the hog pen," he said.

And

"Clint with his shotgun in his right hand just knocks the head of the weakling instantly killing it as he walks towards the litter. He eyes the hog he wants. I watched as he approached this hog. He walked towards it, and it ran off squealing rather loudly. Clint went off running after it," he said.

Billy passed around pictures of the event.

"Clint is chasing after the hog and gaining on him. Clint reaches out with his muscular arms and grabs the hog," he said.

Billy looked around to make sure everyone was paying attention.

"Clint held the hog tight and proceeded to break its neck, killing the hog. I stood there gasping in amazement at Clint's strength. We then walked back to my house and Clint's truck," he said.

Laura was glad Billy's stories were taking her mind off of her own dramatic life.

"We needed to get the hair off this hog, in order to prepare it for dinner. Clint decided it would be easier to burn it off. He laid the dead hog in a bathtub. He proceeded to pour gasoline onto the hog and then threw a lit match in the tub, causing it to blow up," he said.

Meanwhile…

Someone was walking near Keith's dad on his way back from a hike and saw him lying there.

"Can I help you, sir?" someone asked.

Keith's dad had little strength to speak. He just rustled back and forth, hoping the man would understand his body language.

The man stood over Keith's father and saw what was hindering him from moving. He positioned himself to the right of his right leg and loosened his ankle. Keith's dad was now able to move.

The man bent over and helped him up.

"Thank you, sir, but he's my son," his dad said.

He pointed down the hill at Keith lying beside a tree trunk out cold.

The man nodded as he continued to help Keith's dad down the hill to his son. He then leaned down and looked at Keith.

Meanwhile…

"The tub explodes, causing us to react and put out the explosion rather quickly. The hog's fur is all burnt off, but I would not recommend this method. Clint then continued to separate the head from the hog's body by pulling it off. Clint proceeded to separate the meat from the bones. My family as most of you know has a 'bathtub smoker.' We placed the meat of the hog into the smoker and had my dad watch it as we ran off into the woods," he said.

He laughed. Some of kids were grossed out at this point.

"Yes, it is gross. Night came, and my dad switched places with my mom in order get some sleep. However, she added more wood and allowed more air to enter the smoker through a vent, causing the meat of the hog to burn and the flame to spread outside of the smoker. She then woke up my father," he said.

He made motions with his hands to paint a picture of the flames growing.

"My father was able to put the fire out, but our dinner was ruined," he said.

He looked over at his mom.

"Next time, leave it the way dad left it," he said.

Then Billy bowed and walked off the stage.

Chapter 21

Keith had been unconscious for only a short time.

The man leaned over him and took his pulse.

"He's got a pulse. He just looks like he was knocked out. Let's get some blood to the head," the man said.

In a matter of seconds, Keith's eyes opened.

Keith's dad sat down next to Keith and looked into his eyes.

"Don't speak. Just breathe. You took a hard fall," his dad said.

The man stood up and looked around for more people.

"Do you think we can carry him to the ranger's station?" the man asked.

Keith's dad looked up.

"Why? Won't he be all right?" his dad asked.

The man shook his head.

"It looks as if that fall hurt his leg. His leg might be okay, but something is wrong with his ankle. I'm no doctor, but I think he will have trouble walking on it," the man said.

Keith's dad nodded.

"We could try carrying him," his dad said.

Keith could now hear what's going on.

"Can a brother get an explanation? What's happening?" Keith asked.

The two men picked him up.

"Just relax; we are getting you some help," Keith's dad said.

Keith nodded. He had little strength.

The two men carried him a few miles to the ranger's station and knocked on the door. The ranger answered.

"What have we got here?" the ranger said.

The two men laid Keith down on a table.

"He fell and bumped his head on a tree. Could you check his legs?" his dad said.

The ranger nodded as he looked at each of Keith's legs.

"Just relax, son," his dad said.

The ranger looked over at Keith's dad.

"It looks like he sprained his left ankle and scraped his knees. You should have him see a doctor for that ankle," the ranger said.

Keith picked his head up.

"Is it okay for him to walk on it?" Keith's dad said.

"Short distances, I guess. I can get you two back to your car though. I have an off-road vehicle," the ranger said.

Keith's dad nodded.

"That would be helpful. And to you, sir, thank you for all of your help," he said.

The man nodded, smiled and left to find the rest of his group.

The ranger and Keith's dad helped Keith into the ranger's vehicle.

"Am I all right?" Keith asked.

He asked as he was lay down in the car.

"Your ankle needs to be looked at, but otherwise you should be okay," the ranger said.

Keith nodded.

The ranger drove off to the parking lot.

"Thanks for helping us out," Keith's dad said.

The ranger nodded. A few minutes later, they arrived in the parking lot and moved Keith into their car.

Keith's dad drove off to the nearest hospital for Keith's ankle to be checked out. When they arrived, he helped Keith into the building and took a seat in the waiting room.

"Can I help you?" the nurse at the check-in desk said.

"My son needs his ankle checked," his dad said.

She nodded and handed him a clipboard.

"Just fill this out, and we will call your name," she said.

Keith's dad took the clipboard and went back to Keith. He filled out the paperwork and then handed it in.

Two of them waited 45 minutes before the nurse walked over and spoke to them.

"The doctor can see you now. Follow me," she said.

Meanwhile...

Corey's lawyer arrived at the house. The two of them sat in the dining room.

"Corey, have a seat. We will make this painless," the lawyer said.

Corey nodded and sat down.

"Good. Why don't you tell me your side of the story?" his lawyer asked.

The lawyer had already been briefed on the reason that Corey had been in jail as well as the evidence against him. He listened as Corey spoke.

When Corey finished, he nodded.

The lawyer had been taking notes the entire time. This was his 20th assault case. He had gone to court several times, and Corey guessed he was in his forties. The man was a skinny, well-spoken and experienced lawyer. Corey smiled figuring that this lawyer would be able to help him out.

"Corey, I assume you are going to plead guilty?" he said.

Corey stared at him.

"Guilty of what? I mean could you please explain," Corey said.

The lawyer paused.

"Well. You were caught with your pants down so to speak, and if you appear sorry, you could receive a lesser sentence," the lawyer said.

Corey was not amused, but he agreed, since he did not want to spend any more time in jail or on house arrest for that matter, which he thought was his dad's worst idea yet.

Corey nodded.

"Guilty, then," he said.

The lawyer wrote that down.

"Good, that's settled. The girl you attacked and her friends may want to testify against you, but since you are pleading guilty, maybe we won't even have to go to trial," the lawyer said.

Corey nodded.

"Do you have any questions for me?" the lawyer said.

"When is the trial?" Corey asked.

The lawyer picked up his schedule.

"It was delayed and will start in two weeks. In the meantime, I will meet with the prosecution, and then we will meet one more time," the lawyer said.

Corey nodded.

"This should be a quick trial, so don't you worry about a thing," the lawyer said.

With that the lawyer left, leaving Corey with unanswered questions.

Meanwhile...

Keith was lying down awaiting the doctor. The nurse had asked taken some notes on his fall.

Several minutes later, the doctor arrived. He picked up the clipboard hanging on the door and flipped it open.

"Keith?" the doctor said.

Keith nodded.

"It appears that you had a great fall. Where does it hurt?" the doctor said.

Keith opened his mouth to speak as the doctor walked closer. His dad cut him off.

"His ankle," his dad said.

The doctor nodded and began to inspect both ankles.

"The left one is swollen," the doctor said.

He noted that in his chart.

"It does not appear to be broken, just sprained," the doctor said.

He closed the clipboard.

"I will have the nurse give you some supplies for wrapping your ankle. It should heal in around a couple of weeks," the doctor said.

He smiled and left the room.

A few minutes later, after Keith and his dad endured some silence, and then the nurse slid in the doorway.

"Let's wrap you up," the nurse said.

She wrapped his ankle and handed the extras to his dad.

"You should ice it too," she said.

They both nodded.

"We have some crutches if you would like," she said.

Keith's dad nodded.

They helped Keith up so he could start walking with the crutches. They proceeded to the waiting room, where Keith's dad paid the bill.

The two of them then proceeded to the car.

Meanwhile...

Story time had ended at the reunion, and comedy hour had begun.

Laura was thankful that the reunion was keeping her mind off of her situation.

Laura and some of her cousins had separated themselves from the main group. There was around 10 of them ranging from ages 16 to 20.

Keisha looked at Laura as her older brother about Laura's age, Cedric spoke up.

"Let's ditch this joint," Cedric said.

No one had any idea where he wanted to go, but they hopped in cars and followed his car out of the parking lot and through some back roads towards an abandoned building.

Laura wondered what she had just gotten herself into.

"Where are we going?" Laura asked.

Keisha just shook her head.

"I don't know," she said.

Laura seemed annoyed.

"He's your brother," Laura said.

"So. Listen, we are just going to have trust that he knows what he is doing and where he is going. Besides you wanted to have some fun, didn't you?" Keisha said.

Laura nodded.

"But to be on the safe side, don't drink anything okay," she said.

Laura looked confused.

Soon, all three cars arrived at the building. Cedric climbed out of his car and led everyone into the building.

"Are y'all ready to party?" he asked.

The cousins nodded. All of sudden the music became even louder, and a door opened behind him.

"Come on in," a guy said.

Cedric and his cousins walked in. Laura kept repeating to herself, "don't drink anything." She wondered why Keisha had said that.

She walked into a large, decorated building. There were tables covered with plastic cups, filled with different colored liquids, plastic plates and finger foods. In the middle of the building was a dance floor.

Keisha tapped Laura on the shoulder.

"These guys are much older. Remember what I told you," Keisha told her.

Laura nodded.

She wondered if she could eat anything as a young gentleman approached her.

"Hi. I'm Daren," he said.

Laura just nodded. He handed her a drink.

"Thanks. I'm Laura," she said.

She just stared at the light pink liquid in her cup, wondering what do with it.

"It's rather good," he said.

Laura looked up from the cup.

"What is it?" she asked.

"A drink. Don't worry, girlfriend you'll dig it," he said.

Laura didn't respond rather she just looked around hoping someone would rescue her. Keisha walked up.

"Thanks for holding my drink," Keisha said.

She grabbed the cup out of Laura's hand and walked over to another one of Laura's cousins, Cheryl. Unfortunately, Cheryl had already taken a sip of the liquid.

"Cheryl, are you all right? How many drinks have you had?" Keisha asked.

Cheryl counted out loud on her fingers.

"Like five. They taste good, but I still can't figure out what is in them. But that table over there has so many different ones to chose from," she said.

Cheryl was only 16 years old and rather naïve about alcoholic drinks. She had just been thirsty.

"It's also like cool-aid or something. Keisha, where is the bathroom?" she asked.

Keisha shook her head as she led Cheryl to the bathroom. Cheryl threw up a few times. Keisha and another cousin carried her out to the car.

"Stay with her. I'll be right back," Keisha said to her other cousin.

She walked back into the building and grabbed Laura.

"We need to get keys from one of those boys. Cheryl is not feeling well," Keisha said.

"Why?" Laura asked.

Daren just stared at the two girls, wondering why this girl kept distracting his prey.

"She drank too much," Keisha answered.

Laura nodded.

Keish and Laura walked off to find one of the older cousins. Daren followed.

"Where are you going sweet thing? I thought we could dance," he said.

Keisha and Laura kept walking and soon found Cedric. They grabbed him off the dance floor.

"This bright idea of yours just got one of the cousins drunk," Keisha said.

Cedric just shrugged his shoulders.

"Oops. What do you want me to do about it?" he asked.

Keisha shook her head.

"We need to get her out of here. I need a sober driver and a cell phone," she said.

"The only sober drivers are probably you and that girl," he said.

He pointed at Laura.

"I'll give you my keys. I don't know where to get you a cell though," he said.

Keisha nodded and took his keys.

Daren yelled out.

"Hey sweet thing. You can borrow mine," he said.

Laura smiled and borrowed his cell phone to call for directions to the nearest hospital.

Cedric yelled back at Keisha.

"You better not turn us in," he said.

Keisha just kept walking to the car to check on Cheryl. Keisha opened the doors and sat down in the driver's seat.

"Laura. Did you get directions?" Keisha asked.

Laura nodded.

"Is Cheryl okay back there?" Keisha asked.

Her other cousin responded, "I think so." The girls drove off to the hospital.

They arrived not too much later and helped Cheryl out of the car and into the waiting room. Keisha walked up to the check-in desk.

"Excuse me, but my cousin has alcohol poisoning," Keisha said.

The nurse pulled out a chart and then looked up at the girl.

"I'll be with you in just a minute. Please have a seat," the nurse said.

Meanwhile...

Keith and his dad arrived home to find his mom relaxing. Keith sat down on the couch and placed the crutches on the floor beside him.

"What happened to you?" his mom asked.

"I sprained my ankle trying to help dad up from falling. I guess hiking is not something we should to do together," he said.

They laughed.

Meanwhile...

Nate awoke the next morning still in California. He wandered to the kitchen to have some breakfast. As he was walking, he noticed that no one was home besides him.

Nate looked around the kitchen to find something to eat. Instead on the counter he saw a note from his dad.

> Nate,
>
> I was called into work this morning, but my boss ensures me this will be the only time this week. Eat or order in whatever you want. Money is on the counter.
>
> Love,
> Dad

Nate opened the envelope sitting next to the letter. Inside was about $50. Nate picked up the phone and called his mom at work.

"Hi. This is Ms. Williams. How may I help you?" his mom asked.

Nate's mom worked as a senior editor at a magazine in Atlanta.

"Mom. It's me," he said.

"Hey honey. How is everything?" she asked.

Nate sighed as he answered.

"Dad has to work today. He originally told me he had the whole week off," he said.

Nate's mom raised her voice.

"What? I'm calling him right now. I'll call you tonight okay," she said.

Nate nodded and hung up the phone.

Nate's mom dialed her ex-husband. A man answered the phone.

"You left your son home alone with nothing to do. I thought you said you were going to change," she said.

"I'm sorry I think you have the wrong number, but the person I think you are looking for is on vacation," he said.

She hung the phone. Confused, she dialed his cell phone number.

"Hello," he said.

"You left your son home alone. I thought you said you were going to change," she said.

"Hi. Linda. I had something important to do," he said.

"You always have something important to do. If your son comes home disappointed again, I'm ending your privileges, not mention you will owe me extra money for changing the plane ticket. I'm not going to make him stay if he is not happy. At least, I got your check this morning for the plane tickets," she said.

"I'm going home right now," he said.

"Good," she said sternly.

She hung up the phone.

He looked over at this girlfriend, Jamie.

"Want to go meet my son?" he said.

She nodded.

Jamie and Nate's dad dropped what they were doing and went to his apartment.

Meanwhile...

Ginger's family was visiting Niagara Falls, while she was trying to figure out how to tell the truth about her sexuality. She wondered, of course, how Sally was doing knowing the truth. Ginger had waited to share the truth with her parents, but now she figured she might as well just tell them and get the truth out.

She gathered her family into the hotel room before dinner.

"Mom, Dad. I have something to tell you," Ginger said.

She paused. She was trying so hard not to appear nervous.

"I am not like other girls," she added

Her parents look confused. Oh how do I say this, she thought.

"Honey, what do you mean?" her mom asked.

Ginger took a deep breath.

"Mom and Dad, I'm I'm I'm a homosexual. I am attracted to girls," she admitted.

Her mom's eyes filled with tears. Her only daughter, gay? Her dad became angry.

"You're what? That's not how we raised you. We go to church and everything," he said.

His family had an old-fashion, religious background.

"Settle down, Rick. She is still our daughter," her mom said.

He nodded and sat back down on the bed.

"Are you sure?" her mom asked.

Ginger just stared at her mom. She didn't get it.

"Mom, this is not something I can change. You either are one way or the other, and I'm well I'm the other," Ginger said.

Her mom just nodded.

"So no grandchildren?" her mom asked.

"Not unless, I adopt," Ginger said.

Her mom nodded again as tears welled up in her eyes.

"My little girl is all grown up now," her mom said.

Ginger's dad moved to the bed and sat next to his wife and hugged her.

"Ginger, go on now. You have disappointed us," he said.

Ginger didn't move.

"I'm serious. Go take a walk or something. We are not ready to continue this conversation," he added.

Ginger nodded, picked up her hotel key and walked out of the room. She rode the elevator down and walked outside of the building. She walked to the nearest pay phone and dialed Sally.

"Hello," Sally said.

"Hey there," Ginger said.

Sally did not expect to her Ginger's voice.

"I thought you were on vacation," Sally said.

"I am. When is your trip?" Ginger asked.

"In August. Corey's trial is later his month. I think everyone will be back in town by then," Sally answered.

"Good. Then we can fry him," Ginger said.

Sally nodded.

"I told them," Ginger said.

"What do you mean?" Sally asked.

"I told my parents the truth," Ginger said.

"How did it go?" Sally asked.

"All right, I guess. They cried and said that I was a disappointment," Ginger said.

Sally nodded.

"Ginger. I'm here for you. I mean I'm still your friend," Sally said.

Ginger nodded as Sally continued.

"I mean. I'm not sure that I feel the same way and everything," Sally said.

"I better go. This thing is asking me for more money, and I don't have another Canadian coin," Ginger said.

"Bye," Sally replied.

Ginger said goodbye and hung up the phone. She started walking again.

Meanwhile...

Sally lay down on her bed. "She told them," she thought.

Sally took another deep breath as she stared at the ceiling.

What does this mean? What does the future hold for our friendship?

"At least everyone will be here to testify on Laura's behalf in court," she thought.

She smiled on that note.

Chapter 22

Corey's trial was within one week. Each of the kids' vacations were coming to a close. Sally and her family had delayed their vacation until after the trial was over, so she could meet with the prosecution.

Sally got up early and met with the prosecution in his office.

"Come in, Sally. Have a seat," the prosecution lawyer said.

The lawyer was around 30 years old and seemed rather pleased with his career choice.

Sally sat down across the desk from him.

"Are you ready for this upcoming week?" he asked.

Sally nodded.

"Let me brief you on what has been happening," he said.

Sally nodded and pulled out her notebook to take notes.

"Corey has pleaded guilty, probably to avoid a harsh sentence, meaning we might not even have a trial," he said.

Sally nodded even through she was disappointed.

"Instead, what could happen is that the judge would just hear from Laura and Corey. He or she might even hear from more witnesses. That is the judge's decision," he said.

Sally nodded again.

"When will you know?" she asked.

Lawyer picked up this calendar.

"I should know by the end of this week, before the case begins on Monday. Let's schedule a meeting for Thursday," he said.

The two of them scheduled a meeting for Thursday.

Meanwhile...

The defense was to meet with the prosecution in a matter of a day, and the judge was deciding on how she wanted to hear this case.

She had met with the prosecution, the defense and Officer Fuller, who was on duty when the incident happened.

She had handled many assault cases in her time as a judge. Usually, she had no sympathy for the guilty party.

However, the fact is that the guilty party did not succeed in raping the young girl, but what was bothering her was the question of what if he would had succeeded.

She picked up her file and reread the case.

Meanwhile...

Jamie and Nate's dad knocked on his bedroom door. He was napping.

Nate rolled over and responded to the knock. He jumped up and opened the door.

"I thought you were working," Nate said.

They walked down the hall to the living room. All of them sat down. Nate's dad sat next to Jamie on the couch.

"Nate, I lied to you," his dad said.

Nate looked confused, hoping his dad would continue.

"I didn't have to work today," he added.

The anger grew inside of Nate.

"You lied to me!" Nate screamed.

Jamie felt like it was time to defend him.

"It's my birthday, but your father really wants to be a father and settle down," she said.

Nate thought, "Who are you?"

"She is right. I hope that you can forgive me, and the three of us can celebrate her birthday together. Jamie and I are engaged, and she wants to settle down and start a family too. I want you to be a part of that. I really do," his dad said.

He grabbed her hand and held it tight.

Nate was trying to understand everything that was happening.

"Does mom know? How long have you two been together?" Nate asked.

"She knows that I met someone, but she doesn't know that this is serious. We have been together for a few months now," he said.

Nate sat back. He was overwhelmed.

"I'm not sure that I'm ready for any of this. It has always been you and me, and I'm not sure if I'm ready for that to change," he said as he let out his anger.

"Don't be so hard on him," she said to Nate's dad.

He padded her hand.

"It will change and so will I. You can take your time on being ready to accept the new me," his dad said.

He paused hoping that Nate would respond positively.

Nate rather just stood up and walked down the hall.

"I need some time. You two can go celebrate her birthday though. Don't let me ruin your day," Nate said.

He opened the door to his room and shut it behind him loudly. He then collapsed on the bed.

Nate picked up the telephone next to his bed.

His dad was using it. He continued to listen. His dad was talking to his mother.

"I'm concerned about Nate," he said.

"Why?" she asked.

"I just had him meet my fiancée," he said.

"Who?" she said.

"That's right. I didn't tell you either. I have a fiancée, and Nate just met her," he said.

"I guess he didn't take it too well," she said.

He nodded.

"No wonder. You needed to give him the news before you had him meet her. Now he is embarrassed. Can I talk to him?" she said.

"Hold on," he said.

Nate's dad walked down the hall and knocked on his son's door.

"Your mom is on the phone, and she would like to talk to you," he said.

Since Nate was already listening, he just said hello to his mom.

"Hi," he said.

"I heard that your dad just gave you some news," she said.

He nodded.

"He's getting married to some girl," he said.

"What's she like?" she asked.

Nate chuckled.

"She's quiet, but she did defend dad on something earlier," he said.

"She sounds stupid," she said.

Nate laughed.

"I guess that means they will probably get along fine and have several kids. Oh. But he can't even find time to see you," she said.

Nate laughed.

"They want me to be a part of their family," he said.

"What does that mean? You're not moving out there," she declared.

"I guess it means that my dad is supposed to start being a real father," he said.

Nate's mom laughed on that one. So did Nate.

"Honey. Don't get your hopes up. We know your father is not dependable. You go off to college in the fall, and then you will be starting a whole new life," she said.

She smiled and continued.

"So just have a good time and work on putting all of this behind you," she said.

He nodded.

"Thanks. I love you," he said.

She replied with I love you, and they ended their conversion.

Nate felt better and decided he might as well face his dad and the situation. He walked back out to the kitchen.

"Jamie, right?" Nate asked.

She nodded, and they shook hands.

"Dad. I think it would nice if the three of us went on a tour of the city," he said.

His dad nodded.

"Let me get a phonebook," his dad said.

Nate, his dad and Jamie took a tour of the city. Nate was trying to get used to a new member of his family. He was also just trying to take his mom's advice and have some fun. His trip out west would be over soon though.

Meanwhile...

Keith had arrived home and to explain to his mother what had happened. He was lying down on his bed with his leg elevated, and his crutches were on the floor.

The servants had brought him some food, and the TV in his room had been turned on for entertainment.

Keith's mom knocked on his door to check in on him.

"Come in," Keith said.

Keith's mom walked in and sat down in a chair next to Keith's bed.

"How is your ankle?" she asked.

"I don't feel much, because of those pills," he said.

She nodded.

"You know that you will have to appear in court in around a week, right?" she said.

Keith nodded.

"Will you still need the crutches then?" she said.

Keith nodded.

"I have to be on these things for like weeks. Then doc is supposed to check me again and see if I still need them," he said.

She nodded.

"Can I get you anything?" she said.

Keith shook his head and gently closed his eyes. He was hoping when he reopened them that Laura would be sitting there.

His mom kissed him on the forehead and left the room.

Shortly afterwards, Keith opened his eyes and saw an empty chair. He sighed.

Meanwhile...

Laura was having the time of her life not focusing on anything that happened to her prior to the reunion.

Cheryl's stomach was pumped because of alcohol poisoning. She stayed away from the party scene for the rest of the reunion.

Laura didn't though. She was able to split off from the adults and kids for most of the reunion outside from eating meals with her family and sleeping in the same place. Instead Laura and Keisha spent a lot of time together.

A few days after the party that caused Cheryl to slip into a drunken state, Keisha and Laura were invited to join Billy and some other young adults on a day trip to his hometown of Butler. The group included six people, three girls and three guys. Laura, of course, had to obtain her parents' permission.

This day began with a group breakfast, so Laura sat with her family.

"Mom, Dad," Laura said.

She looked at each of them as she said it.

"I was invited to join Billy and some other kids on a trip to his hometown, Butler," she said.

Her parents nodded.

"Billy is one that spoke the other night?" her mom asked.

Laura nodded.

"I don't know. He's much older than you," her mom said.

"Besides, Keisha will have a cell phone and be there the entire time with me," Laura said.

Laura's mom looked over at her husband.

"I guess so. But you will have to check in with us. You need to call us on my work cell phone when you get there, when you leave there and when you return here," her dad said.

Laura nodded. That was rather easy.

"When are you kids leaving?" he asked.

"After breakfast," Laura said.

Her family finished their meal with small talk. The rumors about Cheryl's drunken state had not reached her parents' ears, which was good news for Laura.

After breakfast the six of them climbed into Billy's parents' van and departed on their trip.

Laura and Keisha sat next to each other. This was Laura's first visit to Butler. She could only imagine what it looked like from Billy's stories.

The six of the them were leaving on an adventure.

Meanwhile...

Ginger had been walking in circles around the city for quite some time before someone tapped her on her shoulder.

"Sweetie. Why don't we go get something to eat?" her mom said.

Ginger nodded. She walked off with her family to a restaurant. The family was ushered to a table and sat down.

"You didn't walk very far," her mom continued.

Ginger shook her head. She had walked mostly in circles.

"We thought about what you told us earlier. We may not agree with your decision. But," her mom said.

She paused and looked over her husband.

"You are our daughter, and we do want you to be happy," he said.

Ginger nodded. The tension was killing her.

"If this is what makes you happy, we will support you provided that you take precaution. Please use precaution," he added.

"Homosexuals seem be more likely to contract sexually transmitted diseases," her mom said.

Ginger nodded.

"That's because some of them usually have several partners," she said.

"Right," her mom agreed.

"Just be careful," her dad said.

Ginger nodded.

"I have thought about this way of life a lot, and I'm ready to take it on," she said.

Her parents just nodded, and dinner was soon served.

Ginger breathed a gasp of relief. Her parents still supported her. Some parents of gay children disown them. She considered herself a lucky girl.

Meanwhile...

Laura had arrived in Butler. It was early afternoon, when they stopped for lunch at the town's Subway. The Subway is the only fast food place in the town.

Being lunchtime, it was packed. Nevertheless, the kids jumped in line. They slowly moved to the front of the line.

"What would you like?" the Subway worker said.

Laura smiled at the worker.

"Six-inch Italian sub sandwich, please," she said.

"I'm sorry, but we have run out of bread. Would you like a salad?" the worker asked.

Laura looked confused. How could a Subway run out of bread? In Butler, there is only one fast food place, causing the likelihood of running out of an item to rise.

"I just have the grilled chicken and baby spinach salad with honey mustard dressing," she said.

The worker put together Laura's salad and then took the rest of the orders. The six of them sat down at a table.

"Wait. They have wraps?" she asked.

Keisha nodded.

"They don't refer to a wrap as bread. It is usual that they run out of bread, so I always have a back up. One time, I even brought my own bread from Piggy Wiggly over here," Billy said.

Laura nodded and glanced over at Keisha.

Keisha laughed. She whispered into Laura's ear.

"He's not serious. I'm glad you came. We need to burst your north Georgia bubble," Keisha said.

She laughed again. Billy gave a look to say what are you laughing at. Keisha just smiled.

Laura and the other kids ate their meals.

"Billy, what are we doing today?" Laura asked.

Billy chuckled. This was going to be an adventure.

"I thought we would go four-wheeling after lunch," he said.

Laura looked over at Keisha for an explanation.

"I may be black, but what is four-wheeling?" Laura asked.

Billy chuckled.

"You are not really from around here, are you?" he asked.

She shook her head.

"Oh yeah. You grew up in the suburbs of Atlanta. You would not find a four-wheeler up there," he said.

She nodded.

"In that case, you'll see," he added.

Laura nodded again. She was a little nervous though. She felt so out of place. Everyone had visited Billy's home before. This was all new to her.

They left the restaurant and climbed back into the van to go to Billy's parents' house.

Not too much later, the van drove up on a dirt road. Laura looked out the window. This was the first dirt road she had seen and the first one she had ridden on.

Keisha noticed Laura's expression as she looked out the window.

"Don't tell me this is a first for ya," Keisha said.

Laura nodded, embarrassed.

"You have like traveled out of this country, yet you haven't been in the true south till now?" Keisha asked.

Laura nodded.

"Welcome to your roots, girl," Keisha chuckled.

A few minutes later, Billy parked the car across from a one-floor house. The house was white with several windows. In front of it was a deck with two levels. A grill sat on the deck, and to the left of the deck cut out in the ground was a sitting area. The area was decorated with stones, benches and chairs. There also was a porch swing. Beside the house, sat an above ground dark blue four-foot deep pool. The house was empty, since Billy's family was at the reunion. Down the dirt road stood two more houses, a trailer and what appeared to be a mechanic shop. Next to the van, was a child's play set made out of wood with slides and swings.

Each of them exited the car. This was Laura's first time seeing a sight like this. It looked like a fun place to live, but it certainly was different from the place she called home.

Keisha smiled over at Laura.

"What do you think?" she asked.

"It looks like I'm about to go on an adventure," Laura said.

Billy overheard them and chuckled.

"You bet," he said.

He pointed over at the four-wheeled vehicles parked near the play set as he spoke.

There were three: One red, one green and one yellow. The red was the smallest one, while the yellow looked brand new. The yellow one belonged to Billy's sister and her boyfriend who had come along as part of the group.

Billy grabbed Laura's hand.

"You are riding with me on the baby," he said.

She looked confused.

They climbed on the red one, or the smallest one, "the baby." Billy's sister and her boyfriend climbed on their yellow one, and Keisha and the last guy, who was a cousin of Billy's, climbed on the green one. The rest of Billy's family, including one brother and three sisters had stayed at the reunion.

It was time to four-wheel!

Chapter 23

Corey had a meeting with his lawyer today. The lawyer arrived and knocked on the front door.

They sat down in the dinning room.

"How are we doing today?" the lawyer asked.

"Good," Corey's mom said.

The lawyer sat down across from Corey and his mother.

"I have met with the judge and the prosecution. It seems that just a judge rather than a jury will hear this case. The judge wants to hear from each of those involved, and then she will make her decision," the lawyer said.

Corey nodded.

"A smaller case is better. It is easier to predict one decision versus a whole jury's decision," the lawyer added.

Corey nodded.

"How is it going to work?" Corey asked.

The lawyer laid out his notes in front of him.

"Each of the eight of you, that's including the officer and the teacher, will read a statement describing what happened on the night in question. After hearing from all sides, the judge will take a recess and decide on your sentence," the lawyer said.

Corey nodded.

"So there are no witnesses, and they aren't questioned and cross-examined?" his mom asked.

The lawyer nodded.

"Right. The judge chose to handle it this way instead," the lawyer said.

"Is that good or bad?" Corey said.

"Good. Like I said waiting on a decision from one person makes this less painful. But as for what she will decide. Well let me see," the lawyer said.

His voice trailed off as he looked up something in his notes.

"The judge is female, and she has met both the prosecution and the defense," the lawyer said.

Corey nodded.

"She has also met with Officer Fuller. She had handled several assault cases and usually has punished the guilty party from medium to severely," the lawyer said.

Corey interrupted the lawyer.

"Medium to severely?" Corey asked.

The lawyer nodded. Corey was hoping to get a short sentence and move on with his life.

"Corey, you are being charged with aggravated assault with the intent to rape. She might give you anywhere from three to five years jail time with parole," the lawyer said.

Corey gasped.

"Three to five years?" Corey asked.

"I'll do what I can, but I would prepare for the worst, if I were you, kid," the lawyer said.

He gathered his notes, opened the door and held it open.

"See you in court on Monday," he added.

With that he walked out the door. Corey and his mom left the office and went home. Corey was disappointed with how this was going.

Meanwhile...

Sally was receiving the same news from the prosecution.

It was Thursday, and the trial would be beginning soon. Sally was meeting with the prosecution at his office.

"I have met with both the defense and the judge. It seems that just a judge rather than a jury will hear this case. The judge wants to hear from each of those involved, and then she will make her decision," the prosecution lawyer said.

"Can you explain the procedure of the trial?" Sally asked.

"Each of the eight of you, that's including the officer and the teacher, will read a statement describing what happened on the night in question. After hearing from all sides, she will take a recess and decide on the guilty party's sentence," he replied.

"Tell me about the judge," she said.

Sally took good notes while he answered her questions.

"The judge is female, and she has met both the prosecution and the defense. She has also met with Officer Fuller. She had handled several assault cases and usually has punished the guilty party from medium to severely," he said.

Sally smiled. "Good," she thought. "Corey needs to pay."

"Corey is being charged with aggravated assault with the intent to rape. She might give him anywhere from three to five years jail time with parole," he said.

"Anything else I should know," she asked.

"All of you might want to meet up before the trial and discuss all of this before going under oath on Monday. A trial can be scary for some people. But I wouldn't worry, chances are Corey is going to jail for a while," he said.

"Thank you," she said.

"See you on Monday," he said.

Sally left and went home. She then organized her notes.

Chapter 24

Nate, his dad and his step-mom-to-be had finished a tour of the city and stopped to get something to eat. They were now sitting in a restaurant waiting on their food to arrive. Nate figured he should get to know this lady.

"So how did you get together?" Nate asked.

Jamie looked over at his father and chuckled.

"I'm his secretary," she said.

Nate nodded. "That explains why you are so much younger," he thought.

"So you two met at work then," he said.

Jamie nodded.

"Your father hired me around a few months ago," she said. "We started spending a lot of time together working and not working."

She laughed. Nate was not amused.

"And well here we are," she said.

Nate's dad reached over and put his arm around her shoulders.

"That's the short version. There is a longer one if you would like to hear it," he said.

Nate shook his head. He knew that his father liked to brag.

"You know your father works hard. I always have admired him, and I always wanted to work for his company. Even in school, I dreamt about it," Jamie said.

Nate thought this lady is so dense.

"Where did you go to school?" Nate said.

"UCLA," Jamie said.

The meal arrived then.

"Everyone, dig in," she said.

They began to start eating.

"Are you guys in love?" Nate asked.

Nate's dad gave Nate a look.

"Of course, we are in love. We are engaged," his dad said.

"What I meant was," Nate said.
His voice trailed off. He paused.
"What do you mean?" his dad asked.
He said sternly.
"Calm down. Let him speak," Jamie said.
Nate smiled at her. She seemed nice.
"Well. You didn't tell mom about her, and you didn't tell me. So I thought she might be pregnant, and that was why you two were getting married and didn't tell anyone," he said.
Nate's dad just stared at him.
"How dare you judge me," his dad said. "I realize I may have not been a good father, but I reserve the right to privacy. I don't have to tell you and your mother everything. I'm a man, and I make my own decisions."
Nate just sat quietly listening to his father's lecture.
Jamie interrupted.
"Calm down. He just is trying to cope with the news. But if you must know, Nate, I'm pregnant," she said.
Nate gasped. Nate's father knocked Jamie's elbow.
"When were you planning on telling me that I was going to have a little sister or brother? Is that why you wanted to me to be a part of your family?" Nate asked.
Jamie nodded.
"We want this child to be a part of your life too," she said.
Nate felt overwhelmed. This was all happening so fast.
"That explains a lot. I start college in the fall at UGA, you know," he said.
They nodded.
"However, if you can be a part of his or her life, we would appreciate it. And since, there is a new kid in the family, your father has promised to not let you down either," she said.
Nate doubted that. His father had already let him down on this trip.
"That's right. I'm committed to you, Jamie and this new baby," his dad said.
Nate doubted that too. He had little faith in his father after all of these years.
"When do you plan on telling mom?" Nate asked.

"I thought you could tell her," his dad said.
Nate thought to himself, "figures."
He left the table and walked to the bathroom, leaving them alone. He took a deep breath. He needed a friend. He needed Laura.

Chapter 25

But Laura was off riding a four-wheeler with her cousin, Billy.

The group had been riding for around 10 minutes up and down the main dirt road, before the group decided to become more daring.

The group came across a culvert, one of which was large enough for all of them to fit through on their four-wheelers.

Billy's sister, Lauren, and her boyfriend, Chris, were both old enough to be in college, as was Billy. Laura didn't know their exact ages. But she knew that her and Keisha were the youngest ones there.

Once at the culvert, Lauren and Chris rode down a steep hill on the side of the dirt road, rounded a corner and rode through the pipe.

This pipe had been constructed by Billy's father and was currently filled with water, maybe even home to some water moccasins.

"Next?" Lauren asked.

No one responded.

"It's fun. Just hold your legs up," she said.

Laura looked confused, when Billy turned his head to see if she wanted to attempt the adventure.

"There's water in the pipe," he said.

She nodded.

Billy nodded, and they sped off. Laura was rather scared. She squeezed Billy as they rode down the steep hill, rounded the corner and proceeded through the pipe.

Being that they were on the smallest four-wheeler, it barely rode over the water in the pipe. Laura's pants got rather wet.

Keisha and her partner followed behind Laura and Billy. Once they had made it through, Lauren and Chris sped off down the road.

The rest of the group followed.

Lauren and Chris rode up on the sides of the road. Billy turned his head back to look at Laura.

"Want to try?" he asked.

She just stared at him.

"We'll be fine," he said.

He proceeded to ride up on the side of the road too.

Lauren and Chris rode their four-wheeler up a hill and jumped off down on the road in front of them.

The rest of the group followed. Laura squeezed Billy once again.

All of them landed nicely and continued to ride up and down the dirt road. About 30 minutes later, each of them parked their bikes near the van. All of six of them sat out on the deck.

Billy nudged Laura.

"Having fun?" Billy asked.

She nodded. She was glad they were sitting down.

"I think she had enough new experiences for one day," Keisha said.

Billy chuckled.

"No. I'm okay," Laura said.

"Good. We are camping out later," he said

Laura nodded.

The group relaxed out on the deck just talking for a while. Later they cooked out on the grill and camped out under the stars.

The next morning, they left Butler. They arrived back at the reunion and returned to their families. The reunion had come to a close. It was time for Laura to go home.

Other vacations had come to a close too.

Ginger and Nate were returning home the next morning. Keith was still recovering from his fall.

As the week ended, each one of them returned home safely.

Chapter 26

Saturday morning, Sally knocked on Laura's front door. Laura's mom let her in, and Sally walked down the hall. Laura's door was open.

"Laura. How was the reunion?" Sally asked.

Laura smiled.

"Lots of fun," she said.

Sally nodded.

"The case is Monday. Do you think you can come over tomorrow afternoon around 2 p.m.?" Sally asked.

Laura nodded.

Sally was planning on inviting all of them over, including Keith in order to prepare for the case.

"Would you invite Keith?" she asked.

Laura nodded.

"Great. Bye," she said.

She left then.

Laura sat on her bed. She had already unpacked. She thought to herself, inviting Keith would mean she would have to talk to him. She had not decided on whether or not she had forgiven him. She wasn't ready to make that decision, but she had to call him.

She picked the phone and dialed his number.

"Hello," his mom said.

"Is Keith there?" Laura asked.

"Hi. Laura. How are you?" his mom asked.

Keith's mom yelled up the stairs for him to pick up.

"I'm fine," she said, still dealing with her past incident.

Keith picked up at that second.

"Laura? How was the reunion?" he asked.

"Good. Are you busy tomorrow? Sally wants all of us to meet at her house to prepare for the trial on Monday," she said.

Keith nodded.

"I'm free, but I don't know where Sally lives," he said.

"Oh," she said.

"Can I pick you up with my dad and then you can direct me?" he said.

"I guess so," she said.

"Good. We can talk then," he said.

"Oh. I haven't really had a chance to think about us," she said.

"That's okay. Take your time. I'll wait," he said.

He sounded so sweet saying that.

"See you tomorrow around 1:45 p.m.," he said.

"Bye," she said.

They hung up. She lay back on her bed, but quickly sat back up, when she heard a knock on her door.

"Come in," she said.

Nate walked in and sat down next her.

"Hey there, stranger," he said.

"How was your trip?" she asked.

"Well. Let's see. My idiot of a father is engaged to some woman who he got pregnant and works as his assistant. Plus, they want me to a part of their family," he said.

"Meaning what?" she asked.

"They just want to make sure the baby knows his brother, I guess," he said.

Laura rolled her eyes.

"Your father is a piece of," she said.

Nate cut her off.

"Shit," he said.

Laura nodded.

"Does your mom know about this news?" she asked.

Nate nodded.

"But I found out first," he said.

Laura shook her head.

"So how was the reunion?" he asked.

He nudged her.

"The usual. I did get to visit my cousin Billy and his family's place. I road on a four-wheeler and a dirt road for the first time," she said.

Nate nudged her.

"Are you cultured now?" he asked.

He laughed.
"We camped out under the stars that night," she said.
She said ignoring his comment.
"Billy kissed me," she said with a smile.
"Billy your cousin? The one that is a good storyteller," he clarified.
She nodded.
"But he's your cousin," he said.
"He's adopted. He is like the only white boy in the family. He ran away from home when he was around 16 years old. So we are not really related," Laura said.
"He's what in college? Right?" he said.
"I think so. He is so hot," she said.
Nate rolled his eyes.
"Sometimes you can be such a girl," he said.
"Well. I'm one. Silly," she said.
They chuckled.
"How are you getting to Sally's tomorrow?" he asked.
"Keith is picking me up. Want to ride with us?" she asked.
"Are you two back together?" he asked.
She shook her head.
"We are just friends. He wants us to date and go off to college as a couple," she said.
"What do you think about that?" he asked.
Laura shrugged.
"I don't know. I have trouble trusting him," she said.
Nate nodded.
"I guess I'll ride with you two then. I'll protect you," he said.
She smiled. He always knew how to make her feel better.
"It's good to be home," he said.
Laura smiled back.
"I missed my friends," he said.
"You mean you didn't bond with the new girl?" Laura asked.
"No. She's wrapped around my dad's finger," he said.
They were laughing.
"How did that happen?" she asked.
"She needs his approval," he said.
Laura nodded.
"That's probably the perfect kind of woman for your dad," she said.

"My mom was too strong for him," he said.
"I guess that means you got lucky," she said.
They smiled.
"It's good to be home," he repeated.
"You bet," she said.
After a moment of silence, Nate spoke up.
"Laura, I know you don't want to think about this, but are you ready for Monday?" he said.
"Bring it on," she said.
Nate was surprised by that response.
"I have had time to not think about it and plenty of time to dwell on it. But the facts are that Corey screwed up, and he deserves to pay. I will make him pay. However, whether I am ready for this is not really important, because it's time. Besides, I'll have my homies in my corner," she said.
"I guess," he said.
He hugged her.
That night, all of them slept soundly as Sunday arrived.
Sunday afternoon, Ginger, Keith, Nate and Laura arrived at Sally's around 2 p.m. It was time for the pre-trial meeting.
Sally had placed five chairs around a table in her room. On the table she had her notes from meeting with the prosecution.
"Take a seat, so I can tell you what is going to happen tomorrow," Sally said.
"Yes, sir," Nate said.
All of them sat down.
"This is serious. I have met with the prosecution. It seems that a judge will hear this case. The judge wants to hear from each of us on our side of the story, and then she will make her decision. Each of us, Officer Fuller and Mr. Moore will describe what happened. After hearing from all sides, she will decide Corey's sentence," Sally said.
All of them nodded. Sally moved on with reading her notes. She didn't even notice Keith had crutches.
"The judge is female, and she has met both the prosecution and the defense. She has also meet with Officer Fuller. She had handled several assault cases and usually punishes the guilty party harshly. Corey is being charged with aggravated assault with the intent to

rape. She might give him anywhere from three to five years jail time with parole," she added.

She looked up when she was finished and turned her attention to Laura.

"You want to tell us your side first," she said.

"I guess," Laura said.

She took a deep breath.

"Corey grabbed me at prom as I was coming out of the ladies' room and took me off to some room," she added.

"Be as detailed as you can," Sally said.

Laura nodded and continued.

"Once inside of the room, I let out a scream. Corey told me to shut up and pulled out a knife. He said he was going to give me what I deserved and that he was not afraid to hurt me. He strapped me down, and he placed the knife back into his pocket and reached one of his hands down the top of my dress. I tried to raise my knee to hit him in the groin, but I couldn't. He took the knife back out and threatened me once more saying that he was not afraid to hurt me. With his hands down my dress, he began to touch my breast," she said.

"He did what? He will pay for that," Keith said.

"He then removed his hand from my breast and bent down on one knee. He had the knife in one hand, and his other hand moved up my leg. He reached under my dress and touched my panties. He began to remove them with one hand," she continued.

"Are you serious? What did you do?" Ginger asked.

"I shook back and forth, which caused his knife to fly out of his hand and slide under the desk. Corey punched me then, and my head hit the floor, knocking me out. When my eyes opened, Corey was fixing the position of the desk to hold the door closed. He had removed my panties and his boxers. I tried to sit up and loosen the bands," Laura continued.

She paused.

"I asked him if he had already raped me, and he said, 'not yet,' but that he would. I was able to undo the bands while Corey continued messing with the desk. So I approached him and kicked him really hard, causing him to fall backwards. I pulled my panties back up and fixed my dress. That's when the desk came loose, and Mr. Moore came in," she continued.

"That brother must be trippin'," Nate said.

She nodded. She hated reliving that event. Sally had been taking notes the entire time. She even tape recorded it.

"Thank you. Who wants to summarize what we were doing? Nate?" Sally asked.

Nate nodded.

"Sally and Ginger were in line behind Laura to go to the bathroom. Since Laura came out first, they lost track of her. I saw Corey grab Laura, and I followed them. I hid in a room near them in order to be out of earshot and contacted Ginger and Sally. I filled them in. I waited for Sally and Ginger to arrive with help. Once they arrived, Sally used her screwdriver to open the door enough for the chaperone, Mr. Moore to slide in. Laura slipped out and collapsed in my arms, while Mr. Moore paged the principal," he said.

"We took Laura to a restroom to compose herself. Mr. Moore explained to the principal what had happened, and she called in an officer," Ginger said.

"Good. And Keith where were you during this time?" Sally said.

"Lost. When I realized Laura was missing, I ran off looking for her. I yelled her name up and down halls. Eventually, I found Nate, and all of you explained to me what had happened," Keith said.

Sally continued taking notes, and Laura spoke up again.

"Then, I was running from the past by running up and down floors, and when I came to the bottom floor, Keith picked me up outside and took me to a park so we could relax," Laura said.

"I thought it might help you think," Keith said.

She smiled. Keith can be sweet.

"It did. Then he took me home," Laura said.

"That entire time the three of us were trying to find you," Ginger said.

"I just wanted to disappear after what happened that night," Laura said.

"We know. We understand," Sally said.

She laid her notes on the table.

"It sounds like we have a good understanding of what occurred that night," Sally said.

All of them nodded.

"That's good news. That means the trial will go smoothly tomorrow," she said.

Laura smiled.

"And Corey will be punished," Laura said.

"You bet," Keith said.

Group hug.

"Do all of you know where to go tomorrow?" Sally said.

She handed each of them directions to the court office.

"We do now," Keith said.

Each of them left with directions in hand. Sally yelled at them as they left.

"Be there at 9 a.m.," she said.

Meanwhile...

Corey was nervous about trial the next day. The decision the judge was going to make tomorrow would be life changing for Corey.

He was in his room thinking about all of the possibilities of what could happen tomorrow. His lawyer had recommended that he just plea guilty to the charges, so he could receive a lighter sentence. He knew that was best, but he didn't want a sentence at all.

And with a harsh judge on this case, he knew he could end up in jail for a long time.

Erica knocked on his door.

"What do you want?" Corey asked.

Erica did expect him to be happy to have a visitor, so she was disappointed.

"I want to wish you good luck tomorrow," she said.

"Who is it?" he asked.

"It's me, Erica," she said.

He hopped up and let her in.

"How are you doing?" she asked.

She was dressed in a sundress. It was obvious that she was trying to impress him.

"I'm fine," he said.

"Ready for tomorrow?" she asked.

He shook his head.

"The judge could give me three to five years," he said.

Erica handed him a present as she sat next to him on the bed.

"Three to five? That's ridiculous," she said.

"The judge hates rapists," he said.
"But you are not one," she said.
"I almost was," he said.
"But she deserved it, doesn't that make a difference? That bitch," she said.

Corey shook his head.

"According to my lawyer, the judge will probably side with Laura and punish me hard," he said.

Erica nodded.

Corey looked down at the present that she handed him.

"This will make you feel better," she said.

Corey opened the present. He unwrapped a photo of Erica and a condom.

Erica smiled at him.

"If you are locked up for a long time, you should have something to look forward to. I thought I could be that," she said.

Corey smiled back. He liked Erica because she was easy.

Corey locked to the door to his bedroom and flipped on some music.

Erica slipped out of her sundress and lay down on the bed. Corey undressed himself and slipped the condom on.

He then hopped on top of Erica. The two of them had sex.

Erica had fallen for the bad boy, and she said it was because they were more exciting, but unfortunately, she meant nothing to Corey.

Afterwards, Erica redressed and left Corey's house. Corey picked up the picture and placed it in the garbage.

He lay down on his bed and fell asleep. Tomorrow was a big day.

Chapter 27

All of them arrived at 9 a.m. and sat down on their respective sides.

Corey and his lawyer sat on the right side of the courtroom. His family sat behind him.

Laura, Sally, Ginger, Nate and Keith with crutches sat on the left side of the room along with the prosecution. Behind them sat their families.

The judge walked in and sat her in her seat.

"All rise for the honorable judge, Mrs. Holloway," the bailiff said.

Mrs. Holloway looked around 40 years old to Laura. She could tell that the woman had years of experience on her.

"Thank you. You may be seated," Mrs. Holloway said.

Each of them sat down.

"I'm going to invite each person up to the stand to give his or her side of the story, and then after I have heard enough, I will take a break and make my decision," she added.

At that moment, Erica slid in the back of Corey's side.

"I would like to start with the victim, Ms. Timberwood," the judge requested.

Laura walked up the stand and took a seat.

"Corey grabbed me at prom as I was coming out of the ladies' room and took me off to some room. Once inside the room, I let out a scream. He told me to shut up and pulled out a knife. He said he was going to give me what I deserved and that he was not afraid to hurt me. He strapped me down, and he placed the knife back into his pocket and reached one of his hands down the top of my dress. I tried to raise my knee to hit in the groin, but I couldn't. He took the knife back out and threatened me once more saying that he was not afraid to hurt me. With his hands down my dress, he began to touch my breast," she said.

The audience listened attentively, for some of them this was the first time they had heard the entire story.

"He then removed his hand from my breast and bent down on one knee. He had the knife in one hand, while the other moved up my leg. He reached up under my dress and touched my panties. He began to remove them with one hand. I shook back and forth, which caused his knife to fly out of his hand and slide under the desk. Corey punched me then, and my head hit the floor, knocking me out. When my eyes opened, Corey was fixing the position of the desk to hold the door closed. He had removed my panties and his boxers. I tried to sit up and loosen the bands. I asked if he had already raped me, and he said not yet, but that he would. I was able to undo the bands as Corey continued messing with the desk. So I approached him and kicked him really hard, causing him to fall backwards. I pulled my panties back up and fixed my dress. That's when the desk came loose, and Mr. Moore came in," she continued.

When Laura finished, a scream came from the back of the room.

"That can't be true. She's lying under oath. My Corey is innocent," Erica screamed.

"Quiet. I will have silence in my court. What did Mr. Dawson do? Let's hear from him shall we," the judge said.

She turned her attention to the defense.

"Defense, your client is being charged with aggravated assault with intent to rape. And with Ms. Timberwood's testimony, there is a weapon involved. How does your client plead?" the judge said.

"Guilty, your honor," his lawyer said.

She nodded.

"Corey, would you come up to the stand and tell us your version of the story?" the judge asked.

Corey nodded, walked towards the stand, took the oath and sat down.

"Everything Laura said is accurate and true. I was trying to rape her," Corey said.

Another scream came from back of the room.

"But she deserved it. She was killing the curve," Erica screamed defending her man.

"Young lady sit down. No one deserves to be raped. Go on, Corey," the judge stated.

"I realize what I did was wrong, and I want to pay my dues," he said.

The judge nodded.

"Corey, you can step down," the judge said.

Corey returned to his seat.

"We are going to take a short break before I hear from Nate, Sally and Ginger," she said.

The judge stepped down and exited the room.

Erica ran up to Corey.

"Why are you just letting them punish you?" she asked him.

"If Corey pleads guilty, he can get a lesser punishment," his lawyer answered her.

Erica nodded.

"Unless you are going to be quiet, I suggest you leave," the lawyer said.

"I'll be quiet," Erica said.

"Erica, let's go get some breakfast," Corey said.

She smiled. A date!

Corey and Erica left for breakfast.

Meanwhile...

The judge was in her quarters looking over her notes.

"This is a tough decision," she thought to herself. The question is would he have raped her if he had not be caught. She didn't know why the girl in back thought that Laura deserved it, but she figured he would have finished the deed had he been able to.

Corey had other charges against him in the past including mostly parking and traffic tickets. She figured he had grown up in a home where his parents focused more on work than raising a child.

She knew based on evidence and that he was pleading guilty, she could give three to five years with parole. She hoped that she would choose the punishment that would cause Corey to learn that violence is not a way to solve his problems. She wondered if he even thought what he did was wrong.

Meanwhile...

Laura and her friends were impatiently awaiting the Judge's return. Laura wanted the trial to end.

Meanwhile...

HIS WRATH

Corey had run out to have breakfast with Erica, leaving behind his lawyer and his family.

Corey's father tapped the lawyer on the shoulder.

"What do think his chances are?" his father asked.

"Corey would be lucky if he would receive three years with parole," his lawyer said.

His father nodded.

Corey's father turned and spoke to his wife.

"Is that long enough?" his father said.

She just shrugged.

He didn't think his son felt guilty for what he had done to an innocent girl.

Around 15 minutes later, the judge returned from her chambers. She picked up the gavel and called court to order.

Corey and Erica were no where to be seen.

"Where is the defendant?" the judge asked.

Corey's lawyer was outside on the phone, trying to locate him.

"Your honor. It seems that my son went to breakfast and has lost track of time," Corey's father said.

"Thank you for your explanation. But if your son does not show soon, I will be forced to postpone the rest of this trial until a more convenient time," she said.

Outside the courtroom, Corey's lawyer had finally reached Corey. Corey was one of the few kids his age who owned a cell phone.

"Please tell me you are on your way here," his lawyer said.

"Why?" Corey asked.

"Recess is over, and the judge will be forced to postpone the rest of the trial, which will not help your sentence," his lawyer said.

"Stall. I'll be there," Corey said.

The lawyer nodded and hung the phone abruptly. He walked into the courtroom.

"May I approach the stand?" he asked.

The judge nodded.

"Where is the defendant?" she said.

"He is on his way back. He misunderstood how long recess was," he said.

"No excuse. You should have explained it to him and made sure he did not leave," she said.

"I apologize, but I was not in the courtroom when he left. I hope you will not hold this against my client," he said.

She nodded and sent him back to his seat.

"We will resume in five minutes, with or without the defendant, for his sake, he'd better be here," she said.

Meanwhile…

Corey and Erica had had breakfast and then moved back into Erica's car and drove to make out point.

When the lawyer called him, he was in the middle of making out with Erica. He was planning on "getting some" one more time before he was sent off to jail.

Don't you think he should quit using Erica?

In hopes of getting back in time, Corey jumped off Erica and climbed in the driver's seat and sped off.

Luckily for him, he made it in time.

He walked back in the courtroom just as the judge sat back in her seat. He left Erica half dressed in the back seat of his car. She entered the courtroom around 10 minutes later.

"Nice to have you with us," the judge said.

She picked up the gavel and called the room to order.

"I would like to hear from Sally, Ginger or Nate about how all of you caught the defendant red-handed," she said.

Ginger and Nate looked over at Sally, hoping she would walk to the stand.

Luckily for them, she did.

Sally shared with the judge how the three of them had planned to watch Laura's back at prom due to threats from Corey. She explained the judge their plan and what happened at the prom.

When Sally stepped down, the judge was ready to make her decision.

"Thank you," the judge said.

Sally proceeded back to her seat.

"Would the defense and the prosecution please stand?" the judge asked.

Both sides followed her directions.

"I find Corey Dawson guilty of armed/aggravated assault with intent of rape. I hereby sentence him to three years with parole," she said.

HIS WRATH

Erica was furious.

"No," she screamed.

She jumped out of her seat and run up to the judge.

"Let him go free. My man should be forgiven not punished," she added.

The judge shook her head.

"Sit down young lady. Calm down before I send you to stay overnight," the judge said.

Erica sat down in the nearest seat.

"I have made my decision," the judge said sternly.

With that she stood up and walked out of the courtroom.

Laura and her friends rejoiced. They had punished the guilty.

Part II

Disclaimer: What you are about to read and have read is fiction: some of the events are based on real events, but do not accurately describe the college Georgia Peach is based on or the Atlanta area where Laura grew up. Georgia College and State University is a safe school, and in 2005, it was ranked among the top 20 in the south.

Laura Lynn left her dorm room for her first class of college at 9 a.m.

As she walked, she daydreamed about her summer, and she wished she had more time to spend with her friends before leaving for college. Her high school senior year had pushed her to grow up, after almost being raped and having to reach deep down to forgive Keith.

A familiar young man bumped into her.

"May I walk you to our class?" Keith asked.

He slipped his hand into hers.

Keith's ankle had healed over the summer. The two of them had begun dating during the past week, after they had attended several freshman seminars about the college.

Laura had focused most of the second half of the summer, after the trial, on spending time with Keith's mom, moving past the events of her senior year and getting to know Keith better.

Keith truly meant well and had fallen for her, so she allowed him to come back into her life slowly, and now the two of them were attending their freshman seminar together, since both of them had not declared a major yet.

Their freshman seminar was located in Lanier Hall and was aimed to help them get acquainted with the college while choosing a major.

Keith and Laura walked hand-in-hand to class.

Laura's best friend, Nate, now attends the University of Georgia on a business management track. Sally and Ginger are living together as roommates on mechanical engineering tracks at Georgia Tech.

Corey was serving his sentence in jail, while Erica had begun classes at a local college.

Laura and Keith knew after the year they had together that they were ready to embark on a college adventure.

Chapter 28

Laura Lynn and her roommate, Jasmine, were preparing for the first meeting of their pledge class.

They were members of the Eta pledge class for Gamma Sigma Sigma, a community service sorority.

This organization requires its members to perform 20 hours of community service a semester, attend chapter meetings and socials. This chapter of the sorority is co-ed.

The girls were attending meetings and taking quizzes in order to prepare for the test at the end of an eight-week period. Based on the grade of this test, they may be initiated into the sorority the morning after passing the test in November.

The two of them had chosen this sorority based on their desires to perform community service.

"Is this meeting formal?" Jasmine asked.

"Yep. What are you wearing?" Laura said.

Jasmine had grown up in middle Georgia and attended her first semester of college at Fort Valley State University. Her major was in psychology. They shared an economics class together.

"I'm not wearing this then," Jasmine responded.

She picked up her "doorag" and threw it in her laundry basket. "Doorag" had become one of her nicknames.

"No 'doorag' for you," Laura said.

She chuckled.

Eventually, the two girls were dressed and ready to go.

The first meeting was on the bottom floor of Chappell Hall. The girls left their Bell Hall dorm room to walk across campus for the meeting.

Laura Lynn and Jasmine opened the doors to the room and saw the faces of their future sisters and brothers.

Their pledge mom, Jessica, introduced herself before asking each of the members of the pledge class to introduce herself or himself.

The Eta pledge class had more than fifteen members, one of the larger pledge classes in Gamma Sigma Sigma's history. The class contained mostly girls, but there at least one male member.

The class was rather diverse, including pledges of different backgrounds.

Laura Lynn listened to each of them describe themselves as she thought, "It looks as I may have found a family away from home."

Georgia Peach University was located just over two hours from her hometown, and outside of Keith, Laura Lynn was the only one from her graduating class to choose this school.

Jasmine had already become her best friend.

After introductions ended, Jessica introduced the first study materials, the sorority's mission, its symbols and the Greek alphabet.

Later, the pledges were dismissed to prepare for their quiz next week. Jasmine and Laura Lynn walked back to Bell Hall.

Meanwhile...

Keith was settling into his room in Terrell Hall for the night. Terrell Hall is right next door to Bell Hall.

Both are located on main campus near the academic buildings.

Terrell Hall is where most of the students admitted as part of Georgia Peach University's international academic program live, which allows students to study abroad in the United States.

Keith's roommate, Sul, grew up in India and participated in this program. Sul was about 5 feet 10 inches tall and rather dark skinned. Sul worked in the college's computer lab as a lab assistant. Sul was a sophomore, while Keith, of course, was a freshman.

Sul had come from a rich family in India, complete with servants. Sul and most of the international students, as they were collectively referred to, enjoyed going to clubs downtown.

Milledgeville featured a downtown area of around 20 small shops, six restaurants, two of which had club themes after dinner hours and two clubs.

Sunday was certainly not a night that one would attend a club though. Rather the main nights were Tuesday, Thursday and Saturday. Monday was a trivia night at one of the local restaurants though.

This downtown area was located within walking distance and on the same street as the front of main campus, where Terrell and Bell Hall sit.

Milledgeville is home to about 20,000 people in middle Georgia.

Sul had already chosen business management as his major. Keith and Laura were undecided majors at the moment.

"That girl of yours coming over tonight," Sul said.

"She's got a sorority thing," Keith said.

"She's hot, and she's in a sorority. Nice going," Sul said.

"We went to high school together and came here as a couple," Keith said.

"You'll have to hold on to her, there are a lot of opportunities for new experiences, if you know what I mean," Sul warned.

Keith nodded.

Knock. Knock.

Sul opened the door to see his three friends, Gloria, Mary and Mindie.

Gloria was from Latin America, while the rest of them were from Georgia.

Since there were classes tomorrow, Sul was going to join them for their weekly study group.

Keith, on the other hand, picked up the phone and dialed Laura.

"Hello," Laura said.

She and Jasmine had just walked in the door.

"It's me," Keith said.

"Hey you," she said.

"Fill a brother in. Are you a member yet?" he asked.

"No, silly. I have like eight weeks of classes and quizzes, before my test. But I did meet all of my sisters and my pledge mom," she said.

Keith and Laura spent around an hour on the phone before they hung up. They were growing closer in their relationship.

Laura was able to trust him once again.

Monday morning.

Laura grabbed her morning shake and followed Jasmine to their first class of the day, economics.

As always, they arrived about five minutes late and sneaked in the third row. Mr. Cole never began class on time anyways.

Mr. Cole was in his mid thirties, single and had been teaching economics at the college for five years.

Laura Lynn noticed that one of her pledge sisters, Megan, was in the class. She waved to get her attention.

Megan was a straight A student, and she wanted one in economics to match the rest of the A's she intended to receive. Megan planned to graduate college with a 4.0.

Mr. Cole turned on his projector and began teaching as each of the students began taking notes.

Laura Lynn and Jasmine were now sitting next to Megan.

Mr. Cole was rather attractive for a male in his mid thirties.

As the girls continued to take notes, they realized that this class was not going to be an easy A. This was a decent conclusion after only a few days of school.

After class ended, Megan turned to Laura Lynn and Jasmine.

"Want to be in my study group for this class?" Megan asked.

"Sure," Laura said.

"When does it meet?" Jasmine said.

"Right before every test. I heard that Mr. Cole takes his test questions, from not only the notes, the book, but also the online review tests," Megan said.

"We'll be there. Just tell us where and when," Laura said.

Megan nodded as the girls continued walking to their next classes of the day.

They split up, and Laura waited outside of Lanier Hall for Keith.

Laura had become a diligent college student, much like she was in high school.

College classes were of course harder than high school, but Laura was a go-getter.

Monday passed and Tuesday came along. Classes had finished for the day.

Laura and Jasmine were planning on attending karaoke night down at Buffington's. Their suitemates, Wendy and Jan, were planning on coming too.

About 9 p.m., Laura and Jasmine began preparing for the party.

Laura, the good student, had, of course, already finished all of her homework, allowing her to be able to party on a school night. She was planning on graduating with honors.

In Bell, the rooms are suites, meaning four girls shared a bathroom. The building was only for female residents.

Jan knocked on the bathroom door. Jasmine let her in.

"Joe is mad at me," Jan said.

Joe is a friend of Jan's from her hometown.

"Why?" Laura asked.

"I have a crush on him. So I wrote that in my online dairy, and well he read it," Jan said.

"He should have been flattered," Laura said.

Jan was a rather smart, brunette, petite young lady. She was around 19 years old.

"I won't worry about it. Why don't you come out with us?" Laura asked.

Wendy yelled from the background.

"You know that karaoke always makes it better," Wendy said.

"You bet," Laura said.

The girls continued applying make-up to their faces. They were already dressed for the party scene.

"Laura, you're not going home with anyone tonight are you?" Jasmine asked.

"No silly. It's Tuesday," Laura said.

"And you have Keith," Jasmine said.

"Right. It's more fun to act single at these things, besides I'm sure he acts that way when he goes to those parties with his friends," Laura said.

"I guess it is fair if you are both doing it," Jasmine said.

"Just fooling around, no sex you know," Laura said.

"Exactly. You need to keep your virginity and not get any diseases," Jasmine said.

"You don't get any diseases from kissing," Wendy chuckled.

The girls scream back, "Right."

All of them were ready at about a quarter till 10 p.m. but Jan.

"Jan, are you coming?" Laura asked.

Jan placed her finger on her chin and thought for a minute.

"Let me see if he is still online," she said.

The girls nodded.

"Hurry, because we are leaving in five," Laura said.

Jan walked back into her room and checked her AOL instant messenger buddy list on her computer. Joe was still there. She typed him a message.

"I'm sorry. I should have kept my feelings to myself."
Joe replied.
"I don't have feelings for you in that way. Sorry."
Jan replied.
"I am going out clubbing with my roomies. Bye."
Jan then placed an away message up for her instant messenger.
Laura yelled.
"Jan?" she asked.
Jan walked into the room as Laura was also putting up her away message.
"I have been airported by a rickey."
Rickey was Laura and Jasmine's pet fish.
His name had come from an episode of *Seventh Heaven* on the WB. On this show, the characters do not curse, therefore one of the characters said, "I don't give a rat's rickey" instead. Later the youngest girl on the show said she was airported when someone brought her a present from the airport. The girls just laughed and put the phrases together.
The girls locked their doors and left the dorm. They walked down the street to Buffington's.
Meanwhile...
Keith had a test the next day in one of his classes. He was trying to study, while his roommate, Sul, was getting ready to go to a party.
Sul had been invited to a frat party at the opera house. One of his friends, Jack, was rushing for Phi Kappa Phi.
Sul and Jack left Keith to study.
Meanwhile...
The girls had arrived at Buffington's.
A crush of Wendy's, Jeff and his friend, Rob, were on the dance floor doing karaoke to "ICE ICE, BABY" by Vanilla Ice.
Laura nudged Wendy.
"Your boy is on up on stage," Laura said.
Wendy blushed.
"He's cute," Jan said.
The song ended, and Jeff waved at Wendy.
"Hey you," Jeff said.
Wendy smiled.
"You want your usual?" Jeff asked.

Wendy nodded.

Jeff always bought Wendy a Smirnoff Ice from the bar, since he was 26, and she was 19. Jeff walked over to the bar and got Wendy a drink, while the girls found a booth to sit in.

Jeff pulled up a chair and sat at the end. He placed the drink in front of Wendy.

"Are you ladies going to sing tonight?" he asked.

Laura chuckled.

"Maybe," she said.

"Depends on how drunk I get you," he said.

They shook their heads. Laura did not drink. All of them were also too young to drink.

"Wendy, do you want to sing?" he asked.

She ignored Jeff's comment.

The girls had sung "Genie in a Bottle" by Christina Aguilera one Tuesday night before.

"I don't know," she answered him.

It takes a lot of persuasion for the group to sing in front of a large group. None of them liked confrontations.

"You think about it, darling. I'm going to go over there and talk to Stacy," he said.

Jeff placed his chair back at another table and walked over to Stacy's booth and sat down.

Stacy looked 21 years old and was very attractive.

"What does he want with her?" Wendy asked.

She was obviously jealous.

"She looks easy," Laura said.

"Guys just want sex," Jasmine said.

"Except for Keith. He just wants Laura," Jan chuckled.

"Right," Laura smirked.

Laura wasn't so sure about that. Keith had become more physical since they were going to college now.

She thought back to the last night they were together.

They had both stayed on campus this past weekend.

On Saturday, they were just watching a movie, when Keith leaned over and kissed her. He proceeded to turn the one kiss into several and somehow ended up on top of her.

It was happening rather fast for Laura.

Keith was on top of Laura and moved the kissing from her lips to her neck and to her shoulders.

He lifted his head up and separated the bottom of her shirt from her belly, and then he kissed her belly.

He moved passed her shirt and kissed her legs and slipped her shoes off.

Laura had to admit Keith was a good kisser. But this was going farther than she wanted it to go.

Laura was waiting until her wedding night to have sex.

"Keith, what are you doing?" Laura asked.

He realized that he had crossed some line, based on the stern way she asked.

"Just kissing you," he said.

He smiled and sat up, as she did too.

They sat next to each other and finished the rest of the movie.

Laura wondered what could have happened had she just let it continue.

Jasmine patted Laura's arm and winked at her. She knew what she was thinking of.

"So are we going to sing?" Jan said.

Wendy shook her head.

"Not if Jeff keeps spending time with Stacy," she said.

"We stick together," Laura said.

Sul and Jack had decided to take a break from their party and visit Buffington's. Jack walked up to the girls' booth.

"Hi, Wendy," Jack said.

Jack had a crush on Wendy and Laura. He was a business major with a tall and built physique, but he was rather hairy.

Wendy and Laura looked at Jack as just someone they knew.

"Jack. Your party is next door," Wendy said.

"Don't be so rude. Jack, join us," Jan said.

Jack grabbed a chair and sat on the end.

Jeff stood over Jack's back a second later.

"Taking my seat? Ladies, is this guy bothering you?" Jeff asked.

Wendy nodded.

"Well, you heard the lady," Jeff said.

Jack nodded and left the table frowning.

Laura thought to herself, "poor guy."

Jack was so nice to everyone that he almost came off as annoying. Wendy smiled as Jeff sat back down the chair.

"What did I miss?" he asked.

"Good stories," Laura said.

"I bet. Wendy, you look dry over there," he said.

He grabbed her another drink.

"Thanks," she said.

"So are you girls ready to sing?" he asked them.

Jeff enjoyed seeing people embarrass themselves.

Laura shook her head.

"I doubt it," Laura said.

At that moment, Jasmine's crush, Jeremiah, entered "the buff."

Jasmine nudged Laura's elbow.

"Ow. What?" Laura said.

She realized what was going on as soon as she looked up from the table. They didn't even know his name. They just knew that he played for the college's basketball team, and that he was usually here.

The girls had only been to one basketball game.

"What?" Jan asked.

Jan didn't want to be left out. But in the interest of it being a secret, no one answered her.

Jasmine watched her crush sit down at a table with some other basketball players.

Laura nudged her shoulder.

Jasmine shook her head. She didn't have the nerve to go talk to him.

"We could sing," Laura said.

That got Jeff's attention.

"Sing? Good. I plan on singing again later," he said.

"I guess," Jasmine said.

"What do you want to sing? I can help," Jeff said.

"I was thinking Pink's song, 'Get the Party Started.' It's our party song," Laura said.

"You got it," he said.

He got up and left to go talk to the D.J.

"Are we singing?" Wendy asked.

"I don't know. It just sounded like a good idea," Laura said.

"It could work," Jasmine said.

"It might get his attention," she thought to herself.

"That's not a hard song. But do we know the words?" Wendy asked.

The girls started laughing.

"No," all of them said.

"But it's karaoke," Laura said.

Minutes later they were called up to the stage to sing.

Wendy, Laura and Jasmine left Jan at the table with Jeff to sing the song.

The girls performed it rather well.

As they walked off the stage, Jeremiah walked over to Jasmine.

"Well, my work is done here," Laura said.

Laura and Wendy sat back down at the booth.

"You look very familiar," Jeremiah said.

"We were at the game last week cheering in the stands," Jasmine said.

"I guess. You did a good job up there," he said.

"It is our party song. We play it every night when we get ready to party," she said.

"It sounded like you knew what you were singing. I'm Jeremiah by the way," he said.

"Jasmine," she said.

"Are you coming to the game Saturday?" he said.

"Yeah," she said.

"I'll see you then," he said.

The two parted and went back to their seats.

"Got a date?" Laura asked.

"No. I got a name," Jasmine said.

"Yeah, sister," Laura said.

"It's Jeremiah, and he said he would see me at the game," Jasmine said.

"Saturday?" Laura said.

"Yeah," Jasmine said.

"Sounds like love connection. One point for Laura," Jan said.

"Well, ladies. It's time to check out the party next door. Want to come?" Jeff said.

The girls were not big fans of the Opera House.

"It's a private frat party though," Laura said.

"I know a guy," Jeff said.

The girls glanced at each other.

"Have fun, and take Wendy with you," Laura replied.

"Come on, Wendy," Jeff said.

He put his elbow out for Wendy to lock hers with his. They walked over to the Opera House.

"Maybe, she will get her guy," Jan said.

"That just leaves you," Laura said.

"Listen love connection. I didn't come out for you to set me up," Jan said.

"Excuse me, sister," Laura said.

"I don't need to set up. My life is fine," Jan said.

Laura dropped the subject.

Meanwhile...

Wendy and Jeff got into the party through Jeff's friend.

"Can I get you anything?" Jeff asked.

"My usual," Wendy said.

"One Smirnoff coming right up," Jeff said.

Wendy waited at the table for Jeff to return.

The Opera House was a two-floor club. On the bottom floor, booths were along the left-hand wall. The bottom floor featured two pool tables and an oval bar. Behind the booths were steps and the restrooms. The steps led to the second floor, which had a game room in the back, more restrooms and a dance floor with a bar in the front and a bar and tables on the left side.

The place was rather busy. Jeff had to wait awhile at the bar.

Jack spotted Wendy.

"You shouldn't be sitting all alone," Jack said.

Jack pulled out the chair and sat down.

"I'm waiting for Jeff," she replied.

Jack knew who Jeff was, and he was jealous of Jeff getting all of the girls' attention.

"Where did he go?" he asked.

"To get me a drink," she said.

"How many have you had?" he asked.

"Three, I think," she answered.

Jack was a nice guy even though the girls viewed him as annoying.

"Maybe you shouldn't have anymore," he said.

"I'm fine," she stated.

She ignored Jack's remark of concern.

Jeff appeared behind Jack.

"I thought I told you to leave her alone," Jeff said to him.

"I was just keeping her company. You shouldn't leave a pretty girl alone," Jack said.

Jack smiled at Wendy and left the table.

Jeff handed the drink to Wendy.

"Do you want to dance?" he asked.

Wendy nodded.

Jeff escorted her and her drink to the dance floor for a dance or two.

Meanwhile...

"Do you think Wendy will be okay?" Jan asked.

"I have Jeff's number, Wendy's cell number, and we know where he lives," Laura said.

"I won't worry about it," Jasmine said.

"She's my roommate, and who will go find her if she doesn't come home later?" Jan asked.

"It's only 1 a.m., and we will," Laura replied.

Jasmine nodded in agreement.

"How long do you stay till?" Jan asked.

"Around two a.m.," Laura said.

"When they kick us out," Jasmine said.

"That's not funny," Jan said.

"Girl, you need to chill," Laura said.

Jeremiah walked by their table on his way out. He waved at Jasmine.

"He's sweet on you," Laura said.

Jasmine blushed.

Around an hour later, the girls left to go back to the dorm room. Wendy was not home when they got there.

"Now, what are we going to do?" Jan asked.

Meanwhile...

Wendy had stumbled back to Jeff's apartment.

He laid her down on his couch. He propped her head on his lap and brushed her hair.

"Where am I?" Wendy asked.

"You have had too much to drink. Just relax," he told her.
Wendy closed her eyes, as Jeff's phone rang.
Jeff propped Wendy's head with a pillow and answered the phone.
"Jeff here," he said.
"It's Laura. Is Wendy with you?" she asked.
"She's sleeping on the couch. When's her first class?" he asked.
Laura yelled to Jan.
"When's Wendy's first class tomorrow?" she said.
"11 a.m.," Jan replied.
"Jeff, did you hear that?" she asked.
"I'll drop her off around 10 on my way to class," he said.
"Thanks," she said.
The two hung up.
Jan was worried about the situation.
"Do you think she will be safe there?" Jan said.
"Jeff is a good guy. Besides if anything happens we will hurt him tomorrow at movie night," Laura said.
"What are you watching?" Jan said.
"Jeff said he would surprise us," Laura said.
The girls proceeded to bed in order to rest for another day of college.
Meanwhile... (Earlier that night)
After being turned down by Wendy, Jack walked back over to Sul.
Sul, being the man of the party, had brought along Mindie, Gloria and Mary. Sul had positioned himself in between them—two girls on one arm, one on the other arm.
"Jack, you look glum," Sul said.
"Wendy is after Jeff," Jack said.
"The blonde girl you like?" Sul asked.
Jack nodded.
"I think they will leave together. Wendy is wasted," he said.
"Let's find you someone else then," Sul said.
Sul looked around the dance floor.
He didn't lend out Mindie, Gloria or Mary.
"How about that girl with the nice rack over there?" Sul asked.
Jack shrugged his shoulders and got up out of his seat.
He walked up behind the girl and sat down next to her.

"Are you lost?" she said.

"I'm Jack. Would you like to dance or could I get you a drink?" he asked.

"Jack, I'm sorry, but your pledge dad is my boyfriend, so I can't accept your offer, but Cindy, here, would like a drink. Would you get her a margarita?" she said.

Jack nodded and left the table.

"Thanks. I needed another free drink," Cindy said.

"He seems nice," her friend said.

"Yeah," Cindy said.

Jack returned a few minutes later with her margarita.

"Thank you," Cindy said.

"I'll leave you alone," her friend said.

Cindy and Jack took a liking to each other, and Jack took her home. Meanwhile…

Sul had danced several songs with Mindie, Gloria and Mary along with several other girls.

At around two a.m., the bar began to close, and he could not find Jack.

He grabbed the girls and headed home. He escorted each of them to their rooms and proceeded to his. On his door was a note:

> I took that girl's friend home with me. See you tomorrow.
> –Jack

Sul smiled.

He opened the door to find Keith fast asleep. It looked as if he had fallen asleep in the middle of his notes.

Sul climbed into bed to prepare for another day.

Chapter 29

A couple of weeks later, Saturday night rolled around. Saturday night was ladies' night at Capital City Club in the "ville."

The girls prepared for a big night on the town.

This time though Keith was coming as Laura's date for the night.

Keith and Sul knocked on Gloria's door to grab her for the party. Mindie and Mary went to their hometowns for the weekends. In fact, most of the students drive home on the weekends and only a small percentage stays.

Next the boys headed over to Bell.

Keith called room 107 with the pager system outside of Bell.

Laura's and Jasmine's phone rang.

"Hello," Laura said.

"Sul, Gloria and I are outside," Keith said.

"Be there in a second," she responded.

Laura let them into the dorm.

Bell was an all female residence hall, and all males must be out by 10 p.m. The resident directors and assistants come around promptly and check.

The boys signed in and handed their IDs to the resident assistant on duty. Then they followed Laura to her room.

"Hi ladies," Keith said.

"Doesn't everyone look sexy tonight?" Sul asked.

The girls chuckled.

Sul acted like a big man on campus.

Wendy, Jan, Jasmine and Laura were ready to go.

They gathered together, signed the boys out and got their IDs as they headed for the club.

Capital City was only two blocks from main campus. On Saturdays, there was a small line.

On the inside of the club, there is a long bar on the left side, with high top tables in the front of club. Towards the back is a dance floor with an overhead D.J. Off to the right side are the pool tables, couches and a small bar in the back. In the very back, another room opens which can be used for concerts, but on most days it stays closed.

The fee was free for the ladies, yet all of them did not receive a bracelet, since they were all underage for drinking.

Once they entered the club, the music played loudly as they found a table.

Jan took a seat. She was less sociable in clubs.

The group was there early. It was only 11:30 p.m.

The party didn't start until after 12:30 a.m. Therefore, the dance floor was particularly empty.

However, being a Saturday less people were going to be there later anyways. Saturdays tend to draw more people who do not attend the university. Some of the visitors attend the local military college, or are locals or live in a close city like Macon or Warner Robins.

The group sat down and waited for the party to begin.

"So how was your wild night with Jeff?" Laura asked.

"I don't remember most of it. I woke up on his couch and remember him taking me home an hour before class," Wendy said.

"I made her take a cold shower to wake her up," Jan said.

"A cold shower!" Laura screamed.

"Well it worked, and I didn't miss my test," Wendy said.

The D.J. played trying to get people to dance.

Jeff walked behind their table then.

"Jeff, we were just talking about you," Laura said.

"Thanks for bringing home Wendy that morning," Jan said.

He nodded.

"That's what friends are for. Can I get any of you anything?" he asked.

He pointed at Wendy.

"The usual. But less than last time right," he said to her.

He took orders and walked off to the bar.

"It's good to have friends that are of age," Wendy said.

She wished Jeff looked at her as more of than just a friend though.

The place began to get busier as the clock hit midnight. A few people were dancing.

Jan had been asked to dance by a "local," Travis. Travis had grown up in Eatonton and was a funeral director at the main funeral home in that town.

She was dancing with him when the floor began to get a little crowded. Crowded as in a good number of people were dancing, but there weren't bumping into each other.

Sul was dancing with Gloria and Laura with Keith.

Meanwhile back at the table...

Wendy was drinking and talking with Jasmine.

Jasmine hoped Jeremiah would show up. They had gone to the game and watched him.

At the game...

Laura and Jasmine got front row seats to cheer for their Bobcats. During the game, they screamed and clapped to encourage the team. The Bobcats won the game, and afterwards, Jeremiah waved at Jasmine.

Laura nudged Jasmine.

"Wave back," Laura said.

At that point, she waved back at him.

Jeremiah screamed back.

"I'll see you later," he said.

"At Capital City," she said.

He smiled and followed his team off the court.

"Jasmine you there? You spaced out," Wendy said.

"I was thinking about Jeremiah," Jasmine said.

"I think I just saw him pass by. Should we walk and see if we see him?" Wendy said.

"Hell Yeah," Jasmine said.

The girls began walking around the club. They walked in and out of groups of people. For a Saturday night, the club was hopping.

While they were walking, Jeremiah gently grabbed Jasmine's hand.

"Hey, sweet thing. Where are you headed?" he asked.

"To the dance floor," she said.

"Let's go," he said.

The two of them walked to the dance floor and danced right next to Keith and Laura.

Wendy had found Jeff while she was helping Jasmine search for Jeremiah.

"What have you been up to?" she asked.

"Not much. Want to get out of here and go watch a movie?" he asked.

Wendy nodded.

"I'll meet you outside in five," she said.

She walked off to tell someone she was leaving. Wendy tapped Jan on the shoulder.

"Jan, I'm going over to Jeff's to see a movie," Wendy said.

"Have fun," Jan said.

Wendy left the dance floor and proceeded outside to meet Jeff. Meanwhile...

The dancing couples, Laura and Keith, Jan and Travis, Sul and Gloria and Jasmine and Jeremiah were whirling around the dance floor to all sorts of music, mostly pop and rap.

Travis was a good dancer, which Jan didn't notice, since she was not a fan of dancing. So far, she had just learned what Travis did for a living.

"What caused you to ask me to dance?" she asked.

"Your Green Eyes," he said.

"You're too kind," she said.

Jan was rather flattered by his southern charm. Travis told Jan about how he lived in Eatonton and was a funeral director at his family's funeral home. He was 20 years old, one year older than Jan.

"I was hoping we could go out some time," he said.

"I imagine so," she said.

"So now that you know all about me. Tell me about you," he said.

"I'm a freshman at Georgia Peach, and my major is information systems," she said.

Jan and Travis continued to learn about each other.

"Brown-eyed Girl" began to play over the loud speakers.

Travis sang the words into Jan's ear, substituting brown eyed girl with green-eyed girl.

Laura and Keith decided to take a dancing break and sat down on the couch on the left side of the dance floor.

"I hope you are having a good time," Keith said.

Laura nodded.

"I've been thinking..." he added.

He paused.

"We've been dating for almost two months now and around three in high school. I thought maybe you could spend the night tonight," he said.

Laura was shocked by that invitation.

"I don't know if I'm ready for that," she said.

Keith wouldn't take no for an answer.

"We won't have sex. We will just talk and sleep. If you start to feel uncomfortable, you can leave," he said.

"I guess so," she said.

She had given in.

"When do you want to leave then?" he asked.

It was around 1:30 a.m. The club closed in about 30 minutes.

Laura shrugged not answering his question.

"I was thinking we could just go now," he said.

He was anxious about their relationship moving forward.

"I guess so. Let me tell Jasmine," she said.

Laura left the couch and walked over to Jasmine and Jeremiah.

"Jeremiah, can I borrow your partner for a second?" she said.

Jeremiah smiled and backed away from Jasmine.

"Keith wants me to spend the night," she told Jasmine.

Jasmine knew that Keith and Laura had never spent the night together. She ushered Laura over to a corner.

"Are you ready for this?" Jasmine asked.

"I guess so," Laura said.

Laura had issues with trusting Keith after his incident in high school.

Laura and Keith had spent lots of hours together since they got back together over the summer, but they had never slept in the same bed.

Over the past month, Keith had become physical in their relationship he had tried to kiss her more, and he had even tried to reach up her shirt once. She had been able to talk her way out so far.

"Are you scared?" Jasmine asked.

"Keith might be more physical than I am, but I don't think he would do anything to hurt me," Laura said.

"Take your spray with you," Jasmine said.

Laura nodded.

After what happened to her in high school, Laura began carrying pepper spray on her at all times.

Jasmine hugged Laura and walked off to find Jeremiah.

Laura walked back to Keith.

"Ready?" he asked.

Laura nodded.

The two of them left the building and headed towards Terrell Hall. Meanwhile...

Jasmine could not find Jeremiah. She walked up to another basketball team member. She tapped his shoulder.

"Where is Jeremiah?" Jasmine said.

"He left with some girl," he said.

Jasmine sighed and walked over to Jan.

"Jan, can I talk to you?" Jasmine said.

Jan gave Travis her phone number, and Travis said he would call her. He then left with his buddies.

Jan and Jasmine walked out of the club.

"Laura left with Keith," Jasmine said.

"Wendy left with Jeff," Jan said.

"That just leaves us," Jasmine said.

"What happen to your guy?" Jan asked.

"He left with some girl," Jasmine said.

"His loss," Jan said.

"Yeah," Jasmine agreed.

"I guess it's time to go home then," Jan added.

The girls walked back to Bell Hall.

"Tell me about your man," Jasmine said.

"Travis is a funeral director over in Eatonton. He was sweet," Jan said.

Jasmine smiled. She was glad Jan had met someone.

"I can't believe he just came up and asked me to dance," Jan said.

"Are you going to see him again?" Jasmine said.

"I hope so," Jan said.

The girls arrived at Bell Hall and went to their rooms. Meanwhile...

Wendy was sitting next to Jeff watching a movie. She was becoming rather sleepy though.

She laid her head in Jeff's lap to see his reaction.

"Sleepy?" he asked.

Wendy yawned.

She adjusted her head in his lap. Jeff just patted her head and continued to watch the movie.

HIS WRATH

An hour later it ended, and Wendy was out cold on his lap. Jeff propped her head up with a pillow and went to his own bed to sleep.

Meanwhile...

Laura and Keith had arrived at his door. He opened it for Laura.

Sul and Gloria had gone to a party after leaving the club and won't be back for hours.

Keith sat down on his futon and patted the seat next to him, motioning Laura to sit down.

"Are you tired?" he asked.

They were both wide awake after dancing so much.

She shook her head.

"We could watch a movie or just talk," he said.

"A movie is fine," she said.

"Have you watched *American Pie* yet?" Keith asked.

"Nope," she said.

"It is rather funny," Keith said.

Keith popped *America Pie* into his VCR.

Keith and Laura moved the futon off to the side and lay down on his bed. Keith's bed was a bottom bunk.

Keith and Laura each found a comfortable position

The movie began to play.

About halfway through the movie, Laura was lying in front of Keith, and she could feel something on her back.

In no time at all, Keith had unhooked Laura's bra and reached around to her boobs and then started to caress them.

Laura had mixed emotions. She knew she needed to stop him, but she was also curious.

Laura jumped up off the bed.

"I thought we talked about this. I don't feel comfortable," she said.

"I just thought we could move to the next level," he said.

"What do you mean?" she said.

"Laura, I have been with other girls, and I know you would enjoy it. I promise that we won't have sex," he said.

"I'm not sure," she said.

She grabbed her purse, opened his door and walked down the hallway to the staircase to go downstairs.

Keith ran after her. He caught up with her on the staircase.

"Please stay. I'll keep my hands to myself," he said.

Laura turned around.
"You promise?" she asked.
He nodded.
She smiled.
The two of them walked back to his room hand-in-hand.

Chapter 30

Laura woke up Sunday morning in Keith's arms. He kept his promise, and they just cuddled for the rest of the night.

She smiled as she opened her eyes. It was nice to sleep in someone's arms.

"Morning, bright eyes," he said.

Laura sat up.

"Would you like to eat breakfast?" he said.

Laura nodded.

"Can I use your phone?" she asked.

Keith nodded.

"Sure, sweet thing," he said.

Laura picked up the phone. She called Jasmine.

"Hello?" Jasmine said.

"It's me. Meet us in SAGA for brunch. Grab Jan and Wendy," Laura said.

"Great. I will," Jasmine said.

SAGA was a nickname of the school's lunchroom. Years ago, it was catered by a company whose initials spelled SAGA, and the name just stuck.

About ten minutes later, Keith and Laura left for breakfast.

Meanwhile...

Jasmine knocked on Jan's bathroom door.

"Come in," Jan said.

Jan was sitting at her desk typing on her computer. She was talking to friends on aol messenger.

"Laura is going to meet me to get breakfast. Want to come?" Jasmine said.

Jan nodded.

"I'll call Wendy's cell and be in your room in five," Jan said.

Jasmine walked to her room to get ready.

Jan picked up the phone and dialed Wendy.

"This is Wendy," she said.
She had just awakened.
"It's Jan. Want to meet us at SAGA for breakfast?" Jan said.
Wendy couldn't remember how she got to Jeff's apartment.
"Wendy?" Jan said.
"Sorry. Did I go to Jeff's after the club last night?" she asked.
"You left with him to watch a movie," Jan said.
"Oh. Okay. Last night is a little fuzzy. I'll go wake him up for a ride and see you there," Wendy said.

Jan hung up the phone and got ready for breakfast. She and Jasmine left for breakfast a few minutes later.

Meanwhile...

Wendy got up and walked into Jeff's room.
"Jeff, are you awake?" she asked.
Jeff opened his eyes.
"I guess I should take you home," he said.
"I was hoping you would take me to SAGA to meet my roommate for breakfast," she said.
"Sure," he said.

Chapter 31

Breakfast time.

Laura, Jasmine, Jan, Wendy and Keith sat down at a round table each with their breakfast and ready to dig in. Each had something different to eat: Laura—scrambled eggs with ham and cheese and hash browns on the side, Jasmine—cereal, Wendy—plain scrambled eggs with sausage, grits and biscuits on the side, Jan—oatmeal and Keith—hamburger and fries.

The group tried to meet together like this once week to keep up with each other. Keeping up with people is hard to do with everyone on different schedules.

Keith was a guest to the main group.

"Did everyone sleep well?" Jan asked.

"Someone tell me how I woke up at Jeff's. I don't remember how I got there," Wendy said.

They chuckled.

"I'm serious," Jan said.

"You went home with him to watch a movie," she repeated.

Wendy nodded.

She obviously had too much to drink once again.

"I'm worried about you. Maybe, you should not drink when you go out or not go out at all," Jan said.

"Jan, you only live once, you know," Wendy said.

"BUT," Jan said.

She started to say a comeback when her cell phone rang.

"Excuse me," Jan said.

She picked up her cell phone and proceeded to walk to the corner, so she could hear better.

Kevin pulled out the empty chair at the table. He worked in the Governor's Mansion in Milledgeville.

Milledgeville was the capital of Georgia from 1803 to 1868 before Atlanta became the capital. The mansion was built in 1839, and was restored during the period from 2001 to February of 2005. Eight Georgia governors lived in the mansion, and in November of 1864, Sherman used it as the headquarters for his campaign to "March to the Sea." He stayed there for only one evening before burning Atlanta. Today, the mansion showcases a wide variety of 19th century artifacts and antiques, along with a plan to tell the story of the governors who once called this structure home.

Kevin was in Laura's history class and had a crush on her.

"May I join you?" Kevin asked.

"Sure," Laura said.

This was the first time Laura had seen him outside of class, and the first time Keith had too.

"Don't we have history class together?" she asked him.

"Yes. I'm Kevin," he said.

"This is Jasmine, Wendy and my boyfriend, Keith. The owner of the empty chair is Jan. She'll be right back," she said.

He nodded.

"How do each of you know each other?" he said.

"Jasmine is my roommate, and Jan and Wendy are my suitemates in Bell Hall. Keith and I went to high school together," she said.

Kevin nodded.

"I don't mean to interrupt your breakfast time, but would you like to study together for the history test next week?" he said.

Laura smiled.

"Sure," she said.

She enjoyed study groups.

"Great. Want to meet downstairs Thursday at 5 p.m.? I'll buy you dinner," he said.

"Sounds good," she said.

"See you then. It was nice to meet all of you," he said.

Kevin smiled and waved bye as he left the table.

Downstairs, there was a Chick-Fil-A, The Pit, a sandwich café and an ice cream parlor.

"He's hot," Jasmine said.

She paused.

"Oops. Sorry, Keith..." she said.

Keith was jealous. He stared at Laura.

"He's just a guy in my history class," Laura said.

"He'd better be," Keith said sternly.

"Besides we are meeting in a public area," she said.

"He's buying you dinner," he said.

"I'll use my flex dollars," she said.

Each student at the college can choose to have meal plan which includes a certain number of meals a week at the cafeteria and a number of flex dollars, which can be used in the Chick-Fil-A, The Pit, a sandwich café and an ice cream parlor.

"Okay," he said.

He still didn't like the idea.

"Don't you trust me?" she said.

Keith nodded.

"Then you have nothing to worry about," she said.

Jasmine and Wendy sat quietly while they continued.

Jan returned to the table.

"Dish, girlfriend. Who was that?" Jasmine asked.

Jan was blushing.

"The funeral director," Laura said.

Jan nodded.

"He must like you, since he called the next day," Laura said.

Laura nodded.

"He didn't follow the three-day rule," Laura said.

"What do you mean?" Jan asked.

"Guys usually wait three days to call a girl, and we are supposed wait three days to call them back," Laura said.

"Why?" Jan asked.

"That's just the rule," Laura said.

Jan nodded.

"So what did he say?" Laura asked.

"He wants to take me out to dinner," Jan said.

"When?" Laura asked.

"This Friday," Jan said.

"And?" Jasmine said.

"Well. I'm supposed to go home this weekend, so we are going on Thursday night. He's picking me up at 7 p.m. at Bell Hall," Jan said.

She blushed.

"Nice," Jasmine said.

"Jan's got a date. Jan's got a date," Wendy said.

Now, she was embarrassed.

"Jan, don't be nervous. He already likes you," Laura said.

"We want the 411 afterwards," Jasmine said.

Jan nodded.

"Wendy, are you dating Jeff yet?" Laura asked.

She shook her head.

"I don't remember most of last night, but I don't think so," Wendy said.

"You need to stay sober to get him," Jan said.

Wendy frowned.

The girls continued to eat breakfast.

Once breakfast was over, the girls parted.

Jasmine, Jan and Wendy returned to dorm rooms to rest.

Keith and Laura walked back to his dorm room in Terrell Hall. They sat down on his bed.

"I don't like you having dinner with Kevin," Keith said.

Laura stared at him.

"After everything we have been through, you don't trust me?" Laura said.

Keith paused.

"It's not that. I don't trust him. I think he likes you," Keith said.

Laura shrugged.

"You put me through a tough summer, and I forgave you, the least you could do is trust me," she said.

She glared at him.

"I do," he said.

He mumbled.

"Then don't worry about anything," she said.

Keith grabbed her arm.

"Listen, you're my girl, and I don't want you to go," he said.

Laura gasped.

"What are you doing?" she said.

She pushed him away and walked out the door.

Keith walked out the door behind her and yelled.

"I didn't mean to do that," he said.

Laura walked back to him.

"Did you mean to hit me instead?" she asked.

He shook his head.

"I just don't want to lose you," he said.
He frowned. He knew he had hurt her.
Laura opened the door to his room and sat down on his bed.
"You need to calm down," she said.
Keith nodded.
"I'm not going anywhere. I like you, and you are not going to lose me," she said.
She stared at him waiting for a response.
He said nothing.
"I can't handle you being possessive of me. We're in college. These are the best years of our lives you know," she said.
She paused.
He just stared at her.
"If you can't trust me, maybe we shouldn't be together anymore," she said.
Keith sat next to her.
"You're right," he said.
She stared at him in shock.
"I'm sorry," he said.
Laura just listened.
"Don't ever grab me like that again; otherwise I'm out that door for good," she said.
He nodded.
Keith gently put his arm around her and hugged her.
"Tired?" he asked.
Laura nodded.
They fell asleep on his bed in each other's arms.
Each of them slept the afternoon away.

Chapter 32

Thursday night.
Laura sat in the Chick-Fil-A waiting for Kevin to arrive.
About five minutes later, he walked in and sat across from her at the booth.
"Ready to study," Kevin said.
She nodded.
"Let's get some food first," he said.
The two of them grabbed their food off the line and sat back down.
"Did you have a good week?" he said.
Laura nodded.
"You?" she asked.
He nodded.
"Your friends seemed nice," he said.
He was referring to when he met them on Sunday.
"The best a girl could have," she said.
"What about your boyfriend?" he asked.
"He's good," she said.
"He's okay with us studying, right?" he asked.
Laura nodded.
She didn't want to discuss the subject with him.
"He seemed tense," he said.
"He's fine," she said.
"That's good," he said.
"He's actually taking me out for dinner tomorrow," she said.
He nodded.
He was jealous of their relationship.
"He better take good care of you," he said.
Laura nodded.
She knew it was time to change the subject.
"Ready to study?" she asked.
He nodded.

The two began to study.

Meanwhile...

Travis had just picked up Jan for their date.

Near Sinclair Lake about 20 minutes outside of Milledgeville on Highway 441, there were several fish restaurants.

Travis thought it would be nice to treat Jan to one.

He wrapped a blindfold around her head right after she got in the car.

"Where are we going?" she asked.

She was nervous.

"You'll see," Travis said.

He pulled out of the parking lot and drove towards the lake.

About 20 minutes later, they arrived and parked the car.

Travis undid the blindfold and held the door open for Jan.

"I've never been here before," she said.

She gasped.

Travis smiled.

"This is one of my favorite restaurants," he said.

He smiled. He was a sweet guy.

The two of them walked into the restaurant and were escorted to a table. They sat down for dinner.

Each of them opened the dinner menus.

"Did you have a busy week?" she asked.

Travis shook his head.

"It's been rather dead," he chuckled.

"Very funny," she said.

She had no idea what to order.

"What do you recommend?" she asked.

Travis pointed to some dishes on the menu.

The waitress came over and took their order.

Meanwhile...

Wendy was sitting outside on main campus studying.

It was still warm for fall semester. Several groups of people were outside enjoying themselves.

Wendy was planning going out to see a band called McFly tonight. They were going to play downtown at Buffington's. McFly was a cover band that played songs from 1980s and 1990s throughout South Carolina and Georgia.

The rest of the girls were supposed to meet her there.

She knew she needed to prepare for her biology test, if she wanted to go out that night.

Meanwhile…

Kevin and Laura had been busy studying for the history test on Tuesday.

"Do you want to meet up Monday night to review?" he asked.

Laura nodded.

"Same place, same time," he said.

She nodded again.

"See you then," he said.

Kevin smiled and packed his stuff up. He waved as he left the restaurant.

Laura packed up her stuff and walked back towards her dorm.

She noticed Wendy sitting outside and sat next to her.

"It's getting dark," Laura said.

Wendy nodded.

"I was just about time to go in. How was your study date?" Wendy asked.

"Good," Laura said.

"He's cute," Wendy said.

"He is a nice piece of white chocolate," Laura said.

Wendy chuckled.

"That's just between us though," Laura said.

She nodded.

They walked into Bell Hall and down to their rooms. Jasmine had already begun to get ready.

They needed to get to the bar by 10 p.m. to make sure they got in before it became too crowded.

Thursday was the busiest club night in Milledgeville.

Laura and Wendy walked to see Jasmine getting dressed.

"Look at you," Laura said.

"That's right. Look at me," Jasmine said.

They chuckled.

She was dressed up in a low-necked top and tight jeans.

"We're missing someone," Laura said.

"Jan," Jasmine said.

Laura nodded.

"She's on her date with the funeral director," Wendy said.
Meanwhile...

Travis and Jan had had a nice conversation and were ordering dessert.

Travis ordered them a piece of cheesecake.

"What would you like to do now?" he asked.

"I'm supposed to meet the girls downtown. There's a band playing," she said.

"McFly? I saw a flyer," he asked.

She nodded.

"Would you like to come?" she asked.

He nodded.

It looks like Jan has a boyfriend.

She arrived home not too much later. She motioned for Travis to wait outside.

Jan knocked on Laura and Jasmine's door.

"There you are. Ready?" Laura said.

Jan nodded.

"Travis is waiting outside," she said.

"You've got a boyfriend, don't you?" Laura said.

"I hope so," Jan said.

"I guess this means you'll be spending less time online," Laura said.

She nudged her arm.

Jan just nodded. She was a little embarrassed.

"Well girls, let's head," Jasmine said.

The girls locked arms and walked out of the dorm. Jan locked her other arm with Travis, and the five were off to Buffington's.

Chapter 33

The crew soon arrived at Buffington's. At the door, each of them were carded and marked for being under 21.

The next day, Friday, was a teacher workday, so people had already left campus, allowing for the crowd to be a little bit lighter than usual.

Keith, Sul and Gloria were to meet the crew at Buffington's later.

Once they entered the bar, they realized that because of the crowd, there was only standing room available.

McFly had started playing at 10 p.m.

Travis grabbed Jan's arm and led her to the dance floor. He sure did like to dance.

Wendy located Jeff and sat down next to him. Jasmine and Laura spotted Jeremiah.

"I think you should give him a flat lip," Laura said.

"Maybe," Jasmine said.

They walked off to confront him. Jasmine tapped him on the shoulder.

"Hey sweet thing," Jeremiah said.

"You left with some girl Saturday night," Jasmine said.

"You took too long, babe," he said.

Jasmine just stared at him.

"Jasmine, that makes you better off and this guy not worth your time," Laura said.

She grabbed Jasmine's arm and escorted her away.

Jasmine murmured "loser" under her breath.

They spotted Wendy and Jeff and walked over.

"How have you been?" Laura asked.

"Good," Jeff said.

They were no extra seats at the table so they were forced to stand.

"Can I get anyone anything?" he said.

No one replied, not even Wendy.

Jeff turned to Wendy.

"The usual," he said.

Wendy shook her head to say "no."

Laura thought to herself, "I guess she was planning on talking to Jeff about the future of their relationship. She wants to move to the next level."

The music blared in the background.

McFly was the group's favorite band.

The group was what you could refer to as "groupies." Jeff, on the hand, was more of a fan of the female guitarist.

Meanwhile…

Keith, Sul and Gloria made their way through the line and into the bar.

Once inside, Keith looked around for Laura.

Now, the girls were able to sit down in the booth with Wendy and Jeff. They were across the table from Jeff and Wendy.

Jan and Travis were still on the dance floor.

Keith walked up to the booth with Sul and Gloria behind him.

Keith stared at Laura.

"Have a seat, brother," Jeff said.

Keith just looked at Laura.

"This is Jeff; he's a friend. We can squeeze you in," Laura said.

"Don't bother. You look you are having enough fun already," he snapped back.

Keith was the jealous type.

"Jeff was just talking about the time he did karaoke for the song 'Vanilla Ice.' He knows all of the words," Laura said.

Keith nodded.

He was embarrassed. It was obvious he had overreacted.

"I'm glad you are here," she said to him.

This is the first time Keith had seen McFly.

"I wanted you to witness these guys in action," she said.

She was, of course, referring to the band.

Keith nodded.

"Would you like to dance?" he asked.

Laura slid out of the booth and followed him to the dance floor.

Sul and Gloria also made their way to the dance floor.

On the dance floor, Keith and Laura were in their own world.

"How was your study date?" he asked.
"It wasn't a date, but the study part went well," she replied.
He nodded.
"I'm sorry. I just don't want to lose you," he said.
"You're not going to, unless you keep acting jealous," she said.
He nodded.
"Can I make it up to you?" he asked.
She nodded.
"Stay tonight," he requested.

Laura wondered what he meant by that, but she pushed that thought aside and nodded.

They continued dancing.

Sul handed Keith a drink.

By the end of the night, Keith was drunk, but he hid from Laura. The couples had danced the night away.

Travis took Jan home, and Wendy actually went home with Jeff. Keith walked Laura back to the dorm.

Chapter 34

Keith walked Laura up to his room.

He placed her on his bed. She was exhausted.

Laura simply closed her eyes, and while Keith was lying next to her, he saw a window of opportunity.

He simply reached his hand down into her pants and slipped them off along with her underwear.

Laura's eyes opened.

"What are you doing?" Laura asked.

She gasped.

Keith pinned her arms down and took her virginity.

She screamed.

"No," she screamed louder.

"Stop," she continued.

Sul opened the door at that moment.

Sul picked Keith up off of Laura and threw him against the wall.

"When she says no, it means no," he said.

Laura whispered "thank you" as she redressed herself.

Sul picked up the phone and called 911. He explained to the police officer what had just occurred.

In no time at all, they arrived and picked up Keith.

Sul had requested that he be taken to think about what he had just done.

Laura grabbed her purse and ran back to her dorm, after they turned Keith in for date rape.

Keith was escorted off to the local jail and spent the night in the jail cell.

In the morning, he confessed to raping Laura. He suffered the same fate as Corey, and at one time, they even shared a cell.

Laura arrived back at the dorm.

Wendy had watched a movie with Jeff, and then he took her home. No sparks flew.

Laura spent the night with her true friends.

She suffered with trust for the rest of her life and spent many hours with a therapist, but she graduated college with honors.

Jasmine is in college working on her MBA, and Wendy was just accepted to nursing school. Jan and Travis were married after she finished college, and they run the funeral home in Eatonton.

Chapter 35

Ten years after her high school graduation, Laura attended her high school reunion. It was held at the Fox Theater just like her prom.

As she walked down those halls, she remembered running away from the best friends she ever had.

She entered the main room and picked out her nametag.

She grabbed her food at the buffet line and sat down next to a familiar face.

Sally smiled at her.

"It's good to see you," Sally said.

She pointed at Ginger.

"You remember Ginger?" Sally asked.

Laura nodded.

Sally and Ginger had both become research and design engineers for NASA. They were still the best of friends.

"I heard you started your own marketing company in New York," Sally said.

"I handled marketing and public relations for almost every music group that comes through New York," Laura said.

Laura and Jasmine owned the company together.

Sally nodded as Nate winked at her.

"You know who else lives in New York?" Sally asked.

Laura shook her head and looked where Sally was pointing.

As she turned to look to her left, a young man dropped to her knees in front of her. He opened a little black box.

"Years ago, something devastating happened here, but that night I realized something, and I wished I had said something then," he said.

He paused.

"I love you. I always have. You are my best friend and always will be. Please say you'll be my wife," he said.

Laura just smiled and nodded.

Even though she had not been around him for years, she knew at that moment she loved him too.

Nate slipped the ring on her finger and sat down next to his fiancée.

"Nate owns his own club in New York," Sally said.

She smiled.

They were married later that year. Laura's college friends and high school friends were in her wedding party.

Even though Laura had suffered several years of pain, her life was blessed with a happy ending.

One that had been right under her nose all along...

Moral: Anyone who rapes anyone deserves to be punished. Turn them in.

Advice: Life is unpredictable, so enjoy it!

GC&SU was first called the Georgia Normal and Industrial College. It was founded in 1889 as the sister college to Georgia Technical College to provide a public seat of learning in the state for the education of females. In 1996, Georgia College was renamed Georgia College & State University and designated by the Board of Regents as Georgia's public liberal arts university.

Printed in the United States
59932LVS00006B/96